NO ONE SAW HER GO

SALLY ROYER-DERR

Storm

Ebook ISBN: 978-1-80508-833-2
Paperback ISBN: 978-1-80508-835-6

Cover design: Sara Simpson
Cover images: Shutterstock

Published by Storm Publishing.
For further information, visit:
www.stormpublishing.co

ALSO BY SALLY ROYER-DERR

The Secrets Next Door

The Forever Home

The Innocent Wife

Ohana

The Tracks

High Bluffs Trilogy

High Bluffs

Santa Monica

The Return

To my family

PROLOGUE

My gaze shifts down and I notice a light to the right of my new campsite. I wonder where it comes from? It's higher than a light from a tent or a flashlight, more like a light in a house window. I look around. We moved much deeper into the forest this afternoon, away from the pool, to be safe.

An idea stabs me.

I'm closer to that weird cabin I found a few weeks ago.

I stare at the light, blindingly bright in the black night. It must be coming from the cabin; there's nothing else around here, at least that I know of. Goosebumps prickle on my arms, and a slight breeze ruffles the leaves of the trees. I remember the screaming whispers I heard at the cabin the day I discovered it. *Go away! Go away!*

A twig breaks behind me and I turn, but nothing is there. A screech owl lends an eerie melody to the already creepy night. Dread infiltrates my body and mind, although I don't know why. I'm standing alone in this dark forest. Nobody knows I'm here except Dean. I hope he comes back soon.

Please come soon.

Another twig breaks. I see a movement from the corner of

my eye. I don't know what it is, but I feel the urge to run so I do. I run as fast as I can into the dark woods. My feet are bare against the forest floor and the rough ground digs into their tender flesh, but I ignore the pain. Something is following me. I hear its heavy breathing and its footsteps moving behind me.

This is no animal.

A person is behind me.

A person who doesn't say anything, but moves quickly, gaining on me as I increase my speed.

Sharp sticker bushes prick my bare legs and low tree branches whip my face. Blood runs down my legs. I push myself to go faster, but you can only run so fast in the woods in the dark. At least whoever is behind me isn't using a flashlight. The darkness envelops me in every corner as I move forward. There is no light here.

My heart races, adrenaline fueling me as I continue to run with only moonlight to guide my way. Sweat drips off my face. Who is out here? Who is chasing me? Is it him? I should never have stayed here alone.

Run.

Run.

The forest seems to become still and every sound I make, lumbering through the trees, thunders inside of it. How am I going to hide if I'm making so much noise? Ahead of me is a large hemlock tree with a massive trunk and low-hanging branches.

I'll hide there.

I slip underneath the low branches and stand behind the wide tree trunk.

Please let this person, this thing, whatever it is, go away. Please go away, I continue to pray in my frantic mind.

Now that I've stopped running, the night is quiet, serene almost except my heart that races inside my body. I take a few silent breaths to try to calm myself. I'm going to be fine. Everything will be fine.

A twig behind me breaks, but before I can turn around, a large hand clamps down over my face, and I smell chemicals on a rag that now covers my mouth. I slowly lose consciousness, but I don't fall.

He has me.

ONE

JUNE 2024

Zoey

I turn right onto the paved lane, driving between the towering stone pillars that support the large, curved sign—*Camp Medley*—written in dark green letters with a picture of a green pine tree at each end. Two majestic blue spruce pine trees stand guard on both sides of the sign.

I drive past a spacious dark green two-story house with crisp white shutters. A large wraparound front porch overlooks the sparkling lake and its worn wooden boat dock, which is stacked with bright green and yellow canoes. I pass the small log-cabin-style camp store, where bright red impatiens spill from window boxes that frame a wide white screen door. Four picnic tables sit off to the side, under a large shady maple tree. I continue to the right, to the East Area cabins through the leafy green treelined drive as it winds up into the mountain.

An incoming call flashes on the screen in my car, interrupting my music, and I glance at it.

Mom.

I sigh. I'll call her later. I'm not in the mood to argue. I love her but lately we've been arguing about everything. My grades, going away to school, not coming home enough and even this camp counselor job. She always wants me to be close to her, to keep me safe, she says. My college is only a few hours away and she acts like I left the country, or the planet. She's always suffocating me, although at least now I know the reason.

Growing up, I never knew why she was so protective of me. Then while home for spring break, nursing my wounds from Craig freezing me out, I cleaned the basement, organizing some things, and found a bunch of old photos of Mom and a younger girl.

I walked upstairs to ask her about them. She was in the kitchen cooking dinner and was cutting peppers and onion for a stir-fry.

"Who's this?" I asked, holding up the pictures.

Mom wiped her hands on the dish towel and stared at the photos. Her face fell and she grabbed the pictures from me. "Give them to me. Why are you snooping around?"

"I'm not. I'm organizing the basement, I told you that." I pointed to the picture in front. "I can see that's you, but who's the other girl?"

Mom stared at the pictures. "Oh, I know, but it hurts to see her." Tears filled her eyes.

I was surprised at her emotional reaction. "Who is she?"

"My younger sister, Heather," she said, wiping her tears away. "I should have told you about her. I loved her so much."

I wrapped my arms around her and hugged her tight. I never knew she had a sister and so many questions crowded my mind.

"I'm sorry, Mom," I said.

"I wish you could have known her," she cried. "I wish I knew what happened to her."

We stood in the kitchen for a long time holding each other, and Mom told me everything about Heather and how she had gone missing when she was sixteen. That's when I knew I had to get answers for her about her younger sister.

My aunt Heather.

It was strange finding out that I had an aunt. Mom told me their childhood had been tough, and Mom had moved out with a boyfriend when she was eighteen. Shortly after, Heather ran away with her boyfriend, to stay at a camp, and Mom never saw her again.

After Mom told me everything about Aunt Heather, I became consumed with Camp Medley, not only to find answers for Mom, but to distract me from thinking about Craig. My heart ached for my mother and all the unknowns surrounding Heather's disappearance, but she said it was a relief to finally share everything with me. When I looked on the camp's website and saw camp counselor job openings, I told her I was going to apply and maybe I could find some answers for our family. She wasn't thrilled at first, but warmed to the idea when she saw how determined I was to do it.

I'm thankful for the distraction. The internship Craig and I planned on doing fell through anyway because my grades had plummeted after he took off. Plus, I was surprised to see that the camp wasn't that far from Craig's house. Maybe I could stop by, I thought, and we could talk? Or could I talk to his father? I didn't know, but thought it might be possible.

What happened to Aunt Heather? Mom and I looked through the old pictures together, and I took a few shots of them on my phone to show people at the camp if they had worked there during that time period.

I love cold cases. If I could choose only one area of criminal investigation, that would be it. Aunt Heather's case will be the first I investigate, so a thrill of excitement runs through me now. To finally get answers for Mom is my goal and, hopefully, put Aunt Heather to rest properly.

My first case. Butterflies swarm in my stomach.

I reach the girls' cabins, five nice-sized cabins, each with either a large fern or a basket of bright flowers hanging from its cute front porch. All the cabins are nestled among white pine trees and tall oaks. A large bathroom/shower house sits across from them.

I park in the stone lot next to my assigned cabin, the number listed on my welcome letter, each are numbered, and get out of my car. I pop the trunk, grab my suitcase, but stop for a moment before heading inside to my new home for the next three months.

I sigh, staring at the suitcase. Even though I am excited to solve my first case, this is not where I planned to spend my summer before my senior year of college. I thought I'd be interning at a victims' service crisis center in Harrisburg with Craig this summer, not leading camp sing-a-longs for twelve-year-old girls.

Craig. My heart aches just thinking of him. I'll never understand what happened between us. I miss him so much.

I met him at school, a fellow Criminology student, and we dated for seven glorious months. Then, before we left on spring break, we had a fight over nothing, really, just a dumb fight. He texted me the next day telling me it was over between us; things were getting too serious. He said he was dropping out of school and traveling. I called and texted him repeatedly, but nothing.

I have never heard from him since. He completely ghosted me. Such an important part of my life and then... just gone. Similar, in a way, to how Aunt Heather disappeared from Mom's life. I understand the hurt she feels because I feel it with Craig's absence.

How does someone do that to someone they supposedly love? None of it makes any sense to me. How could he break up with me by *text*?

Craig and I were both Criminology majors at Penn State and hoped to work in Witness Protection after graduation, although I have a strong interest in cold cases too, but regardless, the summer internship would have been good experience no matter which area I choose to pursue.

After the breakup, my grades dropped. I couldn't focus on anything, and they hadn't been great to begin with. I've gotten off track with Craig taking off, but I am going to get back on track with my grades. I still can't believe after all these months, he still hasn't reached out to me, and I sent him so many texts and called him numerous times, it's embarrassing.

I love him and I thought he loved me too.

So, when I saw the counselor job opening at Camp Medley, it felt like fate. I need a completely different environment, and Craig grew up in a town close to the camp, less than a thirty-minute drive away. I know Craig's mom passed away when he was little, but I've been considering looking up his dad. I never met him, but as Craig is Craig Hampton Jr., senior shouldn't be too difficult to locate.

I still see that text in my mind and, of course, it's still on my phone. Why can't I just move on? He certainly has.

I groan and push my thoughts away. I have a case to solve. I remember what Mom told me about Heather. Mom always regretted leaving her, but she had to get out of the escalating situation with their stepfather. She didn't go into detail, but said he was physically and sexually abusive toward her, both of them, but mostly her. She usually stepped in when he bothered Heather, but she told me she couldn't deal with it anymore.

I have never seen Mom like that, so sad and crushed, as she told me about their living circumstances. It broke my heart, and I wanted to help her heal. She is a good mom and my mom. It made me sick to think of anyone treating her like that.

She said she had wanted to take Heather along, but her boyfriend at the time didn't want her to live with them, and she was only a scared teenager herself. While at the camp, Heather sent a few letters to Mom, but after a few weeks the letters stopped, and she never heard from her again. Mom inquired at the camp, but they told her that Heather's father picked her up. Mom was surprised because as far as she knew, Heather hadn't been in contact with her father for years, they were half-sisters, but thought they must have reconnected. At the time, she thought that might be better for Heather, but as time passed and there was no contact, she worried something bad must have happened.

When their mother died about six months later, from an overdose, she saw Heather's father at the funeral, but he told her he hadn't picked her up at camp. He hadn't seen her for years, not since she was nine years old, when he moved out.

I hope to do some investigating and hopefully find out what happened to Aunt Heather. At a bare minimum it will be a good distraction from my own worries. And I have to give my mom some closure too, she deserves it. She deserves to know what happened to her sister.

Suitcase in tow, I walk across the gravel parking space to the front porch. It has a small white sign in the center, above the door, in brown lettering.

Cabin Twelve

I sigh. This summer will be different than I expected, but maybe it will give answers about my missing aunt, a loss Mom has struggled with for years. I'm rather excited thinking about solving this mystery.

And maybe I can stop thinking about Craig.

TWO
1989

Heather

I replace the cordless phone into its base and hurry back upstairs to my bedroom. I pull my backpack from the closet and toss in shorts, underwear, tank tops, T-shirts, a couple of bras, and then I pause, staring at the pretty white bikini with little pink rosebuds. It was Jess's, but she gave it to me before she left to move in with her boyfriend. She never wore it and knew how much I liked it from the moment she brought it home from the store. I touch my ears, rubbing the delicate white opal half-moon earrings she gave me too, a few months ago for my sixteenth birthday.

I miss her so much.

She's my best friend, and my protector since Gran died two years ago. Things were different for us when Gran was alive. Jess and I would stay at her house when things blew up with Mom. We always had a place to stay with her when Mom would disappear for days or if her latest boyfriend was a disaster. We stayed with Gran for months sometimes because it wasn't safe for us to live with our mother. Then she married Harvey. Gran said from the start that Harvey was trouble.

Gran always knew where there was trouble.

I miss her too.

I sit on the bed still holding the bikini, thinking about last night, tears welling inside me. I should have locked my bedroom door, like Jess instructed me to do, but I forgot. How could I forget? Waking up in the middle of the night with Harvey in my bed, touching me, the stink of his cigarette and stale beer breath in my nose, was a shock and a nightmare. He didn't stay long, but I'm sure he'll try again, try more. I can't let that happen. I have to get out of here.

I shake, thinking of the possibility, then wipe the tears away. Nobody is going to save me; I have to save myself. Jess is gone, Gran is gone, and Mom doesn't care. I can't stay here.

I shove the bikini into the backpack along with my makeup bag and a few more personal items. Jess and Gran are gone now, and I need to take care of myself. But I'm not alone. I have Dean and I know he'll always be there for me. We moved here at the beginning of the school year and Dean was the first person I met. I smile as I pack my bag. Just thinking about him makes me happy.

We were on the same bus and as I boarded the first day desperately looking for a seat among the sea of unknown faces, this cute guy with dark blond hair, warm brown eyes and a wide friendly smile called out to me from the back of the bus.

"This seat's free!" he had called.

And I joined him in the back, sitting next to him and returning his smile. A couple months later he was my boyfriend and still is, he's my everything. I feel safe with him, as safe as I do with Jess. He's my favorite person in the world.

He's at Camp Medley now. He's been going there every summer for years, and since he's seventeen now, he'll be a camp counselor for the entire summer.

He's called me every day since he left for camp last week, and this morning I told him what happened with Harvey last night. Well, some of the details. It's not something I want to talk about over the phone, but I'll tell him everything in person. He's going to pick me up this afternoon while Mom and Harvey are at work, and he has a place I can stay at the camp until we figure things out.

I love him. I love him *so* much.

And he loves me. We told each other the night before he left for camp, and my heart soared when he said those words to me. Nothing in this world could ever make me happier than hearing that. Nothing.

I dig in the back of my closet for my hot-pink sleeping bag. I don't think it's meant for use outdoors; I only ever use it for slumber parties, but it's the only one I have. I grab my pillow, an extra blanket and my small boom box.

There's a loud knock at the door.

It must be Dean.

I give my bedroom one last look, grab my stuff and rush out the door.

I hope I never come back to this place.

THREE
2024

Zoey

I toss my suitcase on the neatly made up bottom bunk bed; crisp white sheets and a plain white comforter and two slightly flat pillows adorn it. Then I unzip it to retrieve my container of antibacterial wipes to sanitize the small wooden dresser drawers before placing my clothing inside. I also do a quick wipe of the top too.

One last wipe of the bottom drawer and the cabin door creaks open. A tall girl with long, straight blonde hair and dark sunglasses walks in wheeling a black suitcase.

"Oh, hey." The girl takes off her sunglasses, revealing piercing blue eyes. "Are we roomies?"

I laugh. "I guess so. I'm Zoey, camp counselor for the summer."

"Nice to meet you, Zoey. I'm Melanie, also camp counselor." She glances at the bunks. "I see you took the bottom bunk."

"Oh, I hope that's okay," I reply. "I'll take the top if you don't want it."

Melanie scoffs. "No, I'm fine with the top bunk. Can I borrow some of those wipes? Good idea wiping out the drawers. They probably haven't been cleaned since 2015, and it was probably me who cleaned them then."

"Oh, did you used to camp here?"

Melanie laughs. "Well, I grew up here. My parents own the camp."

"That's fun. Well, this is my first time here, you'll have to show me around."

"Sure, I can do that. By the way, everyone calls me Mel, except my mother, she's the only one who calls me Melanie."

"Okay, Mel." I hand her the wipes. "Let's get these bags unpacked."

Now, we sit on our respective bunk beds and munch on Cool Ranch Doritos. We had picked up our bagged dinner at the dining hall—turkey sandwiches, orange, chocolate chip cookie and a bottle of water—but are still hungry. Tomorrow, the regular meals will start, it's a counselor orientation day, and then the campers will arrive the next day.

"Why do you stay in a cabin if you live here? Why not stay in your bedroom at home?" I ask, popping another chip into my mouth. "I'm guessing your family lives in the big green house at the entrance of the camp?"

"Yeah, we do. Oh, my parents insist I stay in the cabin if I'm going to be a counselor, to be available for the girls. It makes sense. Once camp is over then I'll go back to my room in our house," Mel explains. "Well, at least for a week, until I leave to go back to college."

"It must be fun to live here. You always have the pool and the lake to go to."

Mel shrugs. "Sure, it's fun sometimes."

"Do you have any brothers or sisters?"

"No, just Mom and Dad. Grandma lives with us too, and Aunt Sherry lives in the small cabin with Wynn a little bit down from our house."

"Is Wynn her husband?"

"No, he's her son, my cousin."

I chew my chip and swallow, also digesting what Mel just said. I wonder how long Mel's parents have owned the camp. Maybe they would know something about Aunt Heather.

"Have you lived here your whole life?"

"Yeah, the camp's been in the family for years. It used to be my great-grandparents'. I guess they were the first to buy it. Before that it was a church camp. So, my grandparents ran it and now my parents run it. Mom and Aunt Sherry grew up here too, like me."

"Really?"

Oh, a thrill races through me. I bet they will know something about Aunt Heather. Maybe her mom and aunt even knew her. Oh boy, this might be a fantastic lead for me. I'll have to talk to them at the orientation. My mind races with all the questions I can ask them. When I interviewed for the counselor position, I spoke to a woman called Jennifer. Is that Mel's mom? I ask her.

"Yeah," she says. "Mom does all the hiring for the camp. Dad does most of the maintenance work. He's good at fixing things. My aunt runs the dining hall and the camp store. Grandma used to do a lot around here too, but she hasn't been well. She has dementia so she has good days and bad days. You just never know."

"Oh, I'm sorry to hear that." I crumple my now-empty Doritos bag and toss it in the nearby trash can. I grab a water bottle from the floor and take a long sip. "I'd like to meet all of them tomorrow."

"Sure, they'll be there," Mel says. "I'll introduce you."

I yawn. "Great, don't know about you, but I'm tired."

"Same. Good night, Zoey."

"Night, Mel."

I lie back in my bed, thinking about what Mom told me about Aunt Heather. When they found out her father hadn't picked her up at the camp, that was it. Nobody knew where Heather was, and it seemed that my mom was the only one who cared. She filed a missing person's report with the police, but she didn't feel that they took her seriously. And she was barely surviving at that point too, sleeping on friends' sofas and scraping by. Nobody had any answers other than she left the camp with a man they thought was her father. Heather wasn't a registered camper, she was hiding out at the camp because her boyfriend was a counselor there, but the camp owners had found where she was staying in the woods. My mom spoke to the camp owner and was told Heather had made a call on the payphone, and a few hours later, her supposed father showed up and the two left the camp.

I stare at the wooden bunk above me. Mel's parents must know something, or at least her mom and aunt, since they grew up here. I have to play it cool though. I was going to tell Mel about my aunt's story, but I think I'll wait and ask her mom and aunt some questions when I see them. If something happened here at the camp, they might not want to share that information with me, and I want to see their initial reaction when I ask about her. Body language tells you a great deal about what a person knows about a situation.

FOUR
1989

Heather

I open the door of Dean's blue Chevy pickup truck. His dad bought it at an auction a few years ago and the two of them fixed it up and gave it a new paint job. You'd never know it was almost fifteen years old. They were still working on it when I met Dean at the start of the school year and finished it in February.

He's smiling at me, and I slide over on the bench seat to sit right next to him. He puts his arms around me and draws me close, kissing me gently on the lips.

"I'm so glad you're getting out of here," he says, his warm brown eyes filling with concern. "We'll figure this out. You don't have to put up with that bastard."

I kiss him again and linger in his arms, enjoying his protectiveness and care. I feel so safe with him. I don't know how all of this will work out. I haven't even told Dean about Harvey coming into my bed last night, only about his leering. I will tell him eventually, but I don't want to ruin this moment by talking about that pervert. How could my mother marry someone like that?

Really, I don't want to talk about it ever. And I never want to see Harvey again. And I don't really care if I see my mother again either. She's never taken good care of me or Jess. If we didn't have Gran, I can't imagine we would even have survived, we certainly would be worse off. Although now without her life is pretty bad for both Jess and me, at least we're almost grown up and we can live our own lives now. I'm so thankful to have Dean, and Jess has her boyfriend, but I don't think he's as kind as Dean. Maybe he is to Jess. I hope so.

"Thank you for coming to get me." I lay my head on his shoulder. Dean isn't a big guy, only a few inches taller than me, but he's muscular, strong and has such a warm, calming way about him. Everyone loves being around him. He's so popular in school; he's friends with everyone. He's a good guy and I still can't believe he's mine. He's the best thing that has ever happened to me. The happiest times in my life have been with him.

He pulls away from my mom's house and we begin the forty-five-minute drive to Camp Medley. Dean has been going to this camp since he was ten years old and now, at seventeen, he can be a counselor; it's the perfect summer job for him. Part of me feels guilty pulling him away on his third day there, but I didn't know who else to call.

I can't stay in that house, I hope I never go back there again.

They probably won't even look for me, not at first. Mom will think I've joined Jess. Jess graduated from high school last year and works at a grocery store. Now she has moved in with her boyfriend, and she'll never come back. I don't blame her, I just wish I could go with her. But the last time I talked to Jess she said her boyfriend didn't want anyone else at his house. I have her address, though, so I'll send her a letter to let her know what's going on with me.

Jess knows what a perv Harvey is. She told me when she left to always keep my bedroom door locked at night. I feel so stupid for forgetting.

The radio is on inside the truck. A song is playing by Def Leppard, it ends shortly, and Madonna's "Crazy for You" comes on. Dean puts his hand on my knee, and I lay my hand on top of his. This is our song, the first song we danced to at the Winter Dance at school, our third date.

I look up at Dean, who is already looking at me.

"I love you," he says. His eyes sparkle, and my heart flutters like it always does with him.

I gaze back at him. "I love you more."

Happiness floods my body. Those beautiful words again and it feels so good, so real, so perfect. I can face anything if Dean is by my side. My knight in shining armor.

When we arrive at the camp, Dean drives under the large, curved sign, past a dark green house with white shutters, a sparkling lake with several campers out in canoes and a sandy beach on the left side dotted with swimmers and a few girls lying on beach towels working on their tans. The camp store is next along the road; a few picnic tables sit in front of the log-cabin-style building. Then Dean takes a left and we travel up the mountain, deeper into the lush green forest.

We turn left again, and now the paved road changes to a stone road. We drive past a large bunkhouse where some boys, probably around twelve years old, are playing basketball outside on a small court on the right side of the cabin. They are too absorbed in their game to notice us.

"That's my bunkhouse," Dean says. "Trevor and I are the counselors for the twelve-year-old and thirteen-year-old boys. There are eleven campers in our group."

I nod. "Will you get in trouble for leaving today to get me?"

He shakes his head. "No, Trevor is covering for me and not all the campers have arrived yet, only six now. The rest will come tomorrow."

"Oh, good," I say as we travel deeper into the woods along the stone road. Dean turns right into a small stone parking lot where two other cars are parked. He parks the truck next to a gray Honda. The road ends here, but there's a gravel walking path with a big wooden sign and the word *Pool* in big blue letters and a blue arrow pointing to the path.

"This is where I usually park," he says, pulling his keys from the ignition. "I stopped at home before I picked you up and got a tent from the garage. I think I have a perfect spot in the woods to set it up for you. We'll have to walk in, there's a narrow stone lane that goes up closer to the spot, but Mr. Jefferies, the camp owner, doesn't like us to use it. He's the only one that uses it."

"Okay, we'll walk," I agree, and we exit the truck.

I put my backpack on and hold my sleeping bag, pillow and grocery bag with some granola bars, apples and a thermos of water.

Dean opens the tailgate and retrieves the tent and a small cooler. He looks at me. "I brought a cooler of ice and a few drinks. I figured you'd need it."

I smile. "Thanks, Dean, you think of everything."

"For you, I do." He grins. "Come on, let's go."

We take the gravel path leading to the pool and travel through the leafy green forest. After a few minutes of walking, we come upon a small wooden bridge going over a slow-moving narrow creek dotted with moss-covered rocks. Purple wildflowers cover the side of the creek bed.

"The spot isn't far from the pool, maybe a ten-minute walk, but the forest is dense there, nobody should notice the tent and it's not a place campers use. Plus, there's a bathhouse at the pool, so you have a bathroom, showers and there's a water fountain too."

"Okay, that sounds great. And I brought granola bars and apples, I'm okay for a while."

He frowns. "I'll bring you food from the dining hall, and I work the snack bar at the pool every Sunday, so I'll make sure to grab extra for you."

I smile at him. "I'm so lucky to have you."

He returns my smile. "I'm the lucky one. Now I get to spend the summer with you."

We continue to walk along the path and soon the large rectangular pool comes into view. Kids are swimming, bobbing around on rafts, some screaming as they go down the bright red sliding board into the sparkling water. Dean points over to a foot-worn path to the left and then to a large building at the side of the pool.

"Bathrooms and showers are in there." He hurries into the woods. "Come on, we don't want anyone to see us."

I hurry behind him and we go deeper among the trees. The footpath ends after a few feet and now we walk on the muddy ground littered with branches, rocks and moss. Delicate ferns populate substantial areas as they tickle our bare legs.

"Be careful, there's a lot of rocks here. And watch out for snakes," he says.

I frown. Snakes. I hadn't considered sleeping where snakes slithered around. Oh well, it's still better than sleeping in the same house as Harvey. Several minutes later, we come upon a small clearing in the woods. Dean places the tent and cooler down on the ground. The open patch of ground is blanketed with fallen leaves and soft green moss. More wild growths of the delicate ferns we passed on our walk to the site surround the area, and an opening in the towering trees surrounding us allows some sunlight to filter through. This will be my new home for the summer. Excitement wells up inside me. A calm, peaceful place just for the two of us.

"Here it is, this should work," he says with a sigh.

"It's perfect," I reply, dropping my backpack, sleeping bag and pillow. I wrap my arms around him and give him a long hug. He holds me close, smoothing my hair back, and kisses my forehead.

"You're safe now," he whispers to me.

FIVE
2024

Zoey

I glance at my phone while picking at my breakfast on the plastic dining tray. No messages. I stare at the food again. It's not bad, scrambled eggs, hash browns, piece of toast and a carton of orange juice. I'm just not hungry. I stab a piece of egg and shove it into my mouth, then wash it down with the juice. At least there's air conditioning in the dining hall, which I greatly appreciate.

"Come on, you have to eat more than that," Mel says, joining me. She sits a plastic tray next to me. A container of mixed berry yogurt, small plastic container of granola, and chocolate milk sits on it.

"I should have gotten yogurt," I remark. I eat half a piece of toast. "So, is this better?"

"Sure, I guess." Mel smiles, pulling off the top of the yogurt and adding the granola into it.

"What's on the agenda today?"

"After breakfast we'll get into the camp bus and take a tour of the property. Then there's a meeting in the rec hall and they'll go over the daily schedule, the different special activities that are planned, what to do if there's an emergency or someone gets sick, that type of thing," Mel tells me in between bites of yogurt. "Then we have a pizza party to get to know the other counselors. It's fun."

I nod. "Great, it'll be nice to meet everyone. That's why I took this job; I need a completely different environment."

Mel looks at me. "Why's that?"

I shake my head. "A bad breakup. It's been hard to get over."

She nods. "Sure, I understand. I haven't dated anyone really for over a year. Everything has kind of been crazy for me lately."

"Like what?"

She shrugs. "Just family stuff. I start my senior year in the fall and after I graduate, my parents want me to start running the camp with them, eventually taking it over."

"Do you want to do that?"

"Not really, but they feel it's very important to keep it a family-run camp. I guess it's kind of a legacy." Her gaze drifts away from me and she looks pensive. "And I understand why it's important. It's probably something I'll have to do."

I nod. "Maybe you'll be more excited when you start doing it."

"Yeah, and you'll get over the breakup too," Mel says, gulping her chocolate milk. "Come on, let's get our seat on the bus."

After the tour we head back into the dining hall, where numerous pizza boxes are set up on the counter, all with various toppings, and people quickly line up to make their choice. Mel and I hang back, not in a rush, and luckily her parents walk in as we wait.

Mel introduces me to them, Mr. and Mrs. Thorton.

"Please call me Jennifer," her mom says, smiling at me. She's a pretty, middle-aged woman with straight blonde hair and bright blue eyes like Mel.

"But everyone calls Dad 'Mr. T.'" Mel laughs.

"Yeah, they do. I think it started as a joke, but it stuck." Her dad laughs, his eyes sparkling. He's a handsome older man and seems friendly and good-natured. I enjoy talking to both of them.

"Mr. T it is!" I exclaim.

"Oh, and this is Aunt Sherry, my mom's older sister," Mel says. "And my cousin Wynn."

I smile at Sherry. She looks much different to her younger sister, Jennifer. Short, cropped blonde hair, muscular build, and hard eyes, she looks like a rough sort of person; even when she says hello and smiles, her eyes stay hard and sharp as she assesses me. Her son, Wynn, is a tall, gangly teenager with black hair that hangs limply across his face.

I murmur another greeting to him and the two of them disappear to get some drinks, thankfully. Sherry doesn't seem like a person to mess with, not that I'm planning to mess with anyone, but Jennifer seems like a good person to start with my questions, certainly more friendly than Sherry. Mr. T is called away to help with an issue with one of the sinks in the kitchen, leaving Mel and I with Jennifer. I smile at her.

"Did you grow up here at the camp?" I ask.

She nods. "Yes, I've lived here my entire life."

"Maybe you can help me with something," I say. Nerves flutter in my stomach.

Jennifer looks at me. "Sure, what is it?"

"Do you remember a girl who camped here named Heather?" I ask. "It was a long time ago, in nineteen eighty-nine."

"Oh." Jennifer frowns, thinking. "Well, I remember a lot of girls named Heather. It was a popular name growing up."

"Heather Wills," I reply. "She wasn't a registered camper here but I think she was hiding in the woods. She was my aunt, she ran away from home. She stayed at this camp for a while."

Jennifer stares at me for a moment and the smile disappears; the color seems to drain from her face. She looks down and a few seconds pass before she answers. "Oh, that is a long time ago. No, I don't remember anyone by that name."

I smile at her. "Okay, I just thought I'd ask. I only recently learned about Aunt Heather, but my mom's been dealing with her loss for years. She always wanted to know what happened to her sister."

Jennifer nods, a sympathetic look on her face. "It must have been difficult for your mother."

"Yes, it has. Learning about this family secret explained so much about my mom, like why she's overprotective of me. You're a mother, I'm sure you understand."

"Of course," she agrees. "But I don't think I can help you."

"My mom didn't want me to come here, but I want to get some answers about her sister. You know, to have closure. Imagine if your sister went missing and you never knew what happened," I continue.

Jennifer nods again. "I'm sorry for you and your mother, but like I said, I can't help you."

"Well, do you think your sister, or maybe your mother—"

"No," she cuts me off. "My mother has dementia. She doesn't remember what she ate for breakfast. She won't have any memory of nineteen eighty-nine."

"I just thought—"

"No." Her tone is sharp now. "She will not remember anything. Asking her questions will only upset her. Don't bother my mother."

I glance at Mel. Her eyes narrow when she meets my gaze. I didn't mean to agitate Jennifer, I was only asking a question.

"I'm sorry, I don't mean to upset you. But maybe your sister remembers her?"

"Sorry, girls." Jennifer smiles at us, but her eyes are wary. "I have to take care of something, but it was wonderful to meet you, Zoey."

"Yes, you too," I reply, but she walks away before the words are out. She never answered my question about Sherry. Wow, I really hit a nerve asking Jennifer about my aunt. What does she know about her?

"Geez, Zoey, I didn't know you were going to interrogate my mom," Mel remarks sharply. "Why didn't you tell me about your aunt before?"

"Oh, sorry," I say insincerely. I purposefully hadn't told Mel about Aunt Heather to see her mother's reaction, which, in my opinion, was straight-up suspicious. If Mel had mentioned it to her mother, Jennifer could have prepared herself for my questions. I wanted to see the raw reaction, the body language without any thought beforehand. I'll have to ask Sherry some questions too, although I don't look forward to talking to her for some reason. But for now, Mel needs soothing. Her feathers are ruffled and if I'm going to bunk with her for the summer, I better keep things friendly between us.

I smile at her. "Sorry, I should have told you when we talked last night. It's just such a strange story. My aunt ran away from home and stayed at this camp with her boyfriend for a month or two and then just disappeared. She wrote my mom some letters from here. I just wish I could find out what happened to her for my mom and give her some peace. Finding out about Aunt Heather is new to me, but Mom's been suffering her loss for years."

Mel nods, her face softening. "What a mystery. Do you really think my mom knows something about it?"

"Maybe, she said not though," I reply. Although my

thoughts are much more definite. Jennifer was obviously irritated by my question. My hunch is she knows something, but why is she so secretive? What is she hiding?

SIX
1989

Heather

I open the cooler and grab a Pepsi and take a long gulp of the ice-cold soda. Pepsi is my favorite, and Dean had several in the cooler, along with a container of water, Tastykake cupcakes and Swedish Fish candy. All of my favorites.

The tent is set up and my sleeping bag, pillow and backpack sit inside. The cooler is just outside the zippered tent door. This area of the forest is quiet, a few birds chirp, a squirrel scurries up a tall maple tree and sunlight extends a long finger to the right side of the tent, but everything else is shady and dim in the early-evening hours.

The small clearing where we set up the tent is surrounded by lush, tall green ferns with delicate intricate designs. It provides some extra coverage for the tent just in case someone is walking through the woods, and it's pretty too. Dean said campers don't come out here, and it's isolated, so I'm confident my hiding place will be safe. I take a deep breath and enjoy the calmness in my body. Dean's right, I'm safe here. I feel so free. I don't know what's going to happen but if I'm with Dean, I know things will be okay.

He'll be back tonight after everyone goes to sleep and he'll stay here with me. I think I'll tell him all the details about Harvey then. I don't want to have any secrets from Dean. I want him to know everything about me.

When Gran died two years ago, life got significantly worse. She'd basically raised Jess and me most of our lives. Whenever Mom disappeared for days, we'd call Gran. When Mom moved in with a disastrous boyfriend, we'd stay at Gran's house. Then Gran got sick, but Mom was more responsible at that point. She was working full time at the food-manufacturing factory for over a year, and while we all lived at Gran's, Mom bought the groceries and helped with other stuff too; she was the best I've ever seen her.

Then she met Harvey.

Gran hated Harvey, said he was trouble, but she couldn't do anything about it. She got weaker and weaker every day. I hated seeing such a strong woman become so sick. It made me and Jess so sad; we loved her so much and she always did so much for both of us. After she died, everything got worse at home and Mom started disappearing for a couple days here and there and that's when Harvey would be the worst. We were stuck there, and we couldn't call Gran for help and there was nobody else to ask. Mom and Harvey sold Gran's house and bought a small house closer to the factory where they worked.

Things continued to deteriorate. We told Mom but she didn't believe us. She always said Jess and I made up stories, but we didn't. We were telling her the truth. She just said Harvey paid most of the bills, so we needed to be nice to him, whatever that meant. I often wondered how our mother could be so different from Gran, who was her mother. Gran would never have put us in a situation like that. Gran would fight for us, defend us, but our mother did nothing.

I guess we didn't matter as long as the bills were paid. Then Jessica started disappearing like Mom, a few days here and there, maybe a week.

Dean brings me a flashlight and an extra blanket when he comes back later this evening. The night air is surprisingly cool in contrast to the heat of the day, and I'm thankful for the extra warmth as we snuggle under the blanket together.

"I love you," he says, his breath hot against my cheek as we stare at each other in the dim light of the flashlight.

"I love you too," I reply. I trace his lips with my finger. "I want to tell you something."

"What?"

One of the many things I love about Dean is how he calms me. I know I can tell him anything and he will always love me. He has an unconditional love for me that makes me always feel safe. Relief rushes through me as I begin to talk.

I tell him about waking up with Harvey in my bed and every sickening detail. Even in the low light, I can see the anger in his eyes, but then he stares at me and pulls me even closer to him.

"I'm so sorry that happened to you," he whispers to me. "I hate that asshole."

"So do I."

"What if you tell your mom? Won't she do anything?"

"I've tried before, Jess tried. She says we're lying," I reply. "The only one who ever believed us was Gran, but she's gone."

Dean rolls over on his back and sighs. "You can't go back to that house."

"But what am I going to do?" I ask. I don't ever want to go back there, but where would I go? It doesn't sound like Jess's boyfriend would welcome me to his house.

"Well, you stay here for the next three months with me and

then, I'll talk to my mom and dad. I've only got one year of school left and you have two, maybe you can live with us. I'd have to tell them everything that's going on though, if that's okay."

"Do you really think they would do that?" I ask excitedly. "Yes, tell them everything. No problem. I'd do anything to be with you all the time."

A slow smile spreads across his face. "Yeah, that's a bonus. I'm sure they'd insist you stay in the guestroom, but I can sneak into your room after they're asleep, if you want me to."

"Yes, I want you to, wow, we'd be living together." I smile at the prospect. Hope springs inside me.

"You're my favorite person, I always want to be with you," Dean whispers to me. His hands touch my face gently, his fingers trailing down my face.

The glow from the moonlight allows us to see each other and his face studies mine so intensely. Love soars in my heart for him, and I want to remember everything about this moment and every moment with him.

"You're my favorite too," I say, my lips meeting his.

We kiss and I can't imagine anything more exciting, sweeter and more loving than me and Dean.

Now, tomorrow and forever.

His love is everything to me.

He kisses me lovingly. "And you'd be safe. I'll always keep you safe."

plants and flowers with interest. I'd love to walk through it, but I guess I can't.

"What's this place?" Brittney asks, looking around. "It's so pretty."

We stop and Mel reads one of the signs to the group.

"This is a special place," she says in a stern voice, looking at the girls. "It's very important that nobody goes into this space and disturbs the delicate plants and the bog turtles' home. Very important. This is their home, and we can't disrupt it."

"What if we do go inside?" Diana asks. If anyone is going to sneak into this space, it would be her. She puts her hands on her hips. She always seems to push the envelope for everything, and she's only been here for two days.

"Then you will be asked to leave the camp," Mel says in a sharp voice. "Mr. and Mrs. T will call your parents to pick you up, and you will be banned from ever staying at Camp Medley again. I want to stress the importance of never entering this protected area. You cannot disturb the habitat of the plants and the turtles. And if you do, you will never come back here again. Never."

I shoot her a look, her words surprising me. I understand this is a protected area, but this seems like a harsh consequence for looking at some flowers and a turtle. Her voice is strict, hard and unyielding. She is so serious about this area, almost making it seem a crime you could be jailed for, if someone happened to climb over the fence. Mel is still looking at the girls sternly, then her face softens a bit.

"So, we can enjoy the beauty from here, and there are many other areas in the camp to explore," she says, her voice lighter. "Just a bit farther down this nature path is our sunflower garden and it is stunning in late July when the sunflowers are tall and beautiful. Sometimes they are taller than me!"

The girls start chatting about sunflowers, and we move

along the trail leaving the protected area behind. I follow along but give the secret garden one last glance. A soft breeze ripples around me, and the plants wave in it, accentuating their beauty.

EIGHT
1989

Heather

My eyelids are heavy as I push them open. I stretch my arms and yawn, even though I feel fully rested, more than I have in a long time. I roll over to the other side of the sleeping bag, where Dean slept last night, and sniff it. A hint of his scent still lingers, cologne or aftershave, I'm not sure, but it makes me smile. I miss him already.

I get up and unzip the tent, hurry outside a distance away and pee; there's no way I'd make the ten-minute walk to the bathroom by the pool. I walk back to the tent, pour some water into the thermos cup and quickly brush my teeth. I dig into the paper bag housing the granola bars and apples I brought from home, selecting one of the apples. Half is bruised and brown, so I eat the decent portion then toss the rest into the woods surrounding me.

It's Sunday morning and Dean's working at the snack bar at the pool. I'll hang out there today, I decide. I'm lucky there's a family camp here too, so I can easily blend in since family campers are always changing, usually only staying for a week or so. The family camp isn't as busy this week, so I have to be careful, but Dean says next week and probably the rest of the summer it will be fully booked. I go back into the tent, take off the oversize T-shirt I was wearing, put on my white bikini with pink rosebuds and pull on my cut-off jean shorts. I dig into my backpack, pull out a pink scrunchie and secure my hair into a high ponytail. I slip my feet into my pair of flip-flops and start walking through the trees to the pool area.

The fresh morning air makes me feel good, and the long fingers of sunshine trickle down on me as I walk along the leafy ground and into the large swath of swishy ferns. A large growth of vibrant black-eyed Susans grows next to them. I shove my hands into the pockets of my jean shorts, fingering the cash inside. One twenty-dollar bill, a ten-dollar bill and seven ones. I also have three dollars in quarters. I remember seeing a payphone by the pool and at the camp store, so I plan to call Jess and tell her I'm okay. I'll arrive at the pool a little earlier than Dean told me to meet so I can call her. She'll be so happy to hear from me. I know I need to keep a low profile here, but I don't think anyone will notice me at the payphone for a few minutes. It's a plus that there's also a family camp here too so I could easily be with one of those groups.

I can't wait to talk to Jess; she'll be so surprised to hear I left home. I smile thinking of my sister, we only had each other after Gran's death and we always had fun together. I loved to snuggle in her bed at night and we'd talk about silly things and sometimes serious things, but we always had each other. Then she left, and I was alone.

She had to leave. I know that she had the chance to get out of our house and she took it. I understand why she had to do it, totally. Harvey was awful to her, much worse than with me, and she said it wouldn't be long until I could join her. She left just before Dean and I started dating and, at first, we spoke on the phone every week and wrote letters to each other. But the last few months, her letters have slowed, and it has been harder to get her on the phone. She says she is busy working, and her new boyfriend takes up a lot of her time, but she always thinks of me. I understand, she has her own life to live. Even though we're sisters, we can't live together forever. I wish we could though.

I miss her so much.

Tears sting my eyes.

I reach the small trail and hurry onto it to the pool area. It's still early so only a few people are in the pool and the snack bar is closed. The lifeguard is sitting on his tall chair at the side of the pool, his back to me. I slip on my sunglasses and duck over to the payphone, not wanting to attract any attention. I probably should have waited until it was more crowded at the pool. I'll be more careful next time.

I put the quarter in the payphone and punch in Jess's phone number. It rings three times and then she picks up.

"Hello?"

"Jess, it's me," I say into the phone.

"Hey." I can hear the smile in her voice. "I haven't talked to you in so long. How are you, little sis?"

"I know," I reply. "You never answer your phone."

She sighs. "I'm sorry. I got a new job and I'm not around as much."

"Oh, where are you working now?"

"Just a fast-food place. I still work at the grocery store too," she says hurriedly. "Ted's hours got cut at work and we needed the money. How are you, how are things at home?"

I clear my throat. "That's why I'm calling. I ran away, but I'm safe. I'm staying with my boyfriend at a summer camp. He's a counselor here."

"You ran away? Did something happen with Harvey?"

"Yes, but I'm okay. Promise me you won't tell Mom if she's looking for me. This could really work out. Dean's going to talk to his parents about me moving in with them."

"Really?" Jessica's voice fills with surprise and hopefulness. "Then you'd be out of that house too. Oh, that would be so great for you, Heather!"

"Yes, promise me, don't tell anyone."

"I promise, but send me letters and call when you can." Her voice deepens and for a moment I think she may cry. "I love you."

"I will, and I love you too," I say, holding the phone close to my face. We say goodbye and tears run down my face.

NINE

2024

Zoey

Each table of the arts and crafts room is filled with a brilliant array of different-colored sea glass, fishing lines, various pieces of wood and a few hot glue guns. I've been at camp for a little over a week and today we are making sea-glass windchimes, and the girls are excited. Actually, I am too. I always enjoyed making crafts, although I'm not good at it, but it's fun to try. I would never call myself an artistic person, but a somewhat crafty person.

It's just me today because on Wednesday afternoons, Mel helps her grandmother with whatever she needs. I guess her grandmother was diagnosed with dementia after a series of strokes she suffered and has been slowly deteriorating. Everyone helps with her, and she has a hospice nurse come in the mornings so Wednesday afternoon is Mel's time to help out. She said she usually reads books to her grandmother, and then her grandma falls asleep about half an hour in, then when she wakes, they'll have a snack and watch something on TV. Sometimes they take a walk together, if it isn't too hot outside.

I pick up a few pieces of sea glass and glue them onto various pieces of fishing line, making it easier for the girls to assemble their windchimes. My mind drifts back to Craig as usual. I often think about the dumb fight we had the night before we left for break. We were in a bar close to the college. I went to the bathroom, and when I came back, he was talking to a pretty brunette who I didn't know. Jealousy raged through me when I saw this and I don't know why. I trusted him, but I was acting so childish about it. I've had boyfriends before, but my feelings for them never compared to what I felt for Craig. I know I acted ridiculous.

Turns out he knew the girl from high school, and she was picking up her younger sister from school. I was jealous for no reason and, I admit, I overreacted. We did make up that night and left for spring break on good terms. It was as simple as that. We had an argument, and we made up. We were fine and we were together. No big deal.

At least I thought so.

Then that text arrived and that was it. He was done with me. I will never understand it. How do you break up with someone you love by text? How do you not have a conversation? Even if you don't work things out, you should at least discuss everything. I mean, we loved each other, this wasn't some casual relationship, we were a real couple. Never in a million years could I imagine him breaking up with me in a text. We talked about everything, how could we not talk about this?

A bit of hot glue lands on my finger as I get lost in my thoughts and I yelp, making the girls at the table jump too. It's a short instance of pain, but the thoughts of Craig that fill my mind still hurt.

I loved him.

I still do.

I toy with the idea of visiting his father, again, who only

lives a short distance from here. It's just him; Craig's mom died from cancer when he was in high school, and he has no siblings. I have some time off, so I may just take a drive and see where he lives, but I don't know if I'll knock on the door. I have a feeling it's going to take me a while to summon up the courage to take this trip though.

What if Craig answers? What if he's angry at seeing me there?

But he doesn't have any reason to be angry with me, although he didn't have a reason to break up with me either, at least in my opinion. If I do that, it will probably be humiliating, but why wouldn't he talk to me? That's not his personality.

It's also not his personality to break up via text, so I have no idea.

"You should mix the colors of glass, not use the same color," a male voice remarks.

"Huh." I turn to see Wynn, Mel's cousin, standing next to me. "Oh, hi. Yeah, I only did four so far."

"Want some help?" he asks, smiling at me.

"Sure," I reply, handing him another glue gun.

"Zoey, may I use these?" Christina asks politely.

"Yeah," I say, moving two of the green sea-glass pieces over to her.

"Look at this." Christina points to her windchime. "I'm doing blue, green and white in a pattern."

I smile at her. "That looks so pretty. I can't wait until we hang them up at the cabin."

Christina smiles and nods, continuing to glue her sea glass.

I glance at Wynn, who's gluing red, blue and white pieces of the glass to several pieces of fishing line.

"Are you making one for the Fourth of July?" I ask, noting his patriotic colors.

He grins. "Sure, that works."

We continue to glue in silence for a few minutes.

"So how do you like Camp Medley?" he asks, breaking the pause. His blue eyes search me. It seems all of the family has the same piercing blue eyes. He brushes away his black hair that seems to continuously fall into his eyes.

"Good so far," I say.

"Really?" He raises his eyebrows. "You like it?"

I give him a strange look. "Yes, don't you like it here?"

He laughs. "Not really, but I live here. I know all the secrets."

I laugh, awkwardly. "Oh, okay."

"Some of us are having a party tonight at the pool around midnight," he says. "You should come."

"Doesn't the pool close at eight?"

"For campers, but I can get the key for the gate. We do it all the time."

"Um... we're not supposed to leave the campers alone at night. Is Mel going?"

"Mel's always wandering around at night, don't worry about her," Wynn says in a gruff voice. "And the kids will be fine. They're sleeping."

What does he mean about Mel wandering around? I've fallen asleep by eleven the few nights I've been here so I wouldn't know if she goes out at night, or not. I've been thankful for getting a good night's sleep. My sleep patterns haven't been the best since the breakup. It's been so nice to feel rested when I woke up the last few mornings.

"Maybe," I reply.

"I hope so." His look darkens with interest.

Does he think this is a date if I go to this party? It is not a date. First, I'm not interested in dating anyone right now and, second, Wynn seems kind of... different, he's not my type. I wouldn't want to ever date him. Plus, he's seventeen. No thanks.

"If Mel goes, I'll come with her," I say stiffly.

He looks at me for a moment, flicks his head back again, then lays the glue gun down. He stands there for a few more seconds, frowning, staring at me.

And he leaves the room.

TEN
1989

Heather

I hang out in the snack bar with Dean for about an hour. He doesn't think it's a good idea for me to be out too much during the day because people will start asking questions about me. I don't want that to happen. If I'm going to spend the entire summer here, I want to keep a low profile and blend in with everything.

I munch on the second cheeseburger he made me on the grill. It's juicy and delicious, filling my ravenous hunger. My hair is almost dry after our quick swim before his shift at the snack bar started. After I'm done eating, I'll take a shower in the bathhouse. Luckily there's soap and shampoo dispensers in there because I didn't think to bring either. I stare at Dean flipping hamburgers and rotating hot dogs on the grill.

What would I do without him?

I'd be hitchhiking somewhere, anywhere, or worse yet, I'd be stuck at home with Harvey. Both possibilities are dire.

Dean grins at me from the grill. He points to the soda machine.

"Get some more if you want," he says. "Do you want another burger?"

"No, I'm good," I reply, popping the last bite into my mouth and standing up. "I'm going to take a shower and head back to the tent."

"Okay." He wipes his sweaty forehead as steam rises from the grill. He points to a plastic grocery bag from the counter. "Stop by here after your shower to take that with you."

I open it up to see a couple bags of chips, three bananas and an orange.

"I have a bag of ice for you too," he says.

"Thank you," I say, leaning up to kiss him. "Will you stay with me tonight?"

"Yeah, later after everyone is asleep," he says. "Trev knows I have a girlfriend at camp that I'm going to head out to see, but I didn't tell him any details. He thinks you're camping with your family. I'm sure I can trust him, but I think it's best if we keep it a secret that you're staying in the woods. The fewer people that know you're here, the better."

"Okay." I kiss him again. "I'm hitting the shower."

Lightning bugs dance in the darkness outside of my tent. I have the zippered opening undone and I stare at them careening around, casting their light for all to see. Jess and I used to always catch them when we were kids playing in Gran's backyard. We'd put them in a glass jar and call it our flashlight, until we'd open the lid and let them fly out. It is amazing how such a small insect can make a bright light when several come together. I think it's magical.

I miss Gran. I miss her love, her safety, and her hugs. She had always been our safe haven throughout our lives. I look up at the full moon shining so brightly tonight, streams of moonlight trickling through the trees. Gran loved summer evenings like this, a wisp of cool after a hot, humid day, clear sky full of shiny stars and elegant moonlight. I can feel her here even though I know she's in a better place. We'd sit on her back porch and just enjoy the evening usually drinking some of her home-made iced tea she made from the tea leaves in her garden.

Gran had such a strong faith in God. Not the go-to-church-every-week kind of rigid religion, although she did attend the pretty stone church down the street from her house often and took us with her when we stayed with her. But she always said that it didn't matter whether you went to church or not, because God didn't live there. He was everywhere, even in dark places nobody wants to be in, not just on Sunday morning when you dress up and sing hymns. She said in the darkest parts of your life, even if you feel ashamed or embarrassed, maybe even hope-less, God is right there with you, helping you, comforting you. She said those are the places God is most present as a strong shield to whatever is happening to you, maybe something you can't control. She knew what kind of situation Jess and I were in at home. I'm sure she said those words to help us, bring us comfort when we were alone, but I also think she believed every word.

And I believe her. I always did. She'd never lie to me.

Jess blew off Gran's religious talk, but I understood it, felt it. I still do. I feel the presence of Gran and God in my heart and mind. No, I wasn't alone. I was loved and while terrible things may happen to me, my soul, my spirit, will always be my own. I know this type of thinking may be odd for a sixteen-year-old, but I'm kind of an old soul, that's what Gran would often say. I've always been more mature for my age.

I sigh. When I got back to the tent this afternoon, I finally allowed myself to think about what happened in my bedroom with Harvey. I cried about it, but not for long because what I really need is a plan, a way out. Crying isn't going to help me at all.

I desperately hope Dean is right and I can move in with him and his parents, but what if they say no? I'd end up back in that house with my mom and Harvey. Fear snakes through me at the thought. I cannot go back to that house again.

What if I wake up and he's in my bed again, but it's even worse this time, what if it goes further? I shiver thinking about it. He can easily overpower me, and I have to sleep sometime. And I may not have a choice about it, if Dean's parents don't agree with his idea. Or maybe Mom won't agree, do I need her consent? I think for a few minutes. I could run away, farther, but how would I live? And then I'd be leaving Dean behind, the best part of my life. There's no way I can do that.

I decided something today while I walked through the woods. I can't control if I have to move back into that house or if Harvey does something gross to me, but for now I'm free and can decide who I have sex with for the first time. I want to have sex with someone I love, and I love Dean. Tonight is going to be our night.

It will be our first time and my first time, ever. Dean had sex before with his previous girlfriend, Tara, a bouncy blonde cheerleader who told me they "did the deed," her actual words, which were kind of weird, when we started dating. I guess she wanted to upset me, since he broke up with her to date me.

Dean and I came close, we've done everything over the last year except go all the way. I wasn't quite ready, but now I am. He never pressures me, it's always whatever I want to do, as it should be, and I smile thinking about how surprised and happy he'll be tonight. It will be our night.

As if on cue, I hear twigs breaking as someone walks through the woods, nearing the tent. I lie back on my sleeping bag, stretched out flat on the tent floor and press my head into the pillow. Butterflies fizzle in my stomach.

Dean pokes his head through the open tent flap. "Hey."

"Hey," I reply, rolling on my side, watching him.

He removes his sandals, leaving them outside, takes off his T-shirt, tossing it next to my backpack, and lies down next to me. He kisses me.

"How are you?" he asks. He strokes my face.

"Good." I kiss him again, staring into his eyes. I love him so much. I tug at his shorts. "Why don't you take these off too?"

He smiles and his eyes widen when I take off the T-shirt I'm wearing. I'm completely naked now.

"Oh..." he groans, staring at me.

"Take everything off," I say, putting my body against his chest. "I want to do everything tonight with you. Everything."

"Really?" he asks excitedly. "Are you sure?"

"Yes," I murmur, and his clothes are quickly discarded.

His lips kiss mine, soft and gentle, his hands holding my face and his eyes studying mine in the dim moonlight filtering inside the tent as if he wants to remember this moment for all his life.

I certainly do.

I can't think about anything but him and his hands on my body, his fingers like velvet against my skin. A cool breeze enters the tent tickling our bare skin.

"Are you sure?" he asks again. "We can stop if you want to."

"I'm sure," I whisper. "I want to be with you."

He kisses me again, deeper this time, his lips soft and firm, a slight hint of peppermint lingering as he probably brushed his teeth before coming out to see me. His tongue intermingles with mine and we melt into each other.

My heart beats quickly and I wrap my arms around him drawing him tight to me. My skin against his skin, my lips on his, our hearts beating together. The kissing deepens and his hands touch me in all the ways that are familiar, but it's different tonight, this time we'll go all the way. We touch and kiss, rolling around atop my sleeping bag, teasing and pleasing

SEVEN
2024

Zoey

The campers arrived yesterday, and we got our eight girls settled in and showed them around the grounds. Three girls had camped here previously so they were happy to share all that they know about the camp with their new friends.

This afternoon we're at the lake, the girls are splashing around in the sparkling water and Mel and I lounge on beach towels on the small, sandy beach. The sun burns hot above us and farther out on the lake, past the dock by the green house, two canoes occupied by campers bob up and down in the water.

I slide my sunglasses halfway down my nose and look at Mel, who is slathering sunscreen on her arms.

"How much of that stuff are you going to put on?" I ask.

She laughs. "Oh, I know. I burn easily so I always put it on thick."

"I should probably do the same," I remark, pushing my glasses back up. "I usually burn the first time I'm out in the sun for any length of time."

each other until the anticipation consumes us and all we want is each other. My body trembles.

"Are you okay?" he whispers to me.

"Yes," I reply, pressing my lips against his. "I'm with you."

His breath is hot against my skin, and he whispers in my ear. "I love you so much."

"I love you more," I whisper back.

He is mine.

And I am his.

Forever.

ELEVEN
2024

Zoey

"Here." Mel hands me a bag. I look down. It's my makeup bag. Hers is clutched in her other hand.

"Why do I need this?" I ask. "We're going to a pool party."

Mel frowns. "So? We still want to look good."

I laugh. "Okay, maybe a little waterproof mascara and lip gloss."

"That's the spirit," she whispers as we hurry out the cabin door to the bathhouse. The girls have been asleep for about an hour; it's after midnight now.

We scamper into the bathhouse giggling and knocking into each other. We hurry up to the mirrors over the row of sinks. Mel opens her bag, applies eyeliner, shadow and mascara.

"Wow," I remark. "You're going all out."

"Well, if that blond guy, Brett, is there I want to look good."

"You look good now," I insist.

"Thanks, but I want to look better." She laughs and applies lip gloss. "Come on, hurry up. And maybe there might be someone you're interested in too. There's a lot of cute guys here as counselors this summer, if you hadn't noticed."

I shake my head. I hadn't noticed, I wasn't even looking, but Mel is trying to help me to move on from Craig and I appreciate her efforts. I'm not ready to move on though. "I'm sure there are."

Mel looks at me. "It might be fun. You might find someone you really like and forget all about that other guy."

I shrug and open my bag, brushing off her comments. I put on a bit of mascara, a quick swipe of blush and lip gloss. "Ready."

"You're too fast." She preens in front of the mirror and smooths the right side of her hair.

I zip up my bag and stand next to her. She puts her arm around me, and we stare at our reflections.

"We're besties for the summer, right?" she asks. A bright smile covers her face.

"Besties? What, are we twelve?" I laugh.

"I know, right? Well, we are rooming with a bunch of twelve-year-olds," she replies. "But you know what I mean."

"I know, friends for sure," I say. "This is going to be a great summer."

Mel and I walk down the gravel path following the arrow on a wooden sign with *Pool* written in bright blue letters. The pool, snack bar and bathhouse are located on the far end of the boys' side of the camp, making it a bit isolated. This is the first time I've been here at night. Walking along the path with owls hooting and darkness surrounding us is somewhat eerie, and I'm glad when we top the small hill and lights from the pool area shine in the blackened night.

"There's Brett," Mel says, grabbing my arm. She pulls me

over to the side of the path and points out a cute guy with short blond hair wearing green swimming trunks and a nice six pack.

"He's hot," I say. "Oh, you two would look great together. Come on, let's not hide here, go talk to him."

A smile lights up her face. "That's what I'm going to do."

We hurry down the path now.

"I'll go get a drink," I say when we reach the pool. "You want something?"

"No, I'll get something later. I'm going over before I lose my nerve," she replies.

"Have fun," I say, wandering over to the large blue cooler sitting in front of the closed snack bar. I grab a beer from the limited selection among the ice and pop the lid. I take a sip but don't particularly enjoy it. I'm not a big fan of beer.

"You made it," a voice says.

I look behind me to see Wynn sidling up beside me. He's wearing black swim trunks and a blood-red swim shirt on his rail-thin body, even though the sun isn't out. His pale skin glistens under the night sky, almost like a vampire. He flicks his black hair back.

"I did," I reply, taking another sip of bad-tasting beer.

"Mel moved over to Brett pretty quick," he remarks.

"Yeah, I got ditched, although who can blame her?"

He laughs. "That's your type?"

I smile. "Not really. I don't know the guy."

"So you have to know a guy to go on a date with him?" Wynn is staring at me now. "We've gotten to know each other a bit. Maybe we can go out."

I meet his gaze and raise my eyebrows. "Wynn, I'm not going out with you." Although, for a seventeen-year-old, he's got some game. He certainly isn't shy.

"I'm very charming," he says, flicking his hair back again.

"Not gonna happen," I reply. "Hit on someone else."

"Well, there is a girl who works in the dining hall that I have my eye on."

"There you go," I say. "Is dining hall girl here tonight?"

He surveys the pool. "I don't think so."

I nod. "So, Mel says you'll be a senior in high school this year."

"I guess so."

"You don't seem so sure."

He shrugs. "What does it matter? I'll just end up working at this stupid camp like everyone in my family." He sighs heavily. "I don't want to be stuck here my entire life."

"What do you want to do?" I ask, although I don't really care.

"I don't know, but I don't want to be here." He frowns.

"Why do you hate it here so much?" I ask, tossing my beer into a nearby trash can, sick of its taste.

Wynn stares at me, his blue eyes in an almost penetrating glare, cold and unfriendly, although I'm not sure why. "I'm sure you'll eventually find out."

TWELVE
1989

Heather

Sprays of warm pool water fly into the air as I rise from under the water. Dean's laughing at me as the water splashes onto his face, and he pulls me close to him, his warm mouth kissing mine, slow and soft, then deeper with tongue. It feels so good, our naked bodies pressing together in the steamy pool water, our lips and hands touching each other. We can't get enough of each other.

I crave his kisses and all I want to do is be with him every single minute of every single day. I wrap my arms around his neck, and he lifts me up. I wrap my legs around him, but shiver as a cool breeze hits my skin halfway out of the water. Dean stops kissing me for a moment and moves us back down into the warm water.

"Better?" he whispers.

"Yes," I whisper.

We kiss again, his hands holding me as close to him as possible. Since the first time we had sex in the tent last week, it is all we want to do when we have the chance to be alone. I wish my time with him will never end.

I've never been in love before but can't imagine ever feeling about anyone like I feel for Dean. He fills me with light and love and excitement.

He's my everything.

His body molds into mine, his kisses branding my wet skin. We give each other the pleasure we keep finding in each other's bodies and hearts. Then my thoughts shift to what my body is feeling and that takes over everything.

Only the two of us exist now.

The night air is downright chilly in sharp contrast to the toasty pool water as we scamper up the pool steps, dry off with a towel and slip into our clothes. We're laughing now, hugging each other, trying to get warm.

"Let's sit here awhile," I suggest, perching at the edge of the pool, slipping my feet into the water.

"Okay," he agrees, joining me. He slips his arm around me.

I smile up at him. "I love you."

His eyes twinkle as he meets my gaze. "I love you more."

"I hope you don't get into trouble sneaking in here," I remark. "But it's so fun to go swimming in the middle of the night."

"I won't," he assures me. "It's late, and everyone's asleep. Nobody will notice us."

"I hope not," I reply. There's silence between us. "Did you talk to your parents yet?"

"Not yet." He grabs my hand. "But I promise I will."

"I know you will, you never let me down."

"And I never will."

A twig breaks in the woods behind us, and we turn to look. Another twig, then a scurry along the ground.

"Hello?" Dean and I both call out.

Silence.

Then another twig breaking, farther in the distance.

"Somebody's here," I whisper to Dean.

He nods. "Let's go out the other side."

We hurry to the other side of the pool, slip through the gate, Dean locking it behind us, and move to the woods. We glide through the trees leaving our flashlight off until we reach the tent, both of us breathless.

Standing outside the tent, trying to catch our breath, more scurrying and then a screech. What's making all the noise, animal or human?

"Let's get into the tent," Dean says, and we climb inside. A few minutes later all is silent again.

"Was someone watching us?" I ask as we lie down on the sleeping bag.

"I think it was just an animal, could have been a screech owl, or a raccoon."

"Maybe. I hope so," I say. Animals live in the woods; it could easily be one. But I don't feel reassured.

Dean holds my hand and squeezes. "Nothing to worry about and I'll stay here with you tonight."

"Okay," I say, snuggling into his body, trying to put the worried feeling out of my mind. We fall asleep in each other's arms.

The next day I walk in the woods alone. I don't usually see Dean much during the day because he's busy with his assigned campers. Today they are having a volleyball tournament between the different cabins, so I know he'll be busy all day.

I'm quite a distance from my tent now and see a narrow stone lane a few feet away. This must be the road Dean mentioned when I first arrived here. It's only wide enough for one vehicle. It's quiet here, only birds twittering and the warm, not quite oppressive yet, morning sun filtering through the tall maple and oak trees surrounding me. I walk on the smooth stone road, glad to avoid the uneven, sometimes rocky, untamed forest floor. I certainly don't miss the scratch of the sticker bushes that seem to pop out of nowhere when walking in the woods. It's funny how even though I never went camping or really spent much time out in nature or in the woods before coming here, I feel comfortable and at ease here, my new home.

I walk some distance, lost in my thoughts, then stop and retrieve a drink from my water thermos I keep in the small knapsack hanging on my back. I take a large gulp and look around, then place it back into my bag. I guess I won't get lost because I can always just turn around and follow the road, eventually I'll end up somewhere I recognize. I continue to walk, although now I am considering turning around because the somewhat pleasant early-morning air has thickened its heat. Sweat drips down my neck and face as I move forward on the lonely road. I look ahead and see a clearing not too far away. I'll walk to that spot, eat my orange and head back.

When I reach the clearing, there's another, much narrower path, for walking only, that winds to the right. Tight forest greenery lines each side of the path. Curious, I step onto it and travel its curve until it leads to a small, ramshackle log cabin. It almost looks like a doll house in a horror movie. Curious, I step toward it.

The cabin is a faded, worn wood structure with a small front porch and two dirt-stained windows on the front. The roof looks recently repaired with newish-looking gray shingles. A plain, but sturdy-looking brown door sits at the entrance. I hurry up the path, excitement coursing through me, up onto the rickety porch. An old, worn rocking chair sits to the right of the door and two metal shovels sit to the left.

I peer into the dirt-encrusted window next to the door, but I can't see much. There's a bed in the center of the room, neatly made with a plain white quilt and a white pillow, which seems strange to me in such a dusty little space, yet it appears fresh and crisp, not dirty at all, a couple of chairs, a small table next to the bed and a black metal cabinet against the wall, tightly closed. A large round clock hangs on the wall above the bed. What a strange little place. I turn the doorknob, but it's locked. I turn around and a feeling of dread washes over me.

I look around and study my surroundings. The trees wave in the breeze that intensifies as I stand on the porch, and a few squirrels scurry about on the ground. Why do I feel so uneasy? Is someone here? I stand completely still, listening, but I don't hear any movement. A strong breeze blows my hair back, and it contains a whistle that sounds like *"Go away"* even though nobody spoke the words. My skin pricks and I'm suddenly scared for no reason. I push the uneasy feelings aside. I'm being silly; it's just a little cabin in the woods. I look inside the window again, still wondering what the purpose of this place is.

Go away! Go away! The wind howls now and I can't ignore its call. I whirl around and watch the trees sway harder in the increasing wind. Why is it so windy all of a sudden?

Goosebumps prickle both arms and fear races through me, although I'm not sure why I'm so scared.

Go away! It feels like a message just for me.

I shouldn't have come here.

I run off the porch and down the narrow path away from the strange little house without giving a backward glance.

I won't come back here.

Go away, the wind whistles once again. I listen to its warning this time.

I run faster.

THIRTEEN

2024

Zoey

Mel and I are sitting in the dining hall with the girls. Cheeseburgers, tater tots and carrots are on the menu tonight. The burger and tots are decent, but the carrots are mushy, so I'm skipping them.

"Your cousin Wynn is a character," I remark to Mel.

"Wynn, yeah he's kind of odd, harmless though, he just likes to do his own thing," she replies, shoving a tot into her mouth. "I'm sure he asked you out already."

"He tried."

"He tries with everyone, he has a thing for older girls," she says.

I nod, take a drink of lemonade and push the mushy carrots to the side. "Why do you think your mom acted kind of weird when I mentioned my aunt? Do you think she remembered her?"

I hope that now Mel and I know each other a bit more, she may be a little more sympathetic toward me questioning her mother. I didn't mean any disrespect. I only want to get answers for my mom.

Mel nods. "Yeah, I thought about that. I don't know if she knew her, but she certainly seems to know *something* about her. Tell me more about that story. Why didn't you ever find out what happened to her? It sounds so odd to me, like she just disappeared into thin air. Did your mom ever report her missing?"

"Yes, but it was after their mother's death; she overdosed several months later. That's when my mom saw Heather's dad at the funeral. But when she asked him about picking her up at the camp, he didn't know anything about it. I guess the police didn't take her seriously though. It's a crazy story and I still have questions about everything. I only found out I had an aunt a couple of months ago."

"Wow, poor Heather. So, you said she came here to be with her boyfriend. What about him?"

"That's the thing, the last time she spoke to Heather, she and her boyfriend had argued about something, or he'd promised her something, but it wasn't happening, something like that. Heather wasn't sure what was going to happen and wanted to come live with my mom," I explain. "But Mom said she was barely surviving. Things weren't good with her boyfriend at the time, they were breaking up. She wanted to help her sister, but her life was a mess too."

Mel nods. "That had to be so hard for both of them. Did she ever contact Heather's boyfriend?"

"No, she knew his first name was Dean and that's it. She never met him. Heather only started dating him a month or so after Mom moved out and most of the time Mom stayed at her boyfriend's house. My mom doesn't talk about her childhood much, but she said their family wasn't very connected, everyone was on their own. And I guess especially after their grandmother died, everything really went crazy. She's always said her real life began at twenty-five when she met my dad."

"That's sweet."

I nod. "Yeah, it is, but she has so much guilt about Heather, but she was a kid too trying to survive. I can't imagine living like that, not having a safe place to live and never knowing what's going to happen. It's a sad story."

"Definitely."

"I'm certain my aunt is dead; I can't imagine she'd still be alive, but it would be nice to know what happened to her and put her to rest. Obviously, something happened to her, otherwise she would have gotten in contact with my mom at some point."

"Yeah, you're probably right, but we should be able to figure out what happened at camp. Who was this boyfriend? Who was the man that picked her up from camp, if there was a man?" Mel's eyes widen. "This is a real mystery I think we can solve."

"Would you help me?" If I can get Mel on board, this would be so much easier to investigate. When she nods I smile with delight. "That's amazing, thank you, Mel. Let's work on your mom some more, and maybe your aunt Sherry? They grew up here, right?"

"Yeah, we'll work on them. They must know something about Heather."

I take a bite of cheeseburger. Maybe we will finally get some answers about Aunt Heather. I feel rather excited to be focusing on something other than my breakup with Craig.

The noise in the cabin is at a low murmur as the girls either read or are on their iPad or phone. A little quiet time before dinner. I grab my water bottle and take a drink.

"Girls, we're going to take a run," Mel says. She fastens her hair up in a high ponytail. "If you need anything, go get Sarah or Mae from next door."

"Okay," the girls reply in unison.

Mel and I start on the trail behind the cabin that leads deeper into the woods, providing a gradual incline that makes us work a little harder than some of the other trails.

"I love running," she says as we move along.

"Yeah, it's fun," I agree. Although I never did much running in the past, I've liked joining Mel on her almost daily runs. It's only half an hour, and while Mel is much better than me, she tones down her pace because she says she prefers to have the company. It's become our evening routine before dinner.

"Did you think any more about what we talked about?" she asks.

I glance over at her. "What?"

She's moving faster than me, and I hurry to keep up, getting right next to her again. Her ponytail swings around as her sneakers pound the gravel trail.

"About dating someone new."

"Oh, that," I say. "Not really."

"Brett has a really cute co-counselor, Dave," she says. "I'll introduce you to him."

"Okay," I reply. I'm not interested, but it's nice that Mel cares about me. I tuck the thought away in my mind and we continue on the trail.

"Good night, girls," Mel and I say together, both of us getting into our own beds.

The girls say good night and after a few giggles and a couple of quick bathroom runs to the bathhouse, the cabin settles into a peaceful quiet. One plus of a busy day at camp is that everyone usually falls asleep quickly. A day of swimming, hiking and playing games wears anyone out, except me.

Mel snores softly above me in the top bunk, but I still toss and turn. I've been sleeping fairly decently, better than the last few months at least. But tonight, thoughts of Craig and of Aunt Heather fill my mind.

I miss Craig.

I know that I need to see him one more time just for closure. But how do I do that if he never answers my calls? I'm still mulling over dropping in at his dad's house. It'll be awkward, but I think it's something I must do.

And Aunt Heather. What were her experiences at Camp Medley? Did she sleep in a bunk bed like I am right now? Did she have friends here and why did she disappear? Who did she leave the camp with? Mom said I look so much like her younger sister and from the few pictures she has of her, it's true. Mom's eyes welled with tears when she told me this as she stared at the photos I found in the basement, and I took several pictures of them not only to ask people here at camp if they remember her, but also for me to study. I pick up my phone from the night-stand and pull those pictures up, scrolling through them. We do look similar. I can't imagine being in a situation like she was, and my mom was; they were fighting for survival and unfortu-nately, it seems Heather didn't survive.

I put my phone back on the nightstand and bury my head deeper into my pillow trying to push my thoughts away. Even-tually I drift off to sleep.

I wake up with a start.

I'm staring at the top of the bunk bed, unsure of what I'm doing for a moment or two. I think a sound woke me, but what? I lie still in my bed and then I hear it again. A scraping sound coming from outside the cabin. Dragging and scraping some-thing across the ground.

What is that?

"Mel," I whisper, getting out of bed. I climb up to her bunk, but her bed is empty.

Where is she?

Maybe she went out to use the bathroom. The scraping continues and I have to investigate. There's no way I'm going to fall back to sleep until I find the source of the noise. I do a quick check of the girls, who are all sleeping soundly, then open the cabin door and step onto the porch.

A silvery half-moon hangs high in the starry night, peeking out among the trees surrounding the dark, sleeping cabins. I look to the left side in the direction of the scraping sound. Silence now.

First, I go into the bathhouse across from the cabin to see if Mel is in there and she can go with me to check out the sound. I'd much rather have company to check out eerie sounds in the dark night. I step into the dimly lit structure and call her name.

"Mel?"

No response comes, the space is quiet save for a slow-dripping faucet.

Where the hell is she?

Then a thought occurs, and I smile. She probably met up with Brett, the two of them seem to get along well. A little late-night rendezvous. I guess I'm going to check out this noise by myself. Oh, great.

I exit the bathhouse and continue down the gravel road toward the sound. It's getting louder as I approach a tan maintenance shed, just a short distance from the nature trail we took the girls on a few days ago. The door of the shed is open. I peek into the dark structure. A shiver escapes me and a few goosebumps surface.

"Hello?"

Nothing.

I fumble along the wall, searching for a light switch, quickly finding it and flipping it on.

Nobody is inside.

The scraping sound continues, now it sounds like it's coming from behind the shed. A long drag and then a loud scrape fills the evening air. I turn the light off and turn around.

I scream.

Fear courses through me at what lies in front of me.

What is that? Who is that?

A figure is walking toward me, hunched over, long blonde hair bunched up around the face, so that I can barely see any features. It wears a long brown apron, smeared with dirt, and drags a bright red shovel along the ground. Its legs walk in an uneven, slow gait as it plods forward toward me. My stomach drops, goosebumps prickle my arms and my heart races.

The shovel is making the scraping sound as it is being dragged.

"Hello," I say, hesitant. My hands shake.

The familiar figure stops and lifts its head slowly, staring at me.

But her eyes are shut.

Then they open. Glassy, unseeing eyes staring right through me.

What is she doing?

"Mel," I say. "It's me. Zoey."

Mel turns and walks at a snail's pace behind the shed, the red shovel still scraping the ground, its disturbing sound piercing the otherwise quiet night. She mumbles something under her breath and starts stabbing the ground with her shovel.

"Mel, are you okay?" I ask. She is clearly not.

"I'm so sorry," she says in a shaky voice, still stabbing the ground. Her long blonde hair is in her face again, stringy and dirty. "No, no, no!"

She must be sleepwalking. I remember from a TV documentary about sleepwalking that it's not a good idea to touch someone while they are sleepwalking, and she is carrying that shovel! There's no way I'm touching her. I'll help her but keep my distance. How should I do this?

"Mel, it's okay," I say in a calm voice. "Let's go back to our cabin."

She drops the shovel. She stares at me, eyes still glassy and downright scary. She stands stiff and straight now. "I'm so sorry."

"Everything is fine, Mel," I say.

She bends down and picks up the shovel, then pushes past me, goes into the maintenance shed, puts the shovel inside and takes off the dirty apron, hanging it up on a hook by the door. She walks past me, it was as if she didn't see me, then she continues down the gravel road, walking in a stiff, slow gait, not as she normally walks. I stare at her, my arms a mass of goose-bumps now, my stomach churning.

I feel like I'm in a horror movie. Honestly, I'm that scared. The person in front of me is not someone I know. She doesn't seem anything like Mel at this moment.

I quickly close the shed door and follow Mel. She continues to walk stiffly, sometimes jerkily, in a direct path to our cabin. She enters, and I watch her climb up to her bed and lie down.

What the fuck?

What is going on with her?

I crawl into my bed and lie on high alert. Several minutes later I hear her breathing deeply, calm now, quietly sleeping. I roll over on my side, so many thoughts crowding my mind. Well, I guess she was asleep the entire time. I've never been around someone who was sleepwalking, and it is scary to watch. Thank goodness the girls didn't wake up. They would have been terrified.

I certainly was.

I won't be sleeping anymore tonight.

FOURTEEN

1989

Heather

I pull on my tank top and shorts, then step out of the tent, slipping on my sandals. I pick up the wrapped bacon and egg sandwich and bottle of orange juice Dean dropped off for me and walk over to the old camp chair he brought over the other night. He'd found it in the trash. It's a little wobbly and worn, but it works for me, and it beats sitting on the ground all the time.

The air is cool and fresh this morning, a nice break until the intense heat and humidity that will likely set in later on. I slowly eat my breakfast, my thoughts drifting to Dean as they always do. He'll be busy today but will come see me later tonight, probably at ten or eleven because they have some campfire activities planned. That means I have the entire day to myself. He said the camp is full, especially the family camp section, so I could hang out at the pool or the lake if I want, nobody will question me. I'm going to walk down to the camp store and buy a notebook and envelopes so I can write letters to

Jess. I'll try to call her again on the payphone too, but I haven't had much luck reaching her again. I guess she's still working a lot, and I don't bother to leave a message, I never know when I'll be at a phone. I just have to keep trying to call her. I consider calling my mom, but I don't want to. Why should I bother to let her know I'm safe? She doesn't seem to care any other time. I'm not going to waste the quarter to call her.

I had a horrible nightmare last night, and I woke up shaking and sweating. It was a dream about that strange little house in the woods and the whispers in the trees. I don't want to think about it at all but couldn't get it out of my mind. Why is there a bed in there? Who would want to sleep out there? Everything about it seems out of place and... weird. It's all so creepy. I still try to push away the intruding thoughts. I hate it when you have a dream like that, and it keeps lingering in your mind. It's so annoying.

The birds are singing this morning, calling back and forth to one another, and dew glistens off the tall ferns surrounding me. I think the ferns are so pretty; the other day I wove some together with some long skinny weeds I found, I don't know what they are exactly, but they were sturdy enough to keep the ferns together. I made a few little fern mats that I placed at the campfire to sit on. I like how they look, and it was fun making them. I take the last bite of my egg sandwich and down the orange juice. Then I stand and travel the now-worn trail through the woods to the gravel path.

I travel about ten minutes or so then pass Dean's cabin, but everything is quiet so they must be out on their adventures with the campers. I continue along saying hello to a few people I pass along the path to the camp store.

The store just opened and a guy about my age, maybe a little older, is just turning the sign hanging on the door to *Open*.

"Good morning," he greets.

"Hi," I say, entering the store.

I wander to the back and select a bright blue notebook, two pens and a small box of envelopes. I walk around the store looking at various things because I have lots of time and nowhere to go other than back to the tent. I look through T-shirts and mugs with the camp logo emblazoned on the front, different toiletries, and add a small tube of toothpaste to my basket, mine is almost gone. Then I move on to the candy section trying to decide what I want when a loud, angry voice booms inside the store.

"I told you I want the display in front of the cash register," the man's voice yells. "Not over here where nobody can see it!"

"Okay," the guy at the register mumbles.

"What?" the man demands.

"Yes, Mr. Jefferies, I'll fix it."

"You better, or you'll be looking for a new job," the man says, walking out, slamming the door behind him.

I select two Snickers bars and go up to the register with my items.

"All set?" the guy asks.

I nod as he rings up my purchases. "Who was that guy?"

He rolls his eyes. "Mr. Jefferies. He's the owner of the camp. He's a real dick." His face reddens. "Don't tell him I said that."

I shake my head. "No, I won't."

I pay my bill, thank him and take my bag, then hurry back to my campsite. I don't want to be caught by Mr. Jefferies. Like Gran would say... he sounds like trouble.

The day slips away in a sunny haze as I write a long letter to Jess in my newly purchased notebook and work on a poem or two. I like to write; I always have, and English is my best subject in school. I've written a few short stories, they're not very good, but it's fun and exciting for me. Jess used to tease me that I'm boring. Writing to her seems boring, she's more of an active person than me, but writing is never boring to me. It's the best form of expression and I love every part of it. A day spent writing in my notebook is always the best day of all. Jess doesn't understand that, but I don't mind. I don't think many people do. Unless you love writing, you won't get how exciting it is.

Today I find myself writing a love poem about Dean and how he makes me feel. It's probably not the best I've written, but I like it. I was going to head down to the lake but got so lost in my writing and daydreaming, evening crept up on me before long. My stomach rumbles, reminding me I haven't eaten anything since my breakfast this morning.

I open the cooler and grab a Pepsi; the ice I put in this morning has now melted but it's still cool enough. I have a pack of peanut butter crackers and an apple left, along with one of the candy bars I bought at the store for dessert. I'll save the other one for tomorrow.

I sit on the sagging camp chair watching the trickles of sunlight dim as the minutes pass away and evening wanders in. I take the last bite of candy bar and gulp the rest of the soda, then listen to the darkness closing in around me. The temperature was boiling today, and I welcome the slightly cool break of evening air, although it is still hot.

Sweat drips down my forehead and I wipe it, getting a whiff of body odor as I lift my arm. I look at my watch. It's almost ten and the pool is closed now. I don't want to stink like this when Dean comes over to be with me. I go into the tent and get some fresh clothes from my backpack; Dean threw my clothes in with his laundry this week. I toss them in a small knapsack, pick up my flashlight and move through the dark woods to the bathhouse.

Walking in the dark doesn't scare me, and my tread on the soft ground lends a steady rhythm as the flashlight bobs along in the inky surroundings. The tree frogs hum all around me, adding to the forest melody as I move along, and slivers of the silvery moon trickle in through the trees. The dense woods open to the narrow path to the bathhouse and pool.

I climb over the fence, walk past the pool, over to the concrete bathhouse and enter the structure, flicking on the light as I step inside. Silence envelops the space except for a dripping faucet and a flickering light bulb by the entrance. I go over to the middle shower stall, strip off my clothes, putting the dirty clothes in a plastic bag inside my bag. I hang the knapsack on the hook on the outside of the shower door. I go inside the shower, closing the door behind me.

I turn on the shower, the hot water now running rivers down my body. I reach for the shampoo dispenser and lather my hair, then soap to lather my body. I rinse my hair slowly.

A noise comes from outside the shower door.

I turn off the water, even though I'm still soapy.

"Hello?" I ask.

My voice echoes in the structure.

"Hello?" I ask again.

The water faucet continues to drip. The buzz of the dying light bulb at the entrance fills the space.

Maybe that's what I heard.

I turn the water on again and finish rinsing, this time much faster. After a few minutes, I flip off the water. I stand in the shower for a few minutes but hear nothing unusual. I shake off my fear. I'm just being silly. Just a stupid light bulb about to go out, nothing to worry about.

My hands grasp the knob and open the shower door. A stack of towels sits to the left side and a large bin to deposit dirty towels is beside it. Wearing only my flip-flops, I walk to it, grab a towel and quickly dry my body, then deposit it into the bin. Then I turn to retrieve my knapsack hanging on the hook to get my clean clothes.

No knapsack hangs on the hook.

It's gone.

Panic snakes through me. Someone was in here and they... took my clothes. Why?

I snatch another towel and wrap it around myself then hurry around the bathhouse looking for my knapsack, but don't open any stall door because I fear someone may be hiding inside. But then I stop. Maybe it's just someone playing a joke... Dean? I don't think he'd do this to me though.

"Hello?" I call in a shaky voice. "Dean, is that you?"

My call is met with silence and then the drip, drip of the leaky faucet. I gather up my courage and walk over to the couple of stall doors that are almost closed. I kick them open, one by one with my foot, careful to keep a tight grip on my towel so it doesn't fall off. Empty, nobody hiding inside either of them.

Then a wisp of movement on the other side where the showers are located.

Shit.

I tiptoe around to the other side and stare at the shower stalls, but my stomach quivers thinking about what may be lurking inside of them. No way Dean would do this to me.

Someone else is playing games.

I've got to get out of here.

I run outside now, without a flashlight because that was in my bag too. I scramble over the fence, careful to keep my towel secure, and climb over it. I give a quick backward glance to the bathhouse, hoping nobody is following me and, thankfully, nobody is there, but the light is off inside. I didn't turn off the light. That meant someone else did.

I wasn't the only one in there. Is the person inside watching me now?

I turn and run into the woods.

This time the dark does scare me.

I fly along the path, going deeper into the forest, branches brushing against my bare legs, digging into my tender flesh, and my heart pounds as I keep casting backward glances into the darkness behind me. Who was inside there with me? Why would they hide my bag?

Is someone following me now?

The towel slips and I yank it up. I continue to move as fast as I can, the cool night air whistling in my ears. Then I trip over a rock, and fall onto the dirt. Pain sears through my knee.

Branches are cracking behind me. Footsteps running.

Someone is tracking me. They're coming.

I have to get out of here.

I scramble to get up. I feel blood oozing from my knee, but I can't be bothered with that. Surprisingly, the towel still hangs on me as I try to navigate my way back to the tent, but I'm moving slower now, my knee aching. I still hear footsteps behind me, twigs cracking, or is it an animal?

I hope so. Please, let it be a squirrel or a raccoon.

The movement is gaining on me, I feel its presence gaining on me. Fear courses through me, sweat dripping down my neck and I trip again in my haste, landing on the ground with a thud.

"Hey," a voice calls out.

A cry escapes me.

He rushes toward me.

His form is shadowy until he steps into the silver strands of moonlight streaming through the dark forest. My heart catches and I gulp, my heart racing, and then I relax.

"What's happened?" Dean leans down to me, shining his flashlight, seeing my bleeding knee. He takes off his T-shirt and wraps it around it, stopping the bleeding. "You're hurt. Why are you wearing a towel?"

I tell him between sobs, and he scoops me up in his strong arms.

"You're okay now," he says in a calm voice. "But we'll have

to go back to the bathhouse, there's a first aid kit in there and we can bandage your knee."

He carries me back there and digs in his shorts pocket for his keys. He has a key to the gate since he works the snack bar on Sundays.

"Are you okay to stand?" he asks.

I nod and he places me on the ground, still clutching the now dirty towel. Concern fills his eyes, visible under the dimmed lights surrounding the pool area as he quickly jams the key into the lock and opens the door. He puts his arm around me, and we walk into the structure, silent except for the eternally dripping faucet. He flicks on the light by the door and quickly surveys the area.

"Okay, we'll be fast," he whispers to me. He walks over to the first stall. "First wash off, because you're dirty, then I'll bandage your knee."

I look down at the stained towel I wear and my dirt-caked legs and realize I do need another shower. It's okay, Dean's here now. I'll be fine.

He opens the first stall, and I throw the dirty towel in the bin, step inside and quickly wash away the grime. I turn off the shower and open the door. Dean waits there with a clean towel that he wraps around me, then leads me to the bench by the side and applies antibiotic ointment and a bandage to my knee from the first aid kit hanging on the wall.

His gaze is intense on me. "Where did you take your first shower?"

"On the other side." I point.

He takes my hand. "Let's look before we go."

"My stuff's not there," I whisper. "It's gone. Someone took it."

"Let's just take a quick look, then we'll go back to the tent," he says, taking my hand again.

We walk to the other side of the building, where the dripping faucet is located, its steady rhythm providing an eerie soundtrack as we move along. I look up to the line of open shower doors and walk to the middle one that I used earlier. I grab the door and close it.

My knapsack hangs on the hook.

Exactly as I left it.

FIFTEEN

2024

Zoey

The next morning, I stare at Mel in the mirror over the sink in the girls' bathhouse as we brush our teeth. I'm not sure what to say to her about last night. How do you tell someone they were completely out of their mind when they have no memory of it? The image of her with her hair hanging around her face and dragging that shovel keeps haunting my thoughts. So creepy. Do people remember what happens when they sleepwalk? I continue to brush my teeth thinking about it.

I have to say something.

I spit out my toothpaste and rinse my mouth, then turn to her. "Did you sleep well, Mel?"

She shoots me a confused look. "Yeah, okay, you?"

I nod. "Um, sure." Does she not remember wandering around the camp last night? How is that possible?

She smiles at me, leaning on the sink. "Brett texted me last night. It was after midnight, so I must have been asleep. I only saw it this morning."

Or walking around camp when you were asleep. I have to tell her about last night. "Mel—"

"I need help with my sneaker." Christina bursts into the bathroom. "It's in a knot and I can't loosen it."

"I'll fix it." Mel bends down and works on the knot, easily loosening it.

"Thanks, Mel," Christina says. She turns, her long dark hair bobbing in a ponytail. "Are we soon walking down for breakfast?"

"Give us a minute," I say.

Christina nods and leaves us alone in the bathroom again.

Mel pulls out a lip balm from her makeup bag and applies it to her lips, then tosses it back into the bag and zips it up.

"Come on, we're going to eat breakfast with Aunt Sherry," she says.

"We are?"

"Yes, I told her we want to talk to her about your aunt."

"And she agreed? Your mom was so weird when we asked her about it." My voice colors with surprise. "I'm glad we're going to talk to her, but surprised."

Mel scrunches her face. "Well, she agreed to breakfast. She's a loose cannon, so you never know what you'll get with her." Her voice softens. "But she's always there when you need her. I can always count on Aunt Sherry. But she's a different sort of person, she's not that friendly to outsiders."

"Sounds interesting," I remark. I guess I'm an outsider, so I won't expect a warm interaction, but I'm not here to make friends. I just want to get some answers. I decide to stay quiet on Mel's activities from last night; I don't feel like discussing it. I make a mental note to do some internet searching on sleepwalking though. If it happens again, I'll say something. I don't understand how she can have no memory of it. It baffles me.

We round up the girls and head down to the dining hall. We follow them in the line, grab our trays, place our selected foods on top and join Sherry, who sits at the table closest to the kitchen. I'm not much of a coffee drinker, but today I grab a large one. I think I'm going to need it.

"Hi, Aunt Sherry," Mel says, sitting her tray down on the table, and I follow suit.

"Hey, Mel." Sherry looks at me. Her piercing blue eyes study me. The same color eyes that everyone in the family seems to have. "Hi, Zoey, right?"

"Hi," I reply. I take a big sip of coffee. A *big* sip.

Sherry gives me a tight smile and takes a drink of her steaming cup of coffee. "Mel said you have some questions."

I nod, noting Sherry's avoidance of eye contact and forced smile. I need to play this right. I give her a warm smile. "Thanks for having breakfast with us today, Sherry. I do have some questions and I hope you can help me. My aunt Heather stayed here in nineteen eighty-nine and went missing. This is the last place she was, at least that my mom knew of. I'm trying to find out what happened to her. What she did when she was here, when she left, that sort of thing."

Sherry nods. "Jennifer told me. Yeah, I remember Heather. She hung out here for a little bit. I guess she ran away from home?"

"Right, that's what my mom told me," I reply. I smile at her, trying to gain her sympathy. "I only found out that I have an aunt just a few months ago. My mom never told me about her, losing her was so devastating."

Sherry looks down. "I'm sure it was. It's hard when you lose family."

I nod. "Yes, and that's why I'm here, to get some answers for my mom, you know, to give her closure. So, anything you can tell me is so appreciated."

Sherry presses her lips together. "Well, she wasn't here long. I think her dad might have picked her up," Sherry says, matter-of-factly. She takes a bite of scrambled egg and stares ahead, avoiding my gaze.

"Yeah, that's what we were told, but he never did," I say, twirling my napkin. "My mom went to the police after she found out he hadn't picked her up, but she wasn't taken seriously and she still doesn't know what happened to her sister."

Sherry shrugs, her mouth set in a firm line. Deep lines etched into her face, likely from years of sun damage, my guess by the looks of her deeply tanned face.

"I dunno, maybe she had an older boyfriend."

I shake my head. "No, her boyfriend was a counselor at the camp. His name was Dean."

"I remember him, but they broke up and then she called that guy to pick her up, whoever he was, maybe another boyfriend?" Sherry states. "Like I said, she wasn't here long."

"How long was she here?" Mel asks.

"Um, maybe a couple of weeks, something like that." Sherry takes another drink of coffee. "That's all I know, and Jennifer doesn't know anything else either. Sorry about your aunt, but she wasn't here long and then she left. I don't know any more than that."

"But you knew her while she was here. What did you do together? What was her boyfriend like? Did she seem happy with him? Do you remember anything about the man who picked her up? Who told my mom it was Heather's father?" I rattle off a string of questions.

Sherry lets out a sigh and a look flashes in her eyes. Irritation, anger, worry? I'm not exactly sure, but something.

"Oh, I don't know. We hung out at the lake a couple of times. She seemed happy with her boyfriend, but they broke up, so I guess not that happy in the end. I don't know about the man. I guess he told my mom he was Heather's father. Like I said, she was only here for a couple of weeks. Jennifer and I barely knew her."

I nod, staring at Mel. I'm guessing Sherry is done talking about it but I feel an overwhelming certainty that there's more to the story than she's telling us. My hunch is confirmed when Sherry suddenly stands and grabs her tray, most of her food untouched.

"Okay, girls, I have some things to do," she says and walks back into the kitchen.

I look at Mel, who raises her eyebrows. "What do you think?"

She shrugs. "I'm not sure. Aunt Sherry seemed bothered by your questions, just like Mom."

"Yeah, I don't think Sherry's told us everything." I go over the conversation in my mind. I know she has more information about Aunt Heather and what happened to her, but she's not sharing. Why?

"But why?" Mel asks. "If Heather was here, and they knew her, remembered her, why not tell you everything they remember? Oh, and Mom said she didn't know who Heather was, but Aunt Sherry did? That's weird."

"Exactly. That's what we have to find out," I say. "Aunt Heather was here, we know that much, and there must be more than what they're telling us. Who else would know anything about Heather?"

"Maybe Grandma," Mel offers. "But she doesn't remember much of anything now, with her dementia."

"Right. Let's think more on it. Maybe we'll come up with something."

"Of course we will. We have a mystery to solve!" Mel laughs.

"We're on the case!" I giggle.

Mel takes a sip of orange juice and looks at me thoughtfully. "You know, I might have an idea. A place that might have some clues..."

. . .

The basement is a mess of boxes, old furniture and general junk. Mel and I step off the stairs and she flips on the light. Boxes line storage shelves on two walls and stacks of them are also beside the shelves on the floor. An old paisley-print brown sofa sits by an antique-looking floor lamp, more boxes stacked on one side of it. Yes, a lot of junk.

"I'm surprised your mom didn't mind us looking through this stuff," I remark, walking around the boxes, looking at the dates marked on them. "She acted so odd when we asked her about my aunt."

"Yeah, and that's why we're down here. I didn't ask her," she says. "Why would I? It's my house too. I can poke around the basement if I want to."

"True," I agree. I slowly maneuver my way through the maze of boxes off to the side. There's a lot to sort through. This is going to take forever, although at least they are marked. We have about an hour to search while our campers are with Cabin Eleven at the pool.

"They're labeled by year. We just need to find nineteen eighty-nine and see if anything relating to Heather is inside," Mel explains. "I'm glad we're doing this today. It's a good distraction."

I look at her. "Why do you need a distraction?"

Mel frowns. "I think something's going on with my parents."

"Like what?"

"I think they might be getting a divorce," she says, and sadness colors her voice. "I don't know if it's that surprising, but... I don't want it to happen."

"No, I guess not. Why isn't it a surprise? Do your parents fight a lot?"

She shakes her head. "No, hardly ever, but I always had the feeling something was wrong with them. You know? Like they aren't right together. Things have gotten worse the last couple of years. They barely talk. Dad keeps busy with his projects, and Mom does her own thing. I've really noticed their distance since I've been home for the summer. And I'm not even living in the house now."

"That's too bad. I'm sorry to hear that, Mel," I say kindly.

"What about your parents?" Mel asks. "Do they seem happy?"

I smile. "They do. They're always kissing and hugging. It's kind of sickening sometimes, but sweet. They just really like each other. They have the kind of relationship I want."

The one I thought I had with Craig.

Mel laughs. "That's definitely not my parents. My dad's really distant. He's a great dad, but he's not affectionate like that with Mom. I always thought Mom was more in love than he was. They never really seem like a couple. But, I mean, who ever thinks of their parents as a couple? I don't know, they just seem so separate, they always seem that way. And they never talk about themselves, I barely know how they met. I asked my mom once and she said a party, that was it, no big story like most people have. Like they take care of the camp and take care of me, but that's it. It's more like, I don't know... teammates."

"Teammates?" I repeat. "Well, maybe therapy will help and they can get past whatever they're dealing with now. And even if they get divorced, it might not be that bad. They might find someone who makes them happy. It's probably kind of lonely for both of them if they are so distant with each other. My friend Carrie, from college, went through this recently. Her parents got divorced after being married twenty-five years. It was rough in the beginning, but now she says both of them are so much happier."

"Maybe," Mel sighs. "Who knows what will happen. And I don't even know if they're getting a divorce. It's just they've had a lot of appointments lately and both of them go, which is odd to me. What else would they be going to together, other than maybe marriage counseling? They've never gone to each other's doctors' appointments or anything, and what else could it be?"

I shrug. "I don't know."

"It just bothers me because I know something is going on, something they don't want to tell me about." Mel frowns. "But I guess we all have secrets."

I glance at her, wondering about her serious tone. I wonder what secrets Mel is keeping.

"I hope everything works out, well like you said, we have a distraction today," I reply. "Let's get started."

I walk over to a large shelving unit at the right side under a small basement window. Numerous boxes line the shelves, 1979, 1980, 1981 and so on, but no 1989. Then I spy a box sitting on the floor next to the shelf.

1989.

A rush of excitement races through me. This might hold the answers I've been looking for! I bend down, sit on the floor and open the box.

"Over here, Mel," I say. "I found something."

Mel hurries over from the other side of the room. "Ooh... let's see what's inside."

We open the large cardboard box, and a cloud of dust tickles our noses, causing both of us to sneeze several times.

"There's a lot of dust down here." I laugh.

"I know, it's a mess," she agrees.

We pull a stack of yellowing papers, and a green book, which appears like a yearbook of sorts, with *Camp Medley 1989* stamped in gold letters on the front.

"Oh, maybe Heather will be in here," Mel says, pulling out the book.

I frown. "I doubt it. She wasn't a registered camper here, so she wouldn't be in the yearbook."

"Yeah, but she might be in some of the candid shots. You know, like at the pool or the lake."

"Oh, yeah, maybe," I say.

She hands the book to me. "You look through this and I'll check out the rest of the box."

"Okay," I agree.

I page through the book's faded pages, bypassing the photos of each cabin and focusing on the random photographs, like Mel mentioned. I instantly recognize Jennifer and Sherry, with their long blonde hair and bright blue eyes, so similar to Mel's. They're in most of the photographs. There's probably nothing here. She was hiding out at the camp; I doubt she'd have wanted to draw attention to herself.

"Anything?" Mel asks, still sorting through the box. More dust swirls around her in the air.

"Nope," I say. "Nothing."

"What about this?" Mel puts on a dark green baseball hat with the camp logo on it.

"Lovely." I laugh, still flicking through the pages.

Something catches my eye.

I look closer at the photo that draws me in. Three girls in bikinis, one wearing a white one with little rosebuds. Exactly like the one Mom bought me when I was a teenager. I remember it because she was so thrilled to find it while we were shopping, and while it was cute, I didn't understand why she was so excited about it.

Aunt Heather is the girl in the center of the photo. Her hair is long, dark and wavy, like mine, and her warm brown eyes stare into the camera, a wide smile on her face. She looks happy and carefree, even though she faced a mountain of struggles. I take a picture of the image with my phone.

"Look at this, Mel," I say, and we study the photo together. "Do you care if I rip this page out?"

"Rip away," she says. And I do. I place it on top of the year-book, and we continue to stare at it.

Jennifer and Sherry stand on either side of Aunt Heather in

the picture. The three girls have their arms around one another, appearing as if they were close friends enjoying a sunny day at the lake. The sisters also wear bright smiles, but I wonder about them. They were obviously friends with Heather, not just acquaintances. Do they know more about what happened to her, and if so, why not share it with me?

Later that night we gather around a blazing bonfire with all the cabins participating in s'more making and sharing ghost stories, most silly stories, so we spend a fair time laughing too. Telling spooky stories around a campfire is one of my favorite activities at camp.

Tim, a long-time counselor for the older boys, begins his story and a hush falls over the group. He's an excellent story-teller and I love the voices he makes when telling them. He has all the campers' rapt attention.

"Long ago, Camp Medley was the home of The Man in the Woods," he says in a deep, sinister voice. "Young women were going missing at the camp. They were campers just like you, taking hikes, going swimming and sitting around campfires exactly like this..." He pauses for dramatic effect. "And then one day... they disappeared."

"Ooh," a few campers shriek. A couple of girls put their hands over their ears.

"Legend has it a serial killer roamed the woods of Camp Medley. The Man in the Woods lurks among the trees of the camp, surveying his prey until one becomes the fruit he wants to pick, then he extends his long sinewy arm to pluck that chosen one from the crowd, taking her deep into the forest. Not the forest we know, but his own hidden forest. They are never seen again. Once The Man in the Woods has you there's no escape."

"No!" a few girls cry out, scared.

"I thought he had a hook," one boy calls out. "He hooks his victims in the woods with his weird hook hand."

Tim laughs. "That's one variation of the story. It is an urban legend, so sometimes it changes when different people tell the story, but this is the *true* story."

I look over at our girls, sitting so still and giving Tim their complete attention. A few look terrified. Tim is a gifted story-teller. His gaze sweeps the crowd, then his eyebrows rise, then furrow.

Tim continues in his creepy voice. "You don't have to worry about it now. It's been years since these girls disappeared, but sometimes if you really listen you can hear their whispers in the woods, calling for help. Sometimes their voices are just whispers in the wind, but they will call out to you."

I think of Aunt Heather. Could she have been one of the teenage girls taken by The Man in the Woods? I brush the thought aside, this is just a scary ghost story to entertain the campers, none of it is true. I'm just getting too caught up in Tim's excellent storytelling.

"I've heard those whispers!" one girl exclaims. "I heard them when I was walking through the woods by myself to the pool. It was so creepy!"

"Me too!" another girl confirms. "I thought it was just the wind, but it didn't sound like wind."

Tim smiles and nods. "Yes, we've all heard those whispers here at Camp Medley. It is a bit creepy, but now you know the story behind the whispers, even though it's only for fun. You always have to have a spooky ghost story at camp!"

"What about The Man in the Woods?" a boy asks. "Did they catch him?"

Tim shakes his head. "No, they never found him. Some say he's still lurking in these woods, looking for his next victim... but I don't know, this all happened so many years ago... Me, I think it's the ghost of The Man in the Woods—"

"Stop! Stop!" a shaky voice garbles, interrupting him.

Tim stops talking. An old woman with short gray hair, wearing a long, dark cardigan, rises from a camp chair at the far right of the bonfire. "Don't talk about him anymore. Nobody should ever talk about him! He won't hurt anyone again! He's a monster! A monster!"

"Mom." Jennifer puts her arms around the old woman. "Calm down, Tim's just telling a ghost story."

"I don't know why!" the elderly woman bellows. "Why talk about someone so evil! Evil isn't here anymore! Stop talking about him!"

"That's my grandma," Mel whispers to me. "She was having a really good day and Mom thought she'd enjoy the campfire tonight; it was always one of her favorite camp activities."

"Oh..."

"I guess it wasn't a good idea," Mel says.

"Okay, Mrs. Jefferies, I'm done telling ghost stories. Let's roast some marshmallows," Tim says brightly, trying to smooth things over.

Mrs. Jefferies is still mumbling to herself as Jennifer walks her to the nearby golf cart. A few minutes later, they drive off.

Well, that was weird. Mrs. Jefferies was so disturbed by Tim's story about The Man in the Woods, oddly so in my opinion, but dementia plays cruel tricks in a person's mind, at least from what I understand about the disease. I place a marshmallow on my stick and poke it into the flames, watching it quickly brown and become gooey. I snatch it back and let it cool for a minute.

I replay Mrs. Jefferies's words in my mind. Her words about The Man in the Woods were so odd and seemed strangely... personal. Was this shadowy character more than some made-up ghost story to scare campers?

Is The Man in the Woods real?

SIXTEEN
1989

Heather

I didn't sleep much last night even though Dean stayed with me all night. Everything about last night just freaked me out. Somebody took my bag and then put it back, why? Just to mess around with me? Who would do that? Dean thinks someone was playing a practical joke, but I don't think it was funny and neither did he. I know one thing for sure, I'm never going to the bathhouse by myself at night. I'll only go if Dean's with me. And last week, when we were in the pool, we were certain someone was watching us. Someone is creeping around these woods; even if it's someone just playing tricks, it's not funny.

He left early this morning. He and Trevor are taking the campers out earlier than usual for a long hike. He stopped by about half an hour ago with a Styrofoam container filled with scrambled eggs, sausage, hash brown and toast plus a plastic bag with assorted packs of crackers, oranges, apples, a couple bananas, three individual cartons of orange juice and another bag of ice. He's the best boyfriend ever. Meeting him was the best thing that ever happened to me.

I eat every bite of the breakfast inside the container and drink one of the orange juices. My stomach filled, the warm sun filtering through the trees, and the lack of sleep from last night makes me so sleepy. I crawl back into the tent and lie down. I drift off immediately.

I wake up well rested. I sit up, stretch my arms, and glance at my watch. Wow, it's three thirty. I can't believe I slept almost six hours. I guess I was tired after last night. A scuffling outside my tent distracts me and I freeze.

Someone's here.

The lid of my cooler just outside the tent opens and then squeaks shut. I only closed the zipper halfway, so I soundlessly move toward it and peek outside.

Dean stands by the cooler.

"Hey," I say, scrambling out of the tent.

"Oh, you're awake." Dean smiles, making my heart flutter.

"How long have you been here?"

"About half an hour," he says. "I'm off duty tonight, so I'm all yours."

"I thought you already were," I tease. I wrap my arms around his neck and kiss him.

His smile widens. "You know I am."

We kiss and Dean envelops me in his arms.

"What did you do today?" he asks, pulling away from me slightly.

I laugh. "I slept for about six hours."

He laughs. "You really were tired. I have an idea. Let's go out on a date. Want to go get a pizza?"

"Oh yes, pizza sounds good."

"Pepperoni?"

"Yes, I'm going to brush my hair, then we can go."

I duck back into the tent, pulling my brush from the backpack, give my hair a few swipes and secure it in a ponytail holder. I walk back out to Dean and grab his hand.

"Let's go," I say.

The thick-pan pizza, heavy with greasy pepperoni, tastes so good and I savor each bite. I also appreciate the arctic air conditioning inside the restaurant. A nice break from the heat of my tent.

"I was starving for some good pizza," Dean says, picking up his third slice. "That crap in the dining hall is not real pizza."

I laugh. "This is really good."

We eat in silence for a few minutes. I want to ask him if he talked to his parents yet, but I don't want to pester him. I know he understands my dire need to know if I can move in with them, but he just doesn't seem to be moving very fast.

Dean takes a drink, staring at me. "Why are you so quiet?"

"Did you ask your parents yet?" I ask, my eyes steady on him.

He shakes his head. "No, they're in Colorado for two weeks visiting my uncle. I'll ask them when they come back." He pauses. "I want to make sure it's the right time, I want them to say yes."

I nod. "So do I."

They have to say yes. My mind spins as I think of the possibilities if they don't. Panic rises in me when I think of having to move back home with Mom and Harvey. No, Dean's parents have to say yes. I say a little silent prayer for this outcome. I can't go back to that house, especially if Jess isn't there. I can't do it. Dean's parents will say yes, I'm sure. They're very nice people and they like me.

What will I do if they don't?

SEVENTEEN

1989

Heather

We're back at the tent after eleven. We went out for ice cream after pizza and then went to a movie. It was such a fun night out together. And now we sit outside under the stars, the tree frogs croaking and chirping cicadas encompassing us in their noisy production. We spread out the blanket on the ground and lie on top of it since it is cooler out here than inside the tent. Dean leans over and kisses me. I kiss him back.

Girlish giggling interrupts the nature sounds and our kissing. I look at Dean.

"Someone's here," I whisper to him. We both sit up.

"Yeah," he whispers back.

Footsteps race through the dark woods, followed closely by more giggling, then a shriek. Somebody stumbles and crashes to the ground. Another shriek. More footsteps then two girls emerge from the trees.

"Sherry," one girl yells. "Look at this! A tent!"

"Ooh..." another girl howls with laughter.

Dean and I stare at them, stumbling into our campsite, then he directs his flashlight at their faces.

"Oh, oh," the shorter blonde girl squeals. "It's the cops!"

"It's not the cops, Jennifer," the other blonde girl says.

"Hey, will you two stop yelling?" Dean asks. He turns the flashlight on himself. "It's me, Dean."

The two girls start laughing again, then walk closer to us and plop down on the ground next to us.

"Dean!" Jennifer exclaims. She gives him a big smile. "From Cabin Eight. Why are you out here?"

"It's my night off," he says.

"Who's this?" Sherry asks, looking at me. She moves closer to me; her breath smells strongly of alcohol as she talks. "Who are you?"

Whoa. They are clearly high, as well as drunk. The smell of weed hangs in the air around them. It makes me think of my mom, and I try to hide an involuntary shudder.

"I'm Heather," I say, shooting Dean a look. Who are these girls? And can I trust them to keep it quiet that I'm camping here? They probably won't remember anything about tonight anyway.

Shit.

My mind scrambles. We'll have to move the tent somewhere else. Yes, we'll do that, and hopefully they won't even remember me, they're so out of it. Dean can walk them back to their cabin and they'll go to sleep. They must be counselors too.

"Heather!" Sherry yells my name.

"Heather!" Jennifer chimes in too.

"Um, you two are messed up," Dean says, meeting my look. "Let's walk back to your house and call it a night."

Jennifer plucks a fern from the ground next to her and puts it on top of her head, then starts crying. "Noooo... you won't tell our dad, will you? He will be so... mad."

Sherry lets out a wail. "Please don't tell him."

"I don't want to go home!" Jennifer yells. "Dean, don't make us go home!"

Who are these girls?

"We won't tell your dad," I say. "If you don't tell anyone about the tent out here. And please stop yelling. You're being really loud."

Both girls nod vigorously. "We won't tell."

"Who's your dad?" I ask.

"The camp owner, Mr. Jefferies," Dean answers.

Oh fuck.

Of course he is.

My mind flashes back to when I was in the camp store and the angry man who yelled at the cashier. That was their dad. I'm sure he would be mad if he caught his daughters out getting drunk and high, and if he finds out about me. He didn't seem like a patient man. Can I trust these girls to keep my secret? I have no idea, but I guess I don't have a choice.

"Our dad is so mean, he's so, so, mean!" Sherry says slowly. "Especially to me. Jennifer is his favorite."

Jennifer shakes her head. "He's mean to me too. He doesn't have any favorites."

"No, he's meaner to me," Sherry insists. "You know it."

Jennifer nods sadly. "Yeah. But I'm still not his favorite."

"I don't want to go back. Let's sleep here tonight," Sherry says. She walks over to the blanket Dean and I are sitting on and lies down.

"We can't." Jennifer jumps up. "But I want to dance now."

Sherry jumps off the blanket and the girls dance around, singing to themselves.

"Let them hang out for a while, then I will go with them back to their house," Dean whispers to me.

"Do you think they'll tell their parents about me?"

He shakes his head. "I don't think so."

. . .

They come back the next night, just after dusk while I sit alone at my small campfire. I didn't expect Dean until after ten.

Sherry emerges first from the dense forest surrounding my campsite. Dean said she's the leader of the two, the bolder sister. Jennifer follows along, sometimes, but likes to do her own thing too.

"Hi, Heather." She hands me a Styrofoam container. "I brought you some spaghetti and garlic bread. It should still be warm."

Jennifer is close behind her sister, carrying a brown paper bag. "And there's salad in here from dinner and a bag of cut-up carrots. We were cutting them for lunch tomorrow. Oh, and a fork and spoon. There's a container of chocolate pudding too."

"Thanks a lot." I take the items and open the containers. The spaghetti is still warm and smells heavenly. The salad is green and crisp with a few cherry tomatoes, shredded carrots and cheese sprinkled on top. All I've had today was some toast this morning and two bananas. My stomach rumbles. I pull the fork from the bag and dig into the spaghetti, taking a big bite. "Oh, this is good."

"Hey, sorry about last night," Jennifer says, sitting next to me. "I know we were acting crazy. Dean told us what's going on with you and we promise we won't tell anyone you're here. Stay as long as you want."

I nod. "Thanks, I really appreciate it."

A flood of relief runs through me. I'd been worrying about this all day.

I told Dean he could tell them everything about Harvey, my mom and my sister. I don't have anything to hide, and I want their sympathy so I can keep hiding out here. Looks like my plan worked like I need it to.

I don't have anywhere else to go. I have to make this work.

"Yeah, we usually have dining-hall duty for dinner, so we can bring you food," Jennifer says.

"Thanks, that's great."

Sherry walks over and retrieves a few pieces of wood and adds them to the campfire. "It's not right what happened to you. Not right at all."

An uneasy silence fills the air as Sherry stares into the slow-burning fire.

"Uh, yeah," I say. "Well, we will keep all our secrets right here."

"That's right," Jennifer says. After a pause she asks, "Does Dean stay with you every night?"

"Most nights, but not every night. He'll be out later tonight."

"Dean's a nice guy," Sherry remarks.

"And a really cute guy." Jennifer smiles at me. "How long have you been dating?"

I return her smile. "About seven months. We go on the same bus to school, that's how we met. He's a year ahead of me."

"Is he sixteen or seventeen?" Sherry asks. "I'm seventeen."

"Seventeen." I wonder why all the questions about Dean.

"So, you're sixteen, like me," Jennifer says.

"I am," I reply. I don't understand their interest.

"Well, we should go, we just wanted to drop off the food and tell you your secret is safe with us," Jennifer says, brushing a lock of blonde hair out of her eyes.

Both sisters have long blonde hair and piercing blue eyes. They're both pretty, but Jennifer appears softer and a bit prettier than Sherry, who seems to have a harder edge to her personality. I like her, she's been nothing but friendly to me, but there's a toughness to her that's missing from Jennifer.

"And you promise not to mention we were high last night to anyone, right?" Sherry asks. "If our dad found out, he'd kill us."

"Yeah, we'd be in big trouble," Jennifer chimes in.

"I promise. The only person I talk to is Dean and he won't say anything."

Sherry nods. "No, he won't. He knows what a dick our dad is."

"Thanks, Heather," Jennifer says, grabbing her sister's hand. "We'll come visit you tomorrow."

"Bye." I wave to them as they disappear into the thick woods.

I have some new friends. I smile thinking about their visit. Maybe things will work out here for me.

EIGHTEEN

2024

Zoey

The sparkling blue pool water is a welcome reprieve from the ninety plus degree heat of the afternoon. Even though I'm enjoying it I'm tired of the kids' constant cannonballs into the water and their happy squeals. I'm glad they're having fun, but I'd like a few moments of quiet.

I swim over to Mel, who's lying on a hot pink raft. She lowers her sunglasses as I approach.

"Hey, do you mind if I take a walk?" I ask. "Need a little quiet time."

"Sure, we'll be here until dinner time. The girls are having fun, and I'll work on my tan."

I laugh. "Thanks, I'll be back in a little bit."

"Take your time," Mel replies. She pushes her sunglasses back up.

I get out of the pool, dry off with my towel and pull on my shorts and tank top. I walk past the bathhouse and start to head toward the stone path that we normally take to the pool but notice a narrow path to the side of the pool area and decide to check it out.

The tall trees in the woods around me provide shade from the heat of the day and I move along the path at a leisurely pace, peacefully drinking in the quiet. Craig's been on my mind lately, as usual. I wish I could move on, but everything feels so unfinished between us. I feel as if every emotion possible has traveled through me. Shock, disbelief, anger, sadness, and confusion. I do want to move on, and I have as best as I can, but what we had was real and the Craig I know wouldn't end it in a text. I know he wouldn't.

And why hasn't anyone heard from him? Other than texting. I spoke to his friend Marc before leaving college to come home for the summer, and he had called and texted Craig several times. He received one text from him saying he was going away for a while, traveling. He thought it was odd too, not at all like Craig, who was normally so social.

I agree with Marc, everything about it is so strange and not like Craig. I realize we all have different sides to ourselves, but I can't shake the feeling that something is off about the whole situation. Do we ever truly know a person? I could not have imagined him ever ghosting me like this, as if I don't matter at all. It's just not him.

A text beeps on my phone and I look at it and smile. Mandy, my roommate at college and dear friend. A selfie of her smiling with the ocean behind her. The text reads

Wish you were here!

Her family rented a beach house for the month in North Carolina and I'm glad she's having a great time. I leaned on her so much this year with all that went on with Craig. I don't know what I would have done without her support. I take a selfie of myself in the woods, type a quick reply and hit send.

I continue down the leafy path, past various growths of delicate green ferns lining the path and over an old wooden bridge that provides a walkway over a small babbling creek. I take a deep breath and feel a calmness spread throughout my body. I stand there for several minutes, drinking in its beauty, various thoughts swirling in my mind.

My thoughts settle as I walk on and then they wander to Aunt Heather. I really want to find answers here for Mom and me. Those pictures Mel and I found in her basement linger in my mind. Jennifer and Sherry must know more about her than what they're telling me, which is basically nothing.

What are they hiding?

My pace increases and I see a clearing ahead. I've never walked in this part of the forest and I'm curious. I'm glad I wore my sturdy sandals today rather than my flimsy flip-flops. The forest floor contains quite a few rocks, and I certainly don't need to twist my ankle on an afternoon walk.

I reach the clearing, a wider stone path, more of a road as it could accommodate a vehicle, and I move along it, the line of trees on either side shading my path. I wonder where this leads, maybe another entrance to the camp?

Did my aunt walk this same path? Maybe with her boyfriend or Sherry and Jennifer? How serious was her relationship with her boyfriend? And why was this boyfriend never located? It seems as if he just disappeared too, and like nobody knows anything about him. I had questions about her, and now I have so many more. Maybe Mel and I should poke around more in Mel's basement, but we did go through several boxes and that one photo was the only clue to my aunt. I wonder if the camp has any other storage areas we could check out.

Along the narrow road a small footpath breaks off to the right with dense foliage on either side. I turn and follow it and shortly I come upon an old, dilapidated log cabin. It is a small structure with a sagging, rotted porch that I don't trust to step onto. Its windows are crusted with dirt, and the roof sags on the left side, looking like it might cave in at any moment. I walk over to it, trying to peer into one of the side windows because there's no way I'm walking onto that porch.

There's so much crusty dirt on the window I can't see much. I chip away a small portion of the gunk and peer inside, but it looks like the cabin is empty. I rub my dirty hands on my shorts, regretting picking away at the dirt now as I look at my chipped nails. A strong breeze ripples through my hair, and I welcome its brief coolness. I turn away from the cabin and walk behind it, still wiping my dirty hands on my shorts. I may have to take another dip in the pool before returning to the cabin.

Now the breeze intensifies, ruffling the tree leaves, creating a whistling of sorts. I remember Tim's story at the campfire... *But you don't have to worry about it now. It's been years since these teenage girls disappeared, but sometimes if you really listen you can hear their whispers in the woods, calling for help. Sometimes their voices are just whispers in the wind, but they will call out to you...*

Apprehension fills me as the whistle seems to form a voice of sorts. *Go away*, the voice says. Goosebumps form on my arms and a sick dread fills my body. Are those the whispers Tim was talking about? Could his story have been real?

Go away.

I know it's only my imagination and interpretation of a simple breeze whistling through the trees, but my heart rate increases and panic courses through me and my body's response surprises me. Why am I feeling this way? I stand still looking around the back of the cabin, the cool breeze beating on me now, not in a pleasant way. Why is the air so cool here? A twig snaps behind me, and I whirl around, but see nothing.

Go away.

I hug my arms, now shivering, but I don't know why. How can I be shivering in this hot afternoon? But it's not hot here, it's so cold. I look up to the trees, now swaying in the wind, which intensifies, and nothing feels real around me anymore. That whistling pounds at my ears.

Go away.

Go away.

Goosebumps prick my arms. I don't want to be here anymore.

Quickly, I walk away.

NINETEEN
2024

Zoey

I walk down the feminine hygiene aisle of the grocery store, select a pink box of tampons and stroll up to the cashier, an older woman, probably in her sixties, with long gray hair pulled back in a messy bun and a deep scowl on her weather-lined face. She rings up my purchase, and then stares at my green camp T-shirt.

"Camp Medley, huh?" she asks. "You work there?"

"Yeah, I'm a camp counselor," I reply, digging out my debit card.

"Hmmm... how do you like it?" the woman asks.

I stare at her name tag, perched on the right side of her navy-blue polo shirt. Pearl.

I nod. "Sure, I like it."

Pearl nods. "I used to work there. A long time ago."

"Oh, yeah? What did you do there?"

"Worked in the dining hall. There's something wrong with those people though."

I look at her. "What people?"

to a breakup text only two months later? We were everything to each other; this wasn't just a casual romance; it was serious for both of us. I need closure and the only way to get that is to see him in person. I'm going to go see him next Sunday, or at least go to his house. Even if I can only speak to his father, hopefully he'll understand and have Craig contact me so we can at least talk.

It's the least he can do.

I deserve closure. I can't move on until I receive it.

I close my eyes, drifting off to sleep now that I've made my decision.

TWENTY
2024

Zoey

A scream pierces through my dreamy state, and I start, my body shaking from the unsettling sound. I still my body, my heart racing now, and listen for another, but none comes. I climb out of bed and check the girls, all still sleeping; it's amazing they never wake up until morning. We are lucky to have heavy sleepers. I wish I was so lucky, but no, I wake up at every single sound. I slip my feet into my flip-flops by the bed and glance at the top bunk. Mel's gone.

Again.

Not this again! I don't want to deal with any of this. While it's possible I'm imagining the whispers and don't know why old lady Pearl was staring at me, one thing's for sure, I'm not imagining Mel's freaky sleepwalking episodes. But that doesn't mean I want to wander out in the middle of the night to chase her again. I want to roll over and go back to sleep, which is probably what I should do.

But I can't. She may need my help.

I guess I shouldn't be surprised. A person doesn't sleepwalk one night and that's it; I think it's a chronic condition usually brought on by stressful factors. I don't want to deal with it, but I know I have to. I grimace and hurry quietly out the cabin door. I don't bother to check the bathhouse but go straight to the shed where I saw her before, dragging the shovel. But when I arrive, everything is closed and undisturbed. The darkness shrouds me, and the air holds an eerie quietness as if it's anticipating something soon.

She's not here.

Another scream erupts, cutting into the silence surrounding me, although this one is more muffled, less piercing than the first one. Is she being hurt? Maybe she fell while sleepwalking; that could easily happen here. I hurry in the direction of the scream.

What is Mel up to now? I still don't understand why nobody else wakes up and is looking around for the cause of the scream. Or maybe they heard it, but don't want to investigate? I keep walking at a fast pace in the direction of the last scream. I won't run though. I don't need to hurt myself while I track her down. I turn onto the trail.

Into the woods.

I stop a few steps into the trail, hesitating. I don't want to walk into the dark woods alone. Yes, I'm worried Mel may hurt herself while sleepwalking, but I could just as easily hurt myself by chasing her around in the dark. I should go back to the cabin. Mel must have been sleepwalking before the other night, and she must always make it back to her bed safely. Why am I the only one who chases her around at night? I don't understand how nobody else wakes up. Yes, I know I keep having this thought, it doesn't make any sense to me! Or why she hasn't told me about it yet. Surely, these can't be the first times she's been sleepwalking. I have to talk to her about it. Maybe there's some kind of medication she can take for it.

I stand still for a few minutes, but slowly continue on the path, I can't leave her out here wandering around. She could easily wander off the trail and hurt herself. It would be as easy as a trip over a rock or...

For some reason Tim's story about The Man in the Woods from the campfire the other night springs to mind. I wish I never heard that damn story.

The Man in the Woods lurks in the woods of Camp Medley, surveying his prey until one becomes the fruit he wants to pick, then he extends his long sinewy arm to pluck that chosen one from the crowd, taking her deep into the forest. Not the forest we know, but his hidden forest.

Stop it! Stop it!

I will not think about stupid ghost stories told to scare twelve-year-olds. Grow up, Zoey! I continue to chide myself as I move along the path, cursing myself for not bringing my phone or flashlight. Next time I will be sure to grab one of those. I'm going to have to set up a sleepwalking bag to grab by my bed. Phone, flashlight, snack, water bottle. Oh, I'm getting ridiculous now, but I don't want to be out here in the dark by myself. On second thought, there better not be a next time! The air is cool around me. I'm guessing it's after midnight. Darkness envelops me as I trudge along carefully. There's a break in the trees up ahead and I continue to that area bathed in moonlight.

I quicken my step, while still listening for another scream, something, anything, but only the hum of the forest surrounds me now, wrapping itself around me with its long, slender fingers. A slight rustling sounds on the right side of me. I jump back.

Maybe it's The Man in the Woods.

Maybe I'm the fruit he wants to pluck. Or Mel is.

I need to stop. Now!

The moonlight ahead seems farther than it appeared a few minutes ago but I keep moving toward it. My legs are moving slower now. I'm not in a hurry to see what's ahead of me.

Then another scream pierces the night.

Right next to me, behind me, it feels like it's fucking inside of me.

My pulse races, my heart beats at a frantic pace and I run, but I don't get far. I trip over something lying directly in my path. Something long, heavy and soft. I fly into the ground, gravel splattering around me. I break the fall with my arms and land on my knees with a thud. Little pieces of gravel imbed themselves into my hands.

I turn to see what I tripped over. Moonlight slivers through the trees to allow me to view what lies on the path behind me.

A body.

TWENTY-ONE

2024

Zoey

I scramble up from the ground and stare at the body lying across the trail. It screams again, a bloodcurdling, high-pitched scream. It lies there motionless, like a corpse in a morgue waiting for burial. But one aspect differs from a funeral viewing. This corpse is looking directly at me. A loud breath escapes me.

I want to scream too.

But at least I found Mel, sprawled out on the dirt like she's taking a nap, between screams, of course, with her eyes fucking open looking directly at me! The same creepy look as the other night. What is wrong with this girl?

I stand above her, studying her as she stares at me, but even in the dim light her eyes are glassy and while she looks directly at me, I don't think she sees me. It's eerie and disturbing on so many levels.

I don't want to deal with any of this. I only want to go back to bed.

I want to cry too. I want to run away.

But I can't.

"Mel," I say. "It's Zoey. Let's go back to the cabin."

Her glassy eyes give no recognition to my words, but she rises from the ground and then stands, like a zombie in a horror movie, her body advancing in stiff, slow movements. I curse myself again for not bringing my phone. I could video her and show it to her, then she'd have to believe how scary this is and get some help.

My palms sweat. This is freaky stuff. I just want to get her back to the cabin and into bed. She has to see a specialist or something for this. It's not normal and she's going to end up hurting herself.

Or give me a heart attack. My heart is pounding about a zillion times faster now than it normally does. I take a few deep breaths to slow its rhythm to a calmer pace. It doesn't really help.

She walks down the path with an awkward gait, and I follow. We move slowly and the plod of our feet makes me antsy and nervous. I just want to get back to the safety of the cabin.

The Man in the Woods lurks among the trees of the camp surveying his prey until one becomes the fruit that he wants to pick...

The words of the ghost story repeat in my mind as we slowly march to the cabin. Maybe our death march.

The Man in the Woods will pluck the one he chooses...

Mel continues to walk jerkily. Is that how all sleepwalkers move?

Not the forest we know, but his own hidden forest...

Our pace is so slow I feel as if we will never reach the cabin at this rate.

Once The Man in the Woods has you there's no escape...

If The Man in the Woods would appear now, I'd punch him right in the face.

I wish I never heard that damn ghost story.

. . .

An eternity later, we are back in the cabin. Mel is quiet in the upper bunk, but I'm wide awake in the lower one. I close my eyes and try to fall asleep. But sleep eludes me for another hour or so. All I can do is think about everything strange at this camp. Mel, the whispers I heard, Wynn, the strange lady at the grocery store, Sherry. Honestly, there are more weird things than normal things here.

The next thing I know, giggles and loud whispers wake me up.

"She's still sleeping."

"Is she ever going to wake up?"

"Shhh... girls. She'll wake up soon," Mel says quietly.

I open my eyes and yell, "Good morning!"

The girls squeal and laugh as I sit up.

"We're going to be late for breakfast," Celina says, a worried expression on her face.

I smile at her. Celina is the shyest of our girls and probably my favorite. She looks at me earnestly with big brown eyes and her dark blonde hair in pigtails. I know she doesn't like to be late for anything.

"Don't worry," I say. I grab my toiletry bag and a change of clothes. "Give me ten minutes, then we'll go for breakfast. I promise, we won't be late."

Mel follows me out to the bathhouse. "Hey, did one of the girls play a trick on me? There was a bunch of dirt in my bed this morning."

"Really?" I arch my eyebrows as I quickly brush and rinse my teeth. I turn to her. "Don't you remember what happened last night?"

"We had a campfire and went to bed around ten. Then I woke up with dirt in my bed and I even had dirt in my hair. Luckily, I woke up early, so I took a shower. I'm going to have to throw that bedding in the washer. I'll stop by the laundry room on our walk to the dining hall and throw it in."

"Mel, you were sleepwalking last night. I heard a scream, and I went out looking for you and found you lying on the trail to the protected garden." I pause. "In the dirt."

She stills. "What? Seriously?"

"Yes, seriously. You were screaming and then you got up and walked like a zombie back to the cabin. It freaked me out."

"No way." Mel shakes her head, looking confused and a little concerned about what I'm telling her. "Why am I doing that?"

"I don't know, but it's not the first time I've seen you sleepwalking," I explain. "It's scary and I'm worried about you. A couple nights ago you were down at the maintenance shed dragging a shovel around saying, 'I'm so sorry,' it was really weird." I sigh.

"Oh..." Mel's face goes pale. "Was I really doing that?"

"You need to make an appointment with a doctor, something is not right, and you could hurt yourself when you're wandering around at night. You could easily fall or if you go near the lake, you could drown. Anything could happen."

"Yeah..." Mel gets quiet. "That's not normal and it could be dangerous. I'll make an appointment."

"Promise? I'm worried about you. And I don't want to chase you around in the middle of the night again."

"Yes, I promise, I'll make an appointment. Thank you for taking care of me. I don't know what's going on. All of this is very strange."

"Okay." I give her a quick hug. "Let's go to breakfast."

After a quick breakfast we take the girls to the pool for the morning. I stretch out on my blue striped towel drying off after playing pool volleyball with Mel and the girls. Mel is still in the pool and tries to wave me back in.

"Come on, Zoey," she calls. "Come back in with us!"

I shake my head. "In a little bit."

She laughs and goes back to playing with the girls, although only a few are playing volleyball now, some are floating on rafts, and some are lying on towels like me, drying off.

I settle back on my towel and flick though old messages from Craig, months old now, then I look at my photos of him. One of us at the bar where we met, kissing. Silly selfies in his apartment. A couple photos at a campus party and many other random shots. We spent so much time together; every chance we got we were doing something. In one of the photos he looks at me so lovingly and my heart hurts just looking at it. I miss him so much.

"Who's that?" a voice asks.

I look up to see Wynn standing next to me. I place my phone face down.

"Nobody you need to know about."

He shrugs his shoulders. "Whatever."

He continues to stand there.

"Do you want something?" I ask.

Wynn frowns and leans down. "Some show last night, huh?"

I stare at him. "What show?"

His piercing blue eyes bore into me. "Mel wandering around."

I sit up and stare at him. "You saw her last night, why didn't you help me get her back to the cabin? It was scary, I could have used the help."

"Seemed like you had it covered."

"Where were you? In the woods?" That's why I felt like someone was watching me?

The Man in the Woods plucks the fruit of the one he chooses...

Could Wynn be The Man in the Woods?

No, he's just a kid. That story was about something that happened years ago and it's a made-up story, not real. *It's not real*, I say in my mind again. *Get a grip, Zoey.*

"Just around. It's relaxing to walk in the woods at night. It's not the first time, you know."

"You've seen her sleepwalking before?"

Wynn nods. "Yeah, you don't wake up every time, I guess. She's been wandering around before."

"And you don't help her?" I ask, surprised that I don't wake up every time.

"I have helped when she needs it. Usually, she finds her way back to her cabin. It's kinda weird how she knows where to go, but she's not awake. It's so freaky that her eyes stay open while she's still asleep. Creepy as hell."

I stare at him. He is an odd guy. I start to ask him why he's hanging around in the woods at night so much but change my mind. I don't want to know.

"She's going to make a doctor's appointment," I say instead. "She needs help with this. I'm worried that she's going to end up hurting herself on one of these late-night walks."

Wynn smiles, the corners of his mouth curling up like an old-fashioned cartoon character. "I doubt a doctor can help her."

What a strange thing to say. Wynn is so weird. "Do you know when she started sleepwalking?" I ask.

He shrugs. "I dunno. A few months ago, maybe."

Then he walks away. He may not be The Man in the Woods, but he is creepy. I lift my phone up again and stare at Craig's smiling face.

TWENTY-TWO
2024

Zoey

Sherry pushes the grocery cart down the aisle and loads case after case of bottled water into it, and I follow suit with my cart. The camp's weekly order was messed up and short, but we need more for the obstacle course activity planned for this afternoon.

Mel volunteered me to go along with Sherry because she's teaching a painting class with the girls and I have zero artistic ability, so I'm lugging cases of water with Sherry, who doesn't seem very happy to have me tag along.

She frowns, staring at the carts. "Let's add two more and we should be good. I don't know why this order got messed up. We always order the same thing."

"Okay," I agree, and we each add one more to our respective carts. "Do we need anything else?"

Sherry shakes her head. "No, that's all."

We walk slowly through the store to the cash registers.

"Sherry, I was thinking about what we were talking about the other day."

She nods but doesn't say anything.

"Do you really not remember anything else about my aunt?"

Sherry's mouth becomes a thin line. "No, Zoey, let it be. I already told you everything."

"I mean, anything is of interest to me," I say calmly. I'm not calm though because I'm certain she knows more than she's telling me, which isn't a damn thing. "Even the smallest, most insignificant detail might help my mom get some closure."

Sherry ignores me even though I'm standing right next to her. I know she heard me. I look at her, feeling the anger rise in me. I'm certain she knows something. What's she hiding?

"What do you know?" I ask, looking at her, my tone clipped. I might as well be direct with her. I'm here to get answers. "I mean, that's the whole reason I came to the camp this year. To find out what happened to my aunt to give my mother some peace. Like I said, anything you can tell me would be so helpful, even if it's very small."

She glares at me, obviously not moved by my heartfelt plea, and keeps pushing the cart down the aisle at a much faster pace. I hurry to catch up.

She turns to me. "I don't know anything. Stop asking so many questions. I mean it, *stop* asking questions about the camp. It's not a good idea."

I step back at her sharp tone.

She knows something. Something she doesn't want to share with me.

I glare back at her, but we travel to the register in silence. A middle-aged woman with bright red hair is behind the register.

"Just a moment, ladies, I'm leaving." She pulls out her cash drawer. "But another cashier will be here in a second."

And so, of course, a few moments later, Pearl inserts her cash drawer into the register. Her long, gray hair is loose today. Her deep scowl is still present.

"Hello, Sherry," she says, her voice flat. "How many cases of water?"

"Ten," she replies, her tone just as flat.

Pearl punches in the number and scans one of the cases. She gives me a brief glance.

"Still working at the camp?" she asks me.

I nod. Sherry shakes her head and stares at us both. She swipes her card, and Pearl hands her the receipt.

"Yeah, she's still working at the camp," Sherry retorts. "She'll be there all summer. It's a summer camp and we need counselors all summer." She grabs the receipt and pushes her cart toward the exit.

Pearl stares at me with those unsettling gray eyes. I meet her stare, thinking she is going to say something else to me. I want to ask her more questions about the camp, but I'm mute. Why does she scare me?

After a moment, she turns away and rings up the next customer. I push my cart, following Sherry, but turn to watch Pearl. Why do I feel so compelled to see if she's watching me?

Her head jerks to the right. Gray eyes staring into mine, but her mouth doesn't move. Only her eyes speak to me, although I don't know what they're saying, only that it isn't anything good.

We head down the gravel trail from the volleyball nets to the lake for the tug-of-war contest. Cabin Nine won the volleyball game, but our cabin is determined to win the tug-of-war.

"We'll win this time!" Diana exclaims.

"Go Cabin Twelve!" Christina cheers and all the girls cheer with her.

The girls run ahead of us down to the water. The hot summer sun beats down on us as we assemble on one side of the large, thick rope, and Cabin Nine is on the other side.

"Ready, set, go!" calls a counselor from another cabin.

We start pulling on the rope. Mel is in the front and I'm in the back with the girls between us.

"Pull!" Mel yells and she yanks the rope.

Her pull is forceful, I didn't realize she was so strong. She's putting her all into this and pulls hard again. The girls and I are pulling too, but our strength is barely comparable to hers.

My sandals dig into the sand at the edge of the lake as I pull as hard as possible. Sarah and Mae are on the other side of the rope with the girls of Cabin Nine and they put up a good fight as we maintain a balance with neither group gaining an advantage.

Then the line loosens and Mel screams, "Pull!"

We pull with all our might with Mel's guidance and strength, and finally the other team's side weakens as they tumble into the water.

"Yay!" we all yell, giving each other high fives.

Then everyone throws off their sandals and jumps into the sparkling water.

I look at Mel standing there, flinging off her sandals like me, her face red as a tomato, the muscles in her arms still flexed. She took this little game seriously and damn, she was strong. I need to kick up my workout routine a little bit more.

TWENTY-THREE
1989

Heather

I wonder what Gran would think of me living in this tent in the woods. I know she'd love Dean. How could she not? She'd be happy about me and him but wouldn't like that I'm living in a tent or that Jess and I are separated from one another. I often wonder about what Jess does all day and if she's happy with her boyfriend. She always sounds so rushed and busy when I talk to her on the phone, but I've only gotten a hold of her a few times.

I miss her. And Gran.

She'd tell me not to move too fast with Dean, Gran, not Jess, but that's not going to happen. Everything in my life moves fast now. I don't have a choice. Things would be different if Gran was still alive. Jess and I would stay at her house, but I'd still be crazy about Dean. I'll always be crazy about him.

This summer would be different though. I'd be spending most of it with Gran and Jess, not Dean. And while I don't want to be in this situation, the one plus is being with Dean every day. I love this part, and I never want it to come to an end.

I get up from the camp chair and snatch a banana from the

bag inside the tent. As I peel and eat it, my thoughts go to the fact that eventually all of this will end.

And there's nothing I can do to stop it.

I pick up the phone and dial Jess's number. I glance at the pool behind me, full of chattering, happy swimmers both in the water and lounging on the beach towels. I'm glad it's busy today and I blend in with the crowd.

Two rings and she doesn't answer.

Please pick up, Jess.

On the fourth ring, she does.

"Hello," she says. My heart aches hearing her voice, wishing I could see her too.

"Jess, it's me."

"Heather, it's so good to hear your voice!" she replies, and I can hear the smile in her voice.

"I tried to call before, but couldn't get a hold of you," I say.

"Oh, yeah, I've been busy," she says. "How are you?"

"Well I'm kind of worried," I admit, it feels good to share my concerns with my sister. "Dean still hasn't asked his parents if I can live with them, and I don't know what I'm going to do if I can't move in with him. I don't want to ever go home."

She clears her throat. "I understand. But you can't go back there, it isn't safe."

"Maybe I can come live with you?" I ask hopefully.

"I'd love that so much," she says, then her voice falters. "I just don't think it would work. Things aren't great between me and Ted, and I don't think he'd go for it. I don't even know how long we'll be together."

"Oh..." My voice falls. Worry fills me. What am I going to do if Dean's parents say no and I can't stay with Jess? I don't know what I'll do then.

Her voice warms. "But that doesn't matter. Yes, of course, if you need a place to stay, you'll stay with me. You just let me know once Dean's spoken to his parents. I'll come get you if you need me."

"Really?" Hope springs inside me. I will back the tears that threaten to fall. Everything will be okay. It'll be fine.

"Yes, we have a comfy couch you can sleep on. It'll all work out," Jess assures me. "But from what you tell me, I'm sure Dean will ask his parents. Keep asking him about it and let me know," she says in an encouraging voice.

"Okay, I will," I say. "Thank you for doing this. I know it's not easy for you either."

"You're my baby sister," Jess says in a warm voice. "I love you and I'll do everything I can to help you."

The tears threaten to spill again, although not because I'm upset, but because I can feel her love, hear her love through the telephone. We'll always have each other.

"But keep asking Dean, and let me know, but either way we'll work this out," she promises me.

I promise her and hang up the phone, lingering for a few minutes. She's right, I'm sure he will ask his parents, but I wish he'd hurry up. Summer is slipping away, and I don't know what will happen when it ends, but at least I have a couple of options.

Dean, Jennifer, Sherry and I sit around my small campfire roasting marshmallows and blowing bubbles. Jennifer has brought a bunch of leftover containers of bubble liquid from a children's activity they had at camp today. It's fun to watch the small bubbles form and drift out into the air, the warm glow of the campfire giving us light to see their journey until they dissolve into the night. It's become a regular thing now, Jennifer and Sherry stopping in to hang out with us. Not every night, but often, and it's fun to spend time with them. I'd have to say we've become good friends. I enjoy spending time with them, although I know Dean wishes they wouldn't stop by so often.

I have the Graham crackers and a piece of chocolate bar ready when Dean pulls the long fork with the steaming, brown roasted marshmallow from the fire.

"Here." I glance at it, melted marshmallow running down the fork. "Well, maybe give it a minute. Looks pretty hot."

"Good idea," Dean agrees.

Jennifer blows another stream of bubbles while holding her roasting fork in the other hand. "I love s'mores."

"Who doesn't?" I ask, and we all laugh.

"What did you do today?" Jennifer asks me.

"I wrote a long letter to my sister and walked down to the store to mail it. Then I went swimming this afternoon. The pool was so full, nobody noticed me," I reply.

Sherry nods. "Yeah, the camp's booked up this week."

"I didn't know you had a sister," Jennifer says, her gaze on me. "What's her name?"

"Jess," I reply.

Dean points to the marshmallows, and I slide them off the fork, put one on each cracker, over the chocolate, and place another cracker on top. I hand one to Dean and then take a bite of mine. Ooey gooey marshmallow, melting chocolate and a crispy Graham cracker cause a taste explosion in my mouth. Delicious.

"Is she older or younger than you?" Sherry asks.

"Older. She's eighteen."

"Does she live at home?" Jennifer asks. Again, I find the interest in my life a little intense, but I throw it off.

I shake my head. "No, she moved out about eight months ago with her boyfriend. That's when everything really got bad at home. She was kind of my... protector."

Everyone is quiet for a few minutes, Sherry and Jennifer share a look, then Jennifer breaks the silence.

"Did you hear about The Man in the Woods?" she asks in a creepy voice.

I shake my head, and Sherry laughs.

"Oh, not this again," Dean groans.

Jennifer continues in her scary voice. "He's kind of an urban legend here at Camp Medley. Lurking in the woods, moving around so fast you'll never see him until it's too late..."

"Too late for what?" I ask.

"Until he picks his next victim." Sherry picks up the story, her voice deepening. Her eyes go wide as she studies each of us in the glow of the campfire. "The Man in the Woods lurks around the camp, surveying his prey to find the fruit he wants to pick, then he extends his long sinewy arm to pluck that chosen one from the crowd, taking her deep into his hidden forest."

"Don't listen to them, it's a stupid ghost story," Dean says, looking at me. "They always tell it around the campfire to scare the campers."

"That's because he's scary!" Jennifer squeals.

"Yeah, maybe for a twelve-year-old girl," Dean responds. "Really, it's not that scary. We should think of a scary story to tell that's better than that one. It's so old."

"I like it." Jennifer stands firm. "It's a tradition at camp, our own urban legend, and it *is* scary!"

"Hold on, what's that?" Sherry puts a finger to her lips. Her eyes grow wide.

We silence and listen.

The hot humid air is thick around us, and the hum of tree frogs croaking their melody fills the night air with their song. My heart thumps inside my chest a little faster than normal. Maybe the ghost story isn't that scary, but I'm feeling a little on edge.

"Is that him?" Jennifer whispers as a twig snaps close to us. Then another.

My mind goes back to when my clothes and knapsack went

missing at the bathhouse and I went running through the woods in a towel. We still don't know who was watching us that night.

The Man in the Woods lurks in the woods of the camp surveying his prey until one becomes the fruit he wants to pick...

Could it have been him? Am I the fruit he wants to pick? Thinking about that night still scares me; I still don't know who was hiding and took my bag. *The Man in the Woods?* I'm being silly now; it was someone playing a prank, not an urban legend, but a real, live person.

The snapping stops. All of us are still. And around us only...

Silence.

"No," Sherry whispers back, pointing. "Over there."

We look in the direction she points at.

"No, over here," she shouts. "Boo!"

And she and Jennifer burst out laughing. Dean looks at me and rolls his eyes, but I laugh too. A silly ghost story by a campfire is fun.

"You're idiots," I say.

"I know," says Jennifer. "But you weren't sure for a moment."

"Okay, you got me," I agree with her, even though they didn't. A silly story doesn't scare me.

The Man in the Woods isn't real.

Monsters in real life are much scarier.

TWENTY-FOUR
2024

Zoey

The morning moved quickly with the daily routine. Breakfast at the dining hall, a short hike on the trails followed by a dip in the pool and back to the dining hall for lunch. I hadn't slept well last night and I was tired and wishing we could go back to the cabin for an afternoon nap, but no such luck.

This afternoon, we are having a Christmas in July day at the East Lodge. A brightly decorated Christmas tree stands in the center of the activity room, decked out in twinkling white lights and bright, shiny red ornaments. A sparkling silver star sits atop the tree, lending a festive brightness to the room. The activity tables have red tablecloths on them and each table has a large bowl of mini candy canes and wrapped chocolate candies to munch on while we do our craft. The plan is first to make two bead ornaments, a wreath and a candy cane shape, then a snowman activity, and finally bake cutout sugar cookies.

I always thought Christmas in July was a strange thing to do, but Mel and the girls seem excited about it, so I can get into it for them. Plus, crafts and cookies are a fun way to spend an afternoon. I sit with Diana and Celina, and we construct the wreath ornaments. These two girls always seem to be partners for everything, and I find it funny because their personalities are so opposite. Diana is very extroverted while Celina barely speaks to the counselors, but they get along very well.

"Where are the red bows?" Diana asks, searching around the table.

"Here." Celina grabs one from the dish. It's a tiny red ribbon. "We can glue it on to the beads when we're done with the wreath."

Diana nods and they go happily about their work. I place my wreath on the side and glance around the room. The East Lodge is large with a huge stone fireplace in the center of the massive room. Mel said it's often used for large group functions or corporate meetings throughout the year. I am thankful that it has air conditioning and am more than happy to stay here during the hot afternoon.

All of the other cabins are in attendance too, doing the activities on a rotating schedule. We will do the snowman activity next, and then baking cookies will be last on our list. Sherry and Jennifer move around the room, but I notice they mostly stay away from me, which isn't very helpful if I want to dig for more information. I'll try to be a little more friendly and relaxed with them. Even though that's my intention, I always seem to burst out with rapid-fire questions, further irritating them.

"We need more green beads," Mel says, surveying our table. "I'll get some from Mom."

"Oh, let me," I offer and make a beeline over to Jennifer.

"Hi, Jennifer," I say in a friendly voice. "We're short on green beads. Mel thought you had some extra over here."

"Sure." She hands me a small box of beads. "That should be enough."

"Okay, thanks," I say, lingering. "This is a fun activity. Have you always had Christmas in July day?"

Jennifer looks thoughtful. "Maybe the last ten years or so."

I nod. "Oh, so not when you were younger."

She shakes her head, giving me an odd look.

I pull out my phone from the back pocket of my shorts and pull up a picture I took of the yearbook photo of the three girls at the lake. "I found this. That's my aunt Heather in the middle."

Jennifer frowns, staring at the picture. "Where did you get this?"

"Oh, I found an old yearbook," I reply, watching her.

She continues staring at the photo, her jaw rigid. "I remember her vaguely. Pictures can be deceiving, though. There are many pictures of us with camp friends. Often someone you only knew for a few weeks or so."

"But you didn't say you were friends. Please, anything you can tell me about her would be great," I say, meeting her gaze. I'm not going to get anywhere with Sherry, but maybe I will with Jennifer. She seems like the more stable sister. "It would mean a lot to me. I'm only trying to get answers for my mom. It was so difficult losing her sister, as you certainly could imagine. I'm sure if Sherry went missing, you'd want to know what happened to her."

Jennifer hands me another box. "Here, take another box of red beads too." She leans closer to me and whispers in my ear, her hand digs into my arm. She stares at me with cold, hard eyes and something else. Anger, or maybe fear? "Stop digging, there's nothing to find. You have to stop asking these questions."

Then she walks away from me.

I clutch the bead boxes in my hands. Her words and reaction tells me everything I need to know.

Whatever secret Jennifer and Sherry hold...

It's a big one.

. . .

The warm afternoon is perfect for a canoe ride on the lake. Brittney, Diana and Celina are with me, while Mel is hanging on the sandy beach with the rest of the girls. The water sparkles around us and the lake is full of canoes today, leaving the dock by the big green house with shiny white shutters empty. Luckily, we have one of the newer canoes and it's slightly larger than the older ones.

I show them how to use the paddles and we glide around the lake. The girls are really into using the paddles themselves, so I let them take control and bask in the warm sunshine, enjoying the bright summer day.

I push my sunglasses up and smooth my hand over my freshly braided hair. Normally I wear it loose or in a ponytail, but I felt like braiding it today. I sigh. Craig always liked it when I braided my hair. He said it made me even more beautiful than normal. He was sweet like that. I sigh, he was a lot of great things.

He would have liked to be out here in the canoe, enjoying the sun and fresh air. We took a few hikes together in the fall. He's more of an outdoorsman than me but I enjoyed spending time with him anywhere.

Funny how there are so many studies into the psychological functions of how the human brain works. What type of learner are you? What makes us choose certain actions? How do we perceive reality and what creates those perceptions in our mind? Yet, we can't explain a simple question of clicking with someone. It just happens. A few conversations, some time spent together, and you think about when you'll see that person again. You can't wait to see that person because you connect with them on every level.

I clicked with Craig and he with me. It was a stronger connection than with any other guy I dated in the past and I miss that closeness. If I'm honest, I miss everything about him. I wonder if he ever thinks of me too. At least a little bit.

He must have those thoughts too, even though he broke up with me. He must sometimes think of all the good times we had together. I couldn't have imagined the strength of our relationship. We loved each other. We spoke those exact words to each other, and I meant them so much.

But I guess he didn't.

Mel waves to me from the beach area and I return the wave, as do the girls. I like Mel a lot, but what in the world is going on with her sleepwalking? It's so *damn* creepy. I'm glad she decided to make a doctor appointment. I don't want to have to follow her around in the dark all summer. And I don't even want to think of Wynn stalking around the woods at night. Something about him is unsettling. I'll just focus on Mel for now. And her mother and aunt.

"My arms are tired!" Diana exclaims. Sweat runs down her forehead and she swipes back her long, dark hair.

"Here, I'll take a turn," I say, taking the paddle from her.

"Let's go back and go swimming," Diana says, looking at the other girls.

"Is that what everyone wants to do?" I ask.

"Yes!" they all exclaim.

I nod and we direct our canoe back to the dock.

"You're slower today," I remark to Mel as we take our daily jog. "Everything okay?"

"Yeah," she says. We move along through the woods at a moderate pace. "Just kind of a weird day."

"Why?" I ask.

"My parents had another one of their appointments today. I just want to know what's going on with them," she says. "Plus they're on my case about working here after I graduate next year. It sounds like they want to retire soon or something."

"Oh, I guess that was a surprise to you."

"Yes, kind of," she says. "But how would that work? Eventually Wynn and I running everything? I don't see it happening."

"Maybe, when you're both older," I suggest. Although that seems like the last thing Wynn wants to do.

"I mean, I get it." Her voice wavers. "I know we have to keep it in the family and that means I'll have to take over, but I'll be lucky if Wynn sticks around."

We run in silence for a long period of time, both lost in our thoughts.

Sweat still drips down my back even after ten at night. We're standing outside our cabin, but I really want to go to bed because I'm tired of listening to Kristen from the next cabin over complaining about her co-counselor, Cari, who honestly is kind of a jerk, but I don't want to deal with listening to all the details. I don't really care. I have bigger issues to deal with at the moment.

"So, I told her to stop telling me what to do. I'm not a camper and I'm an adult. She's not my boss! I certainly don't need her to tell me anything," Kristen continues. She shoves a handful of popcorn into her mouth from the bowl that we all share.

Mel nods. "Cari is pushy."

"And do you know what else she did?" Kristen pauses for dramatic effect. "Wore my favorite T-shirt without asking because she was doing laundry. I mean, I probably would have let her wear it, but still, she could at least ask."

"Yeah, she should have asked you," I agree. I pretend I'm interested, but I'm not. Bickering over a stupid T-shirt is so childish to me. It certainly isn't a real problem.

"She's always sneaking out with Brett in Cabin Seven too. That guy is such a player, and I told her he was, but she doesn't listen to me," Kristen huffs and then stands up. "I mean, yeah, he's hot, but he's not worth it."

Mel shoots me a look. She's been sneaking out to see Brett sometimes too, but I guess she's not the only one. I wonder how upset she'll be about this news. I'm not sure if she thought things were serious between them or just casual. I'm sure I'll find out when Kristen leaves.

"Okay, I have to get back to my cabin," Kristen says. "Thanks for listening to me complain."

"No problem," Mel says. "Anytime."

"Bye, Kristen," I say, and she walks away, back to her cabin, probably to argue with Cari. Although, I think I'd like to squabble about T-shirts rather than chasing my co-counselor around the camp in the middle of the night.

Mel and I are silent until she's out of sight, both of us mulling over Kristen's words. I'm sure she's upset about Brett. She probably didn't know she was one of many who was spending time with him.

"So, Cari's sneaking out to see Brett too," Mel says in a despondent voice. "I thought that we were seeing each other."

I raise my eyebrows. "I guess he's seeing her too."

Mel lets out a deep sigh. "It's not like we ever said it was exclusive. It's just a summer fling. I don't know why I'm surprised the way things have been going for me. Nothing ever works out for me."

I grab a handful of popcorn and ask, "What's going on?" Then I proceed to eat my snack and take a sip of the soda sitting beside me on the porch.

A dark look covers Mel's face for a moment before she speaks. "Oh, you know, just life," she says vaguely.

I study her as I chew my popcorn, detecting the sadness in her voice. I researched a little about sleepwalking and stress is a big factor that increases its occurrence. Isn't stress a factor in everything negative? Maybe more is going on with Mel than she's telling me, there must be more going on. I know she's not thrilled about eventually running the camp and now Brett, but those don't seem like major stress factors. I wonder what else she's dealing with right now. Maybe I can help her figure things out and that will help her sleepwalking. I understand that some things she may not want to talk to me about, we haven't known each other very long, but I would like to help her if she's willing to let me.

"You can talk to me about whatever," I say to her. "I'm a good listener."

Mel lets out a rueful laugh, then sits silent for a short while.

"There's some things you can't talk about, even if you want to talk about them," she finally says. Her voice deepens sharply. "Some things can *never* be talked about."

She stands up and stamps on her empty soda can sitting on the ground, crushing it flat. She stomps on it with her foot a few more times, staring intently at it. She stops and continues to look at it for a few minutes while I watch her. She's not herself tonight; her behavior is odd for her normally cheerful self. She looks up from the can, and turns to stare at me, a strange look crossing her face momentarily, then she smiles at me.

An unusual smile that completely unnerves me.

"I'm going to bed," she says, her weird smile fading away.

"Good night," I say. I feel her gaze on me until she disappears inside the cabin.

An owl screeches in the quiet, steamy evening, now close to eleven. I should go to bed too, but I don't want to right now and my mind dwells on the conversation I had with Mel. My skin pricks with goosebumps when I think about the smile she gave me only a few minutes ago. I'm not sure why it disturbs me so much, but it does. Something about it was so... unsettling.

And what was she talking about? Clearly, something huge is

bothering her, but why can't she express it? My curiosity is piqued now, and I really want to know what's going on with her. And maybe if she talks about it, her sleepwalking will improve, if she can relieve some of that stress.

Is there anyone at this camp who doesn't have secrets?

I flush the toilet and walk out to the line of sinks to wash my hands. I soap my hands and rinse them off, then grab a paper towel from the dispenser. I was so relieved when I woke up needing to pee and noticed that Mel was sleeping quietly in her bed. No chasing her through the woods tonight. I toss the paper towel into the trash and head back to my cabin. I stop outside in the still night and take another step, heading back to my cabin.

But something stops me.

A movement on the edge of the woods next to the parking area for our cars—the five cabins around the bathhouse share the same parking location. I'm not exactly sure where the movement originated, but I saw movement, brief and quick. I sink back into the shadows, hoping they hide my presence.

And I watch.

There's not much to see. Some branches are moving and someone coughs, then a figure emerges from the back of the cabin. I shrink back as far as possible into the darkness.

Who is it?

The figure, wearing a dark hooded sweatshirt, walks to the front of our cabin, stares a moment, then goes round the back again and disappears into the woods. A strong wind blows their hood back, revealing short, blonde hair.

Sherry.

TWENTY-FIVE
1989

Heather

The hot sun blazes in the cloudless sky above our beach blankets stretched out on the grainy sand by the cool, sparkling lake. The lake is full today with canoes and swimmers; only one more canoe is available at the dock by the big green house. It feels good to be lying here in the hot sun, a nice change from always being in the woods, and I enjoy the beautiful day. Sherry and Jennifer lie on either side of me. They helped with a special BBQ lunch at the dining hall because today is the Fourth of July and they had a few hours off until the bonfire tonight, where everyone would roast hot dogs and make s'mores before the fireworks later.

I slip my sunglasses down over my eyes, adjusting my white bikini, and stare out into the lake at Dean, who is swimming and now is floating halfway in the lake on a huge yellow float with a few of his campers.

"Is that Dean out there in the red shorts?" Sherry asks, sitting up on her towel.

"Yeah." I smile. "He's so..."

"Hot," Jennifer chimes in, then giggles and looks at me.

I laugh. "He is."

I stare at Jennifer. She obviously has a crush on my boyfriend, but I don't care. I know Dean loves me; she doesn't have a chance. I look back at Dean. And she's right. He is hot. He leans over on his side on the raft and waves at me, his wet dark blond hair glistening in the sun. I wave back.

The girls laugh.

"Do you think he's The One?" Jennifer asks, her eyes sparkling.

I nod. "He's definitely The One."

Sherry smiles. "Have you had sex with him yet?"

"Sherry!" Jennifer exclaims. "That's really personal." But the way she looks at me, I can tell she wants me to answer.

"Oh, sorry," Sherry says, her tone still curious. "You don't have to answer if you don't want to."

"That's okay, yeah we have sex." I smile and give Jennifer a smug look.

"How is it?" Sherry asks; her eyebrows arch.

I look back to Dean, now sitting up on the yellow raft, his dark sunglasses on, but I know he's looking at me.

"It's great. Everything about Dean is great."

"Sounds like you're in love," Jennifer says, her eyes wide.

"I'll love Dean until the day I die," I say with absolute certainty.

"Wow, it must be good sex," Sherry remarks.

"Sherry had sex with a guy last year," Jennifer says. "She said it was terrible."

"I didn't say terrible," Sherry quips. "But I'm not in love with that guy. We did it four times and none of those times was very memorable."

"That's more than me," Jennifer adds quietly. "I've never had sex."

"How many times did you and Dean do it?" Sherry asks.

The questions are getting very personal, but I figure they're just interested in what a great relationship looks like. I think for a moment. "I'm not really sure. I stopped counting."

"See, that's what happens when you're in love," says Jennifer.

"In love until the day I die." Sherry laughs. "Come on, Heather, really?"

"Yes, really," I say firmly.

"Where was your first time?" Jennifer asks. "Was it super romantic?"

My voice softens. "It was here, in the tent. And it was romantic because it was with him."

"Ooh... I love that," Jennifer swoons.

"And you've only been here like, what, three weeks or a month," Sherry said. "And you've already lost count. You must be doing it all the time."

I laugh. "The more you do it, the more you want to!"

We all laugh, and I look up to see Dean walking out of the water. His dark blond hair slicked back and water running down his strong, muscled chest to his red swim trunks. My heart flutters and heat grows in my body. After all this sex talk, the only thing I can think about is being alone with him in the tent tonight.

Maybe we'll skip the fireworks.

We stay for the fireworks. Huddled together on my striped beach towel, eating a burnt hot dog cooked over the bonfire and drinking an icy drink from the cooler. I'm wearing one of Dean's sweatshirts because the night air has a chill to it. I lean back on him, his arms around me as bright red, white and blue flames are exploding into the sky.

Jennifer and Sherry are farther down the beach toward their family house with the slowly dying bonfire that has some campers still making s'mores as the fireworks pop above them. Jennifer looks in our direction and waves.

"I think Jennifer has a crush on you," I say to him, waving back.

Dean chuckles. "Yeah, she has for a while."

"You were never interested in her?"

"No, I mean she's nice, I like her, but not like I like you." He holds me close and kisses my cheek. "I love you."

A rush of emotions floods me from his words. He's my security, my love, my home. He's everything I ever want.

"I love you too." I turn my head and kiss him.

"You're not jealous, are you?" Dean asks; his face wears a teasing grin.

"Nope, I know you're all mine."

"Damn right." His voice lowers. "I'd do anything for you."

I snuggle into him, and we watch the fireworks. I wish we could stay here forever, just Dean and me, always. There's nothing I want more than to be with him forever.

"I was thinking," he says. "I'll ask my parents about you staying with us when they get back from Colorado, but if they say no maybe we can do something else."

"Like what?" I ask.

"Like get married," he whispers to me.

I turn around. My heart leaps with joy. "Are you serious?"

"Yes," he says with certainty. "I want to be with you forever."

I stare at him. It's as if he was reading my thoughts from only a few minutes earlier. To be with him forever is all I ever would want. Is this really happening? "Can we even do that? Wouldn't we have to be eighteen?"

"Probably, but I turn eighteen in October, and you turn seventeen in March. We can just run away together now and get married when you're eighteen."

"But how would we live? We'd need money."

"I have a friend who lives in New Jersey. He's a couple years older than me and works in his dad's garage as a mechanic. I bet I could get a job there, I got really good at understanding cars when my dad and I fixed up my pickup. We'd be okay. It would work until we save up some money."

"Oh, wow, that sounds amazing. It would be you and me in our own place. I can get a job too," I say, excitement rises in me. All these possibilities are running through my excited mind at a rapid pace. It's almost like a dream come true.

"Yeah, and then when you turn eighteen, we can get married," Dean says. "And we'll always be together."

I wrap my arms around him and hug him tight. "Oh, Dean, I love you so much. Yes, yes, let's do it!"

Zoey

I have the afternoon off, not for anything fun, but a dentist appointment. Normally, I'd push it off, but I need to have a cavity filled so I want to get it out of the way before I go back to school next month. Going to the dentist isn't my favorite thing to do, I doubt it is for anyone, but a necessity.

I drive my car out of the camp and decide to go a longer route to the dentist rather than hopping on the interstate. Craig used to take this back way home from school sometimes too; when Mom told me the name of the camp, I remembered he'd mentioned it in the past. I'm early so I want to stop at a cute shop I saw that sold handmade benches and pottery. My mom's birthday is coming up and I'll probably find a nice gift for her there.

I accelerate as I go up the sharp hill, then crest it and continue down the other side. I pump the brakes, but nothing happens. Pump again.

Nothing.

Panic seizes me as I careen down the hill. I don't have any

way to stop or slow down the car. I'm flying now and another car is ahead of me, not too far away. I'm going to crash into it if I don't do something.

What can I do? I don't have any brakes!

An open field sits to my right and large hay bales occupy it. I swerve, choosing to run into them instead of the car ahead of me. I slam into the bales, one by one, and pull the emergency brake. My car spins in the open field and the air bag ballons in front of me.

My neck snaps back, side to side and lands cushioned in the huge balloon. I'm shaken, but okay. I sit in the now unmoving car, thankful for its now sudden calmness and thankful to be alive.

"You're sure you're okay?" Mom asks me for the millionth time. She fusses with the blanket and goes over to the cabinet at the side of the hospital room, retrieves another blanket and covers me with it.

"Yes, Mom," I insist. "I feel fine. The doctor checked me out and said I was fine. They're only keeping me overnight to be extra safe."

"I know, I know." She smiles. "You know how I worry about you. How did this happen?"

I shrug. "I don't know."

Mom looks at me. "I don't think you should go back to that camp, Zoey. You should come home. I mean, you heard what the police said, it's a possibility that your brakes could have been tampered with. It's not safe to go back."

I shake my head. "No, I'm staying. I'm learning more about Aunt Heather and I'm going to find out what happened to her. I'm sure I can find the answers soon. And the police also said the brakes could have loosened on their own, they have no evidence of tampering."

She is driving me nuts! I understand why she'd be worried about me after the car accident, but she suffocates the life out of me, treating me like a baby.

"But why were your brake lines loose? I told you to make sure your car is serviced. I can't take care of everything for you." Mom frowns. "When was the last time you had an oil change, is your car inspection up to date? I assumed you took care of those things now."

I grimace. "Yes, I had my car inspected a couple of months ago when it was due. I don't know why my brakes were loose," I reply. She's driving me crazy and I don't want to think about this anymore.

"I want to know what happened to Heather too, but I don't want you getting hurt. Do you think this happened because you're asking questions about her?"

"I don't know, Mom. It was probably just a weird thing that happened to my brakes," I say. "The police said brakes can loosen on their own."

Mom frowns. "Yeah, if you're not maintaining your car. Please come home. That's the best thing to do."

"No, I'm going to finish out the summer," I say. "I'll be fine. My car will be in the shop for a while. I won't be driving anywhere."

Mom shakes her head. "You know you'll get a rental car until your car is finished. Insurance pays for it."

"Oh, yeah, that's right." I smile at her. "Seriously, don't worry about me, I'll be fine."

"I still don't think it's a good idea."

I love my mom, but sometimes she will not let a subject rest.

"How about this, I'll put a small camera out by my car and check the footage periodically. If someone is brave enough to mess around with my car, I'll have it on tape," I say. "And I won't drive my car if I see it was tampered with. I'll call the police."

"Maybe. If you do go back, you'll need to set up a camera, but why bother? Just come home and be done with all of this." Mom frowns at me.

I take a deep sigh as Mom prattles on about coming home for the rest of the summer. There's no way I'm going home. If my brake lines were loosened on purpose, I know exactly who did it. The short-haired blonde woman lurking around our cabin the other night.

Sherry.

And if she did this, I must be getting close to finding out what happened to Aunt Heather. Sherry's scared for some reason. I rattled her cage. It reminds me of a case we studied in class about a group of boys that had murdered an elderly woman in a robbery. The boys had a pact to keep their secret, but one was showing signs of going to the police. One of his other friends had a suspicion that he was involved with the incident and kept asking questions. His brake lines were cut shortly after while driving with this friend to a party and ended up having a head-on collision, but both survived and he told the police everything that had happened.

And I want to know why she's so rattled.

A couple days later, I'm fully back into the camp routine. I walk up from the lake with the girls while Mel and Sherry are standing by an old gray pickup truck, talking. Sherry glances up, sees us, then whispers something to Mel, who looks over at us too and waves with a tight smile across her face.

Did we interrupt something?

"Can we help you with something?" I ask.

"I want a popsicle!" one of the girls cries.

"Ice-cream sandwich for me!" Christina calls out, laughing.

I grin. "Okay, whoever wants to get ice cream, go get it. We'll wait out here at the picnic tables."

All the girls go inside chatting about which kind they will choose.

Mel laughs. "You can't compete against ice cream."

"Yeah, true," I agree. "So, what are you two doing?"

"Oh, we just got some new shipments of T-shirts and sweat-shirts for the store," Mel explains. "We're taking them in."

"I'll help you carry them inside," I offer.

Sherry clears her throat. "Surprised you came back here after the accident."

I nod. "Yeah, my mom wanted me to come home."

"Maybe you should," Sherry says flatly. Her eyes appraise me, then flit to Mel.

I stare back at her, keeping my gaze cool and level. "Did you hear what happened?"

She nods. "Heard you had an issue with your brakes."

"Thank goodness you're okay!" Mel exclaims. Her uneasy gaze moves from me to Sherry.

"Yes, it was a scare," I reply. I continue to stare at Sherry. "Do you know anything about brakes, Sherry?"

She meets my gaze, those clear, blue eyes seeming to bore into me. Uh... I may have gone too far poking the bear with that one. Anger flares in her eyes.

"What exactly do you mean by that?" she demands in a fiery voice.

"Nothing, Aunt Sherry," Mel interrupts in a breezy voice, trying to break the tension. She picks up a box from the bed of the truck. "Come on, let's take these boxes inside."

Sherry holds her gaze for another moment before picking up a box, and she walks into the store without another word. I watch her disappear, just as she disappeared into the woods that night.

I'm going to find your secrets.

But I better be careful while I do it.

. . .

Wynn leans against the store's porch railing, chugging an energy drink and staring at us. He does his customary hair flip and then continues his stare.

"Why are you always lurking around?" I ask him, carrying a box of T-shirts. I sit it on the picnic table. Sherry and Mel are still inside the store.

He glances at me out of the corner of his eye. "Maybe you're the one lurking around."

I frown at him. "No, I'm the one working. Why don't you get a box from the truck and bring it inside?"

"You're not my boss," he says, draining the drink. He smashes the can on the railing and tosses it into the trash can in the corner of the porch.

I look at him. Maybe I should be friendlier to Wynn. He is Sherry's son so maybe he knows something. Or if I become friends with him, perhaps I can get closer to Sherry. Either way, it's a win for me. He's a little odd, but who isn't odd in this camp? Some days I feel like the only sane one here. Only some days though.

I smile at him. "I never said I was your boss. I just thought you'd want to help me."

Wynn stares at me, his surly attitude slowly dissipating. He cocks his head to the side. "Really?"

I laugh. "Really. Then we'll have a chance to talk."

I watch him consider my words, then he's beside me, lifting the box I placed on the picnic table. He does his usual hair flip again and grins at me.

"I'll take this in and then we can get the others together," he says, disappearing inside.

I smile back at him. Oh, this will be easy.

Mel and Sherry come outside and grab the remaining two boxes.

"I'll take this in, and I think the girls all have their ice cream," Mel says.

On cue, a line of girls emerges, each holding various flavors and types of ice cream.

"Okay, great. Um... do you mind if I take a short walk with Wynn before we head back to the cabin?"

"Really?" Mel asks, surprise colors her voice. "Yeah, sure. I can take the girls back when they're finished with their ice cream. Just head back to the cabin when you're done with your walk."

"Okay, great," I reply.

A few minutes later, Wynn and I are walking on the trail leading to the sunflower garden. We walk along in silence for a few minutes.

"So, tell me about yourself, Wynn," I say.

He glances at me. "You sound like a guidance counselor. Tell me about yourself. What are your life goals?"

I laugh. "Yeah, I guess I do kinda sound like that. Well, another subject... your mom doesn't seem to like me much."

A chuckle escapes him. "She doesn't like many people."

"Why's that?" I ask. Excitement courses through my body. Maybe Wynn is the one I should have been talking to all along. It makes sense he would know about most things that are going on around here.

Wynn looks thoughtful. "I don't really know. I do know she has a lot of secrets, and I don't know most of them. The ones I do know, I'm not supposed to."

"Really, like what?" I ask. Could it really have been this easy?

Wynn narrows his eyes at me. "Do you think I'm that dumb? I know why you wanted to go on this walk now. Just for information."

"No, of course not," I quickly say. "It's just... I do wonder why your mother seems so cold to me."

He laughs. "Cold might be the best you get from her. You

don't want her to be angry with you. Yeah, consider yourself lucky if she's only cold to you."

I stop in the path and face him.

"Why do you say that?"

He lets out a loud sigh. "Come on, Zoey, isn't it obvious? My mother is, well she's unhinged. You obviously know this, or you wouldn't be giving me the third degree."

I continue to stare at him and repeat the same question I asked earlier. "Why do you say that? I mean, it's kind of an odd answer about your own mother."

He meets my gaze. "You're full of questions, but if you pay attention, you'll find out. I will say to be careful. She may be unhinged, but she's smart too. And, yes, I'm her son, so I should know what I'm talking about. She's not a person to mess around with. And if for some reason she has a problem with you, you should take the threat seriously."

And with that, he turns and heads back down the path at a swift pace, leaving me alone in the woods to ponder his words.

Mel takes the girls to the pool later and I take the opportunity to complete a task. I tell her I'll catch up with her later because I have to use the bathroom. I don't, but I do want to set up a tiny camera I purchased at Walmart after I left the hospital, before returning to camp. If someone, I'm certain it's Sherry, is going to mess with my car again, I'll know about it. I take Wynn's warning seriously. I won't stop looking for answers, but I will be more careful how I go about doing it.

I pull the white bag from the duffel bag sitting under my bed. I read the instructions last night in bed using the flashlight on my phone. I take the tiny camera and walk outside the cabin. First, I survey the area, but nobody is around. This is the best time of day to do this, everyone is usually at activities, the pool or the lake.

I stand at the side of the cabin where the parking area is located. I look at the cabin wall and there are several notches that the camera would easily fit into. I usually park my car in the same spot, so I search for the best notch to hide it in. One that I can easily hide it inside and that it won't be noticed by anybody.

I choose the one farther to the left as it affords the best view of my car. I take the stepstool I brought outside from the cabin and quickly survey the area.

Empty. I need to move fast.

I put the stepstool in place and scramble up it. I lodge the small camera into the notch, making sure it's pointed directly at my car. Then I move down the steps and take the stepstool inside.

I pull my phone from the back pocket of my shorts and click on the camera app. A perfect view of my car.

I'm watching you now, Sherry.

Zoey

The East Lodge is lit up with multicolored strings of lights and a rotating silver disco ball in the center of the room. A DJ is set up at the front of the room, filling the area with blasting music. A refreshment table is set up to the left side of the DJ, covered in a crisp white tablecloth with a bowl of fruit punch in the center, pitchers of ice water on either side and various plates of cookies, cupcakes, brownies and cannoli. A fruit tray and veggie tray complete the table.

"I love the annual camp dance!" Mel says, touching my arm as we walk inside the building. Her face is beautifully made up with much more makeup than she normally wears. She looks great. "It's so fun!"

I'm wearing more makeup than usual too and a cute red dress with gold sandals. It feels good to be dressed up after weeks of wearing shorts and camp T-shirts. The girls are thrilled to be wearing fancy clothes, well at least for camp, too, and all their chatter while we got ready for the dance revealed they were also nervous about dancing with the boys. Well, more excited than nervous. Mel and I had fun listening to their concerns.

Mel also keeps trying to get me to talk more to Brett's friend, Dave. And as if on cue, Dave is standing by the DJ and waves to us.

"Oh, Zoey, there's Dave!" she says excitedly. "He is so fun. You should definitely go talk to him."

I smile. Dave's okay. He's a cute guy, nice to talk to, but I'm not interested in anyone right now. Even though I've told Mel many times, she still seems to think I need a boyfriend at camp for some reason.

"Maybe," I say noncommittally.

"Oh, he's talking to Sarah now." Mel frowns. "But she's so boring, don't worry about her."

"I'm not worried," I reply. "Brett's over there." Hopefully I can divert her attention away from me and Dave.

"Oh, where? How's my hair look?" she replies, adjusting her white dress.

"Over by the punch," I reply, staring at her. "So you're still seeing him? What about Cari? And, yes, your hair looks great."

"Yeah, there was nothing going on with her, I asked him. Thanks, Zoey." Mel smiles, her gaze darting over to him again. "He's coming over."

"Have fun," I say. I wave to Brett as he approaches and go to grab a cookie. I watch them as they walk off together. Mel is gullible to believe Brett, but I guess we all believe what we want to sometimes.

I pour some punch in one of the red plastic cups and select a peanut butter cookie. Most of the girls are out on the dance floor jumping around to the heavy beat vibrating through the room. A few boys join them, but most are hanging in the back by the entrance.

"Nice dress," a voice says behind me. I turn and Wynn is standing there in tan cargo shorts and a black polo.

"Thanks, you look nice too," I reply. I take a sip of punch. And he does.

"Are you going to dance tonight?" he asks, his eyebrows rising.

"Probably later, you?"

"I'll dance when you do." He grins at me.

"Okay, I'll look for you on the dance floor," I reply.

"Under the disco ball."

"Sure."

"That was my mom's idea. She thinks it's retro cool." Wynn uses air quotes.

"Well, it's fun," I remark. "You know I wanted to ask you something on our walk the other day."

"More questions about my mom?"

I shrug. "Sorry, but yes. I think your mom may have done something to my brake lines. I'm sure you heard about what happened to my car."

He nods. "I have."

"So... do you think she could have done it?"

He stares at me. "Why would you ask me? Do you trust me? Don't you think I'll tell her what you're saying? I mean, she is my mother after all."

"Will you?" My goodness, I hope not. I might not wake up tomorrow, but for some reason I don't think he'll say a word to his mother about our conversation. I think the only loyalty Wynn has is to himself.

He's quiet, his blue eyes flitting from me to the floor. It's probably only a few minutes but feels like an eternity.

"I won't. I don't think she would do something like that, but she's unpredictable. There's a lot about her that I don't understand." He pauses. "I think she can be dangerous though. But I don't know a lot of things, just suspicions really."

"Of your own mother?" I ask. I'm surprised by his response.

Wynn is a little odd, but much more perceptive than I originally thought.

"I'm being honest with you." Wynn lowers his voice. "I like you."

I smile, knowing I need to use his attraction to me to gain information about Sherry, but I still need to maintain boundaries with him. I'm not interested in him at all.

"I like you too," I reply. "I really like talking to you."

A slow smile spreads across his face, and we stand silent for a few moments. I'm being honest in that statement. I do enjoy talking to him; he's an interesting sort of person.

"Come on, Zoey." Mel grabs my hand, pulling me away from Wynn. "We have to do the chicken dance."

She whirls me onto the dance floor, and we do all the motions and shake our tailfeathers, making our girls squeal with laughter and we do the same. We stay out and dance two more songs before going to retrieve a drink. Wynn is gone. I'm not sure if he left or is just lingering around somewhere.

"I'm going to the lake with Brett after the dance," Mel tells me. Her eyes are bright as she guzzles her punch. "I won't be back until late."

"Sure, no problem," I say. "Is it a party?"

"Yeah, a party of two." She winks at me. "You know what I mean."

"I do, have fun," I reply with a grin.

"Oh, I will." Mel fills her cup again. "Don't wait up for me."

I smile at her, glad to see her happy. She has a lot on her mind, like I do, and sometimes you must let everything go. Just living your life without analyzing everything.

Something I struggle with daily.

The cabin is quiet, the girls are asleep, but Mel isn't back yet. I've been lying on my bed trying to think of the name of a case study we had in my Theories of Crime class about a missing girl in western Pennsylvania. Cassidy or Cassie? I pick up my iPad from the nightstand next to the bed and start searching.

She was fourteen and ran away with her sixteen-year-old boyfriend. The family never reported her missing, that only happened after the boyfriend was found on a construction site several months later. He had been shot and dumped into a ravine, but there was no sign of the girl. Cassidy, that was the girl's name.

I search for a bit but it seems no new information has come up on the case. It reminds me of Aunt Heather's case, and it happened in the early nineties before Amber alerts. In both of these cases though, neither girl was reported missing in a reasonable timeframe.

I swipe through my search results, looking over the information again, wishing it would somehow give me a direction with Aunt Heather's case. She broke up with her boyfriend and another man picked her up. Who?

Mandy and I always watched *Dateline* at college when it was on. Obviously, I'm a true crime fanatic and she loves mysteries too. And it's always that tiny detail that leads to a full reveal, often lying in plain sight.

I'm missing something here. Was there another guy in her life that nobody knew about? A secret boyfriend?

I ponder the thought for a few moments and then close the cover of the iPad.

TWENTY-EIGHT
2024

Zoey

Celina surveys the various pizza boxes lined up on the counter in the dining hall. I do the same and choose ham and pineapple, not my usual, but on occasion I like a change.

"What are you going to pick?" I ask.

"I don't know. I might just get plain cheese," she says, frowning. "I don't like lots of stuff on my pizza."

"Sure, plain cheese is good," I say. "I'm going for the pineapple and ham. Oh, there's meatball too."

"I'll try the meatball!" Celina says, grabbing a slice.

I laugh at her excitement. I guess she likes meatballs.

The pizza party is for the two cabins which won the scavenger hunt yesterday, and we are one of the lucky winners. I grab a paper plate, take a slice of pineapple and a slice of meatball.

Mel walks up and snags a slice of supreme. She looks at me and motions at an empty table at the side of the room. She grabs two water bottles and walks over to it while I follow.

"I was thinking," she says as we sit our food down on the

table, "there's a storage area in the back of the garage at our house. Maybe we should look through it and see if we can find any clues about your aunt in there. I don't know what we'll find, but there's so much junk in there, there may be a clue or two."

"Sure," I say. "Let's look in there. You never know, we might find something."

"Okay." She nods. "Let's do it tomorrow afternoon. Mom and Dad have another appointment together, so they'll be out. And Aunt Sherry will be busy, so nobody will question what we're doing in there."

"Sounds great." I take a bite of pineapple pizza, chewing slowly, then swallow. "So, you're still sure they're seeing a marriage therapist?"

"I'm not sure about anything. They didn't really say, but something is going on with them. They've been acting so secretive lately, and having all of these appointments, it's unusual," Mel says. "It's driving me nuts."

"Maybe just ask them," I suggest.

Mel frowns. "I have and they just brush it off, oh, it's only an appointment. I am going to find out one way or another."

I nod and take a drink of water.

"And what about you? Brett said Dave's really interested in you."

I look at her. "Really? I've barely spoken to him."

"Zoey, come on, you've got to start dating sometime and Dave is so great! He really likes you. Give him a chance," she says. Her eyes go wide. "I promise you will have so much fun with him."

I shrug. "I don't know why you're so insistent on me dating Dave."

"Because we're friends," Mel says. "I want you to be happy."

"Okay, I'll think about it," I reply. "Anyway, tomorrow we check out the garage, right?"

"It's a plan." Mel smiles at me and takes a bite of pizza.

The next day we slip into the garage located at the side of the big green house with the shiny white shutters. Mel leads the way to the storage room in the back of the concrete structure. She opens the door, and it makes a loud squeak, then flips on the light switch. It's a continuation of the basement. Boxes, old chairs, some broken lawn equipment and spiderwebs dominate the space. I sneeze as soon as I step inside. The air is stale and it feels as if it's been months since any fresh air entered the area. It's a large space, just four concrete walls, and the entrance door, no windows. Without the overhead lighting, it would be pitch black in here.

"Eww..." I say as I walk into a long spiderweb. I swipe it off my hair and wipe it on my shorts.

"Yeah, it's a mess in here," Mel says, walking around, kicking some boxes out of her way. She glances at the door to the garage that's partially open.

"Where should we start?" I ask, sneezing one more time.

Mel shoves a few boxes around then pulls out some from the back. They're coated with a thick dust. "These boxes look like they've been here for a while. Let's look through them. Like I said, I don't know what's in here or if anything will help you, but we can just poke around."

"Okay." I open one of the boxes. Some old clothes are inside. A few pairs of girls' shorts, a pair of bell-bottomed jeans, a fringe vest, a T-shirt with a peace sign on the front, and some old sandals. An old backpack lies under the clothes, and I open it. Toiletries that are cracked and yellow with age lie inside. Deodorant, toothpaste, a yellowed toothbrush, an old pink hairbrush and a makeup bag. I unzip the bag and inside is a bunch of expired makeup, dried up and brittle. Why would anyone keep this junk?

A faded photograph lies under the fringe vest. I pick it up. Two teenage girls wear shorts, camp T-shirts, long striped tube socks and sneakers. They have their arms around each other, smiling broadly at the camera. I turn it over, *Nadine and Marie, 1974* is written on the back.

Who are these girls?

I look at the contents of the box again: Everything is of a personal nature. Why would someone leave these items behind and why would someone store them? I place the photo in my pocket. I pick up the fringe vest and inspect it. A small pocket is on the side. I slip my hand inside and pull out a scrap of wrinkled paper.

The cabin at midnight

I frown at the words. They don't really mean anything. There's lots of cabins here and someone was meeting another at midnight, but the nature of these saved items is unusual. I shove the note inside my pocket with the picture, then take a few pictures with my phone of the other items in the box.

I've been listening to true-crime podcasts for a few years, my favorites being *Cold Case Files* and *Up and Vanished*. Nobody just disappears, there's always a story to be told, but unfortunately those stories are not always revealed, to the anguish of their loved ones. Other stories though with a thorough investigation uncover the reason and the steps that led to a disappearance, and with that information the knowledge of the person's whereabouts is revealed, either living or dead. The right piece of the puzzle is all you need to complete a picture.

Nobody would leave these items voluntarily. I think there's more of a mystery here than only Aunt Heather going missing at the camp. Could others have run into foul play too?

I look up, seeking Mel, and it doesn't take long. She's staring at me, that creepy-ass smile on her face. Then her smile read-justs and she's herself again. She's a mystery in some ways too.

"Did you find anything?" she asks cheerfully. She walks over to me.

I show her the stuff in the box, and she gasps. "Oh, how weird. Who would leave things like this behind? It's really strange, right? Do you think some of this belonged to your aunt?"

I shrug. "Maybe, there's no way for me to tell, but it's an interesting find."

We pick through the boxes for another half an hour, but don't find anything else that would relate to the case. Sweaty and dusty now, we decide to call it quits and head back to the cabin.

We stop at the camp store and get sodas, then sit down on the porch when we get back to the cabin, drinking and talking about our finds. The girls' laughter spills out of the cabin. They're playing card games, which keeps them busy for a while.

The image of the clothing and personal items is still vivid in my mind.

Mel stands up. "I'm going to get some chips. Do you want anything?"

I shake my head, and she disappears into the cabin.

I pull out the old photograph from my back pocket and stare at the teenage girls. Instead of answering questions, I only have more.

TWENTY-NINE
1989

Heather

We sit on the bed of Dean's truck, snuggling on the blanket we had at the fireworks. Everyone was tired after swimming and eating all afternoon and went to bed, but we wanted to continue our conversation from earlier.

"I mean, I'll ask my parents first, but I'm not letting you go back to that house," he says, determination lit in his eyes. "No way is that going to happen."

"I can't go back." I shake my head. "Running away with you would be amazing, but dropping out of high school?"

"I'll get my GED eventually," he says. "I never wanted to go to college anyway. I want to work with my hands, on cars, whatever, fixing things. And I can do that now."

"You're so good at it too," I say, wrapping my arms around him.

"Do you want to go to college?"

I sigh. "I don't know. I'll get my GED too and then we'll see."

"What do you think you'd want to do as a job?"

I'm quiet for a moment. What do I want to do? I don't know, I'm sixteen. I love to write, maybe I could be an author? But I don't have a clue how to do that. I'd probably have to go to college. How does an author make money by writing stories? That's not a real job, is it? I mean, I know authors write books, but I don't think regular people like me could be a writer, could I? It seems like a fantasy job. Not like working in a factory, or a grocery store or an office. I can do those jobs and make money but it's not what I want to do.

"You like to write," he says softly. "I saw your notebook and the one you keep in your backpack at school."

I nod. "I do."

"What do you like to write?"

I smile. "Poems and stories."

"Maybe you can write for a newspaper or something," he suggests.

"Maybe one day. I could get a job but keep working on my writing."

Dean kisses me. "Yes, we can do anything as long as we're together. I know we can."

I lean against his chest and listen to his heart beating. He's all I want. Emotion wells inside me. I'm so lucky to be here with him, to have someone like him in my life. He's my home and excitement runs through me thinking about the possibility of our future.

Our future together.

The path to the pool seems shorter today for some reason and I soon emerge from the trees and head toward the pool entrance. It's so hot today and I can't wait to take a swim. But then I stop and shrink back among the trees again. Dean is standing by the side of the pool, but it's not him I'm watching now.

It's Jennifer.

She stands in front of Dean talking to him. She's standing very close to him, as close as you can to someone without touching them. She tosses her long blonde hair back and pushes her chest forward, wearing her cute yellow bikini. She extends a hand and lightly places it on his bare chest for a moment, then he brushes it away.

She smiles and laughs, her eyes fixed on him. She says something I can't hear from here, and Dean shakes his head. She continues to stare and smile at him.

She's totally coming on to him.

It's obvious she has a crush on him. I knew that right away, but come on, she knows we're together. And I thought the two of us were friends.

Guess I thought wrong.

Maybe all those late-night visits to my tent aren't about seeing me, but rather seeing Dean. Bringing food and stuff to his poor pathetic girlfriend living in the woods. Maybe these girls aren't my friends at all.

Anger seeps through me as I continue to watch her talking to my boyfriend. Although I can't hear what she says, her body language is enough for me to determine what she's up to here.

She wants him.

Of course she does.

I stride over through the pool entrance and walk over to them. I grab Dean's hand, wrap my arms around him and give him a big kiss, and then turn toward Jennifer.

"Oh, wow." He grins at me.

I smile at him. "I just missed you."

Jennifer stands awkwardly beside me. "Yeah, that was some kiss."

I stare at her, my hand now on Dean's chest.

He's mine and you better back off. I don't say it with words, but I'm sure my eyes relay the message to her.

"That's how it is when you're in love," I say to her. My gaze meets hers.

"Oh..." She looks away now. "See you guys later, I'm going to swim."

Dean and I watch her walk away. He kisses the top of my head and whispers to me.

"What was that all about?"

I look up at him. "She was hitting on you."

He shrugs. "So what, I don't want her."

I smile. "Who do you want?"

He kisses me. "You. I want you. It's always you."

I have so much time to daydream during the day and now even more fills my dreams. What will life look like once Dean and I get away from here? Excitement fills me as I think about all the possibilities.

And my writing. Could I really be a writer one day? A real writer. We were going to move to New Jersey and that's so close to New York City where I imagine all the writers and creative types live and work. Maybe we could eventually move there, get a cute apartment in SoHo, I like to say that name, or any part of the city. Not that I even know much about SoHo or any of the neighborhoods; I've never been there, but I've dreamed about it, even before all of this happened.

The thought of such a big change in my life makes me look forward to the future and what I can do in it, in a completely different way. I'll be in a new place with Dean. It's what I've always wanted.

This is really going to happen!

My thoughts go to the other day at the pool with Jennifer. There's been a weird vibe between us since then and they haven't stopped by my tent the last couple of nights. A big change for them because they usually stop by several times a week. Sometimes every evening for a bit.

And I'm fine with that. Even though I thought they were my friends, and maybe they are, I could be overreacting. But I'm getting anxious now to start my new life with Dean. I don't want anything or anyone messing it up. I'm glad I was able to stay here at the camp, but now I want to move on with Dean. I'm done with the camp life now. I want a real life.

I sit on the camp chair and pull my orange apart, placing a segment into my mouth. I wish there was a way to fast forward with Dean and me living in a little apartment. Him working at the garage and me working somewhere and writing stories in the evenings. I want it so badly I can taste it.

THIRTY
2024

Zoey

My phone buzzes and I pull it from my back pocket. Mom again. She's dead set on me coming home for the rest of the summer. I understand why she's worried. I'd be worried too if I had a daughter and she was in a car accident. Maybe I should be more worried about myself. She even said her and Dad would pay me the amount I'd earn working at the camp. I shake my head and put my phone back in my pocket.

I haven't shared my discoveries about the other girls that went missing from the camp too, or how I'm certain that Jennifer and Sherry know details about Aunt Heather's disappearance. If I had, she'd probably come out here and refuse to leave until I went home with her. No, I started this investigation and I'm going to complete it.

I can't go home yet.

This isn't about money. I mean, I do need the money, I'm a college student after all, but this is about finding the truth. While I'm curious about Aunt Heather, it's really a gift to Mom. And honestly, I don't feel like I can leave this camp without uncovering the truth. I need to uncover the truth for all of us, especially Mom. I also need to prove to her that I can do things on my own. I can't have her hovering over me all the time.

I want to give her answers about her long-lost sister. Even though she kept Aunt Heather's existence a secret from me all these years, I can tell looking back that the pain always lingered with her. Mom aches to know what happened to her and I want to, and have to, give her answers.

I'm so close.

Close enough to cause danger for me, but I'll deal with that issue. I'm certain something shady happened at this camp and I'd bet money on it that Sherry and probably Jennifer know exactly what happened.

Did they *kill* her?

It's not the first time I've had this thought. I haven't decided what I think about it though. I can't imagine Jennifer hurting anyone. Sherry though, yeah, I think it's possible she could have done something like that. But what would be her motive? Did it have something to do with Aunt Heather's boyfriend, Dean? And what about the man who Heather apparently left the camp with?

I have no idea what the truth is, but I'm sure that even if she's not a killer, Jennifer knows more than she's admitted so far. Maybe I should try talking to her again.

The thought lingers in my mind.

That's exactly what I should do.

I have my camp chair set up under a shady hemlock at the back of the cabin. We're having a lazy afternoon. Mel took some of the girls to a basket-weaving activity, but others wanted to stay at the cabin, some reading, some taking naps, and I'm going to do some research on my phone.

I get comfortable and type in some keywords. *Missing girls. 1974. Camp Medley. Nadine and Marie.* I'm not exactly confident I'll get any hits on this story since it happened years before the internet was around.

But I get lucky.

An article, written in 2004, by a local newspaper detailed the disappearance of the two girls, and one of the girls' mothers, Nadine's, continued to ask police to reopen the cold case, even though police declared it a runaway situation in 1974. Louise Rivers, Nadine's mother, insisted that her daughter was not a runaway: She was never in contact with her or any of her friends or family. Louise said in the article that Nadine would never do this, never cut all ties with everyone she knows. She was certain something had happened to her daughter and she wanted answers. I scan the article, but no new details catch my eye, other than Nadine's mother's name.

Maybe I can contact her. I type in her name and my hopes are quickly dashed. Louise Rivers passed away in 2013. I read the obituary and see that Louise had another daughter, Gayle, Nadine's sister. I type in her name and find she lives about two hours away, and unbelievably, a phone number is listed for her. A landline.

Should I try calling? The answer is immediate: yes.

I call the number, and it rings once, twice, three times and then a woman answers.

"Hello?"

I clear my throat. "Hello, is this Gayle Rivers?"

"Yes, who's calling?" she asks.

"My name is Zoey Montgomery. I'm a counselor at Camp Medley and I'm investigating the disappearance of my aunt from the camp in nineteen eighty-nine. In my research I learned about your sister, Nadine." I pause. "I wonder if I could ask you some questions, or if you could share her story with me?"

She's quiet for a moment. "Your aunt went missing from the camp too?"

"Yes, and I've been searching through some of the camp's storage areas. I found a photo of Nadine and Marie and a box of personal items."

"Personal items?" Gayle repeats quickly. "Like what?"

"Um… clothes, a brush, that sort of thing. I took a couple of pictures. If you give me your cell number, I'll text them to you."

She does and I do, keeping the line open still.

Gayle lets out a deep sigh. "That fringed vest is Nadine's. She loved that thing, and she wouldn't have left it behind. We always knew she didn't run away. I wonder if this will be enough to reopen the investigation of her disappearance."

We talk several minutes longer. She tells me more about her sister, and I tell her about my aunt. Gayle is going to talk to the police about getting a search warrant for the camp, and she says she will be in touch with me soon.

I click off my phone and hope springs in me. Maybe, with Gayle's help, we'll find answers for all the missing girls.

THIRTY-ONE
2024

Zoey

Movie night is one of those perfect starry nights with a slight chill in the air making a sweatshirt over a T-shirt a cozy necessity. Mel and I work the popcorn/candy stand while Brett and Wynn handle the drinks and the cotton-candy machine. Wynn looks thrilled as he spins fluffy pink and blue sugar.

Mel is over by the back of the table talking to Brett while I fill bags of popcorn and hand them out to the campers. Their voices carry over to me as I do so. It doesn't seem like things are going very well with them.

"And you think that's okay?" Mel's voice rises. I glance back and she's pointing her finger at Brett, who's backing away from her. "I will not be treated like that."

"Geez, Mel, we're not *married*, we're not even a couple," he retorts. "This is just a summer hookup, you know that."

"Do I?" Mel's face is bright red. She clearly did not know that, even though she had a clue about his activities. And if I remember correctly, I think she did say that they were a summer fling, but maybe she wanted it to be more. "Do I know that?"

Brett shakes his head. "Whatever, I'm done."

He walks back to Wynn and helps him hand out freshly spun cotton candy, without so much as a backward glance to Mel. She stares at him for a moment and then runs into the woods.

"Hey, Wynn," I say. "Take over for me. I'm going to talk to Mel."

Wynn shrugs. "Okay."

I wipe my buttery, salty hands on my shorts and hurry into the woods searching for Mel. She's just a few feet in, sitting on a bench in a meditation garden off the trail, her face in her hands.

She's crying.

I walk over and sit next to her and put my arm around her. She glances up at me and wipes her eyes.

"I don't know why I'm crying about him," she says. "He's such a jerk."

I nod. "It's still upsetting."

"Yeah, it is." Mel sighs and sits back on the bench.

We sit in silence for a few minutes, then Mel starts talking at record speed about Brett, Cari and what a jerk he was to her. I let her rant because sometimes that's all we want to, or need to do, to feel better and move on. There's something cathartic about saying the words out loud.

By the time we're done, her tears have dried and there is a hint of a smile on her face. I'm glad I followed her into the woods. She just needed someone to talk to, to work out her thoughts about everything with Brett. By tomorrow, she'll barely remember him.

"Want to go back to the movie?" I ask.

"I guess so." She looks at me. "Thanks for listening to me, Zoey. You're a good friend."

"Sure, no problem." I smile at her. "We're friends, good friends."

She nods but then gives me an odd look. "It's too bad..."

"What's too bad?" I ask.

Mel shakes her head. "Um, it's just too bad we won't know each other long."

I frown. That's an unusual thing to say. "Why?"

"Well, when summer's over, we'll go our separate ways," she stammers.

"Uh, yeah, sure," I reply. "But we can still keep in touch with each other."

"Of course." She hugs me and grabs my hand. "Let's go back to the movie."

We walk back down the trail in the darkness and back into the movie area. Her words still ring in my ears and I'm still not quite sure what she meant by them, just add it to my list of never-ending questions.

The photograph of my aunt with Jennifer and Sherry lies on my bed beside me. I lean on my side staring at it, the flashlight from my phone directed at it. Aunt Heather looks older in this picture than the other ones Mom has. I guess most of them are from when she was fifteen and younger and, in this shot, she's sixteen, so she *is* older.

I smile looking at her. Beautiful long, dark wavy hair, warm brown eyes and a sprinkle of freckles on her nose. I turn my phone on picture mode facing myself. There's a definite resemblance with me, but she's much prettier, in my opinion. I have the long, dark wavy hair and brown eyes, but no freckles. I do have a few of their ugly cousin, the mole, only on my arms, though. I wonder if that's why I feel such a connection to her, because we have similar looks? That might be a part of it, but I think it was my mother's pain that created that connection for me.

Once I found out about Aunt Heather, Mom was hesitant to talk about her, angry even that I was digging into the past, but then she started talking about all her memories of her younger sister. I loved hearing stories of Mom and her sister growing up. I know there were many unhappy memories too, but Mom told me those sparingly. Mostly she talked about when they lived with their grandmother, Gran they called her. She talked about the things they did together, the secrets they shared and how lucky she felt to have a sister like Heather. She was her best friend. She said she was a creative person, enjoyed writing stories in her notebooks and drawing pictures. She and Gran liked to do crafts together sometimes, but not my mom; she thought it was boring. I enjoy crafting sometimes and used to be into scrapbooking when I was younger, so I guess I shared that creativity with Aunt Heather. Listening to all the stories only strengthened my desire to solve her mystery for Mom and myself.

After learning about Heather, I thought even more seriously about my choice to pursue a degree in Criminology. Before, no other career path held any interest for me. Now, I want to seek out answers, justice for those who are unable to do so. Studying Criminology is fascinating to me. Understanding the psychology and personalities of criminals and the reasons why they commit crimes has always held my interest. The research methods and how they relate to the law, honestly, everything about it draws me in. And in one more year, I'll be in the field helping people and making my own impact in the world.

From the scant details Mom gave me about her childhood it was such a difference from mine. I know that her mother had a problem with addiction and had a lot of men in and out of her life. I know she eventually married a man who was abusive toward my mom and Heather, but that's about it. And I understand why she wouldn't want to tell me all the details. I don't think Mom will ever tell me everything. Only she and Heather know those details. Well only her, probably.

I'm certain Heather isn't with us anymore.

It's funny though how a person's life can change so much if the right people or right opportunities come into your life. Like my mom, she got a job as a receptionist in an insurance office and that's where she met my dad. If she never got that job, she probably never would have met him.

The right place and the right time.

Or the wrong place at the wrong time.

Unfortunately, I think that's what happened to Aunt Heather.

I know that summer internship would have been good experience and help me land a job after graduation, but being here digging around and learning more about Aunt Heather has strengthened my desire to crack cold cases. Of course, I must crack this one first.

And I'm certain I will.

I sigh. What will my life look like five, ten years from now? Investigating cold cases, finding answers for people's loved ones, finding answers for the lost ones, the abused, the murdered, the forgotten. Getting answers for the family they left behind is important, but getting answers for the individual is even more important to me. Everyone has a story and if they can't tell it themselves, then it's my job to tell it for them.

And my personal life? Who knows? Will I fall in love again? Will I want a new relationship, feel the way about someone I still feel about Craig? I want to, but I don't know if I ever will have those feelings for another person again. I feel like I'm at such a standstill in my life right now. I want answers to everything, and it seems like the more I want the answers, the more elusive they become for me. And it's frustrating.

I hope Gayle can convince the police to get a search warrant for the camp with the pictures I sent her of Nadine's vest. Something is going on at this camp—more than one girl has gone missing and nothing has been done about it. People don't just disappear; they have to be somewhere. Maybe the girls never left this camp.

I lie back on the bed as Mel snores in the bunk above me and the girls sleep, soft breathing filling the cabin. I continue to stare at the picture. I know Sherry might be dangerous, but what about Jennifer?

She seems like the levelheaded one between the two sisters. I mean, obviously, but she knows something. Is she only protecting her sister, or is there something more going on? Does she have her own secrets?

I open the nightstand drawer next to the bed and pull out the 1989 camp yearbook. I flip through the pages. Aunt Heather's boyfriend was a counselor here and his name was Dean. His picture must be in here someplace. How many counselors named Dean could there be in this yearbook? I don't know why I never thought of it before now.

I hold my phone close to the pages, studying the names. Then one appears, Dean Thorton. I stare at the picture of a good-looking teenage guy with dark blond hair and a friendly smile. I quickly go through all the other cabins and the counselor's names. Only one Dean. This was Aunt Heather's boyfriend. I stare at the pictures, a million questions running through my mind.

Mr. T, Mel's father.

Jennifer's husband.

THIRTY-TWO
2024

Zoey

On Sunday, my throat is scratchy and even though I don't feel like stopping at the small grocery store where Pearl works, I have to do so. I need some cough drops. Today I'm finally driving to Craig's house. I've been toying with the idea since I arrived at camp and it's something I need to do. So a quick stop at the store for cough drops as it's the closest place to get them and then off to his house. For some reason, the camp store doesn't stock them. I'm still reeling from the revelation that Aunt Heather's boyfriend at the camp is Dean Thorton. This story is getting stranger and stranger. I'm certain Jennifer, Sherry and Dean know exactly what happened to Aunt Heather. All three of them had some part in her disappearance, I'm sure of it. I won't tell Mom yet though. If I do, she'll come out here and demand that I leave the camp. Even I must admit, I'm feeling a bit scared for my own safety.

Could Dean have been seeing Jennifer behind Aunt Heather's back, and the two girls got into an argument, a fight, over him? I know Sherry would instantly take Jennifer's side, maybe things went too far, resulting in Aunt Heather's death? I was certain Aunt Heather was dead from the first time Mom told me the story in our kitchen, otherwise she would have contacted Mom, but even so, getting those details will be difficult and especially difficult to share with Mom. I know I'm getting close to the truth.

But that theory doesn't explain the other missing girls. My thoughts continue to spin with probable possibilities of how the two stories connect and, unfortunately, I don't have any solid answers at this point.

I survey the selections in the small medicine display at the front of the store and pick two cherry-flavored packs. I walk slowly to the only open cash register.

Pearl's register.

She stands with a scowl on her face, and I wonder if that's how her face always looks as she wordlessly scans my purchase.

"Still at that camp?" she asks without looking at me. She stares at the cough drops as she places them into a small bag.

A chill creeps up my spine. What's this woman's problem? "Uh... yeah." I say it in barely a whisper as if someone was eavesdropping on me. My hand shakes. I feel so unnerved by this old woman.

Her gray eyes now bore into me as she looks up from the bag. "I told you that's not a good idea. You really should leave, for your own good. That camp is nothing but trouble; those people aren't right. You should run while you can."

I swallow hard; my hands become clammy. "What does that mean? Why did you say that?"

Pearl's gaze softens slightly, and a sigh escapes her. "Sorry to scare you, but you should leave that camp."

"Why?"

Another customer is behind me loading pasta, a bag of apples, and boxes of cereal onto the conveyor belt. Pearl stares at me for a moment, begins to say something, then shakes her head.

"Four dollars and twenty-nine cents," she says.

I pay the bill and continue to stare at her, my hands still shaking, wishing she would say more. "Pearl, would you like to meet at the coffee shop next door sometime to talk about the camp?"

She gives me the receipt. "Sure, I'm finished with work at five."

"I'll see you there," I reply, taking my bag.

She doesn't say another word and begins scanning the next customer's groceries. I walk out of the store and to my car. I don't bother to give a backward glance like the other times.

I guess I'm coming back at five.

Pearl is so strange, but I must know whatever it is that she wants to tell me. It must be something serious or she's just playing games with me. Maybe she's just a lonely old lady who likes to make up drama, and I'm falling for it. Regardless, I have an uneasy feeling about her. And if she does know something, I should at least hear what she has to say.

Run while you can.

The words echo in my mind as I start my car and drive out of the parking lot, heading to Craig's house. Today I will find out the truth.

About everything.

I take the third exit off the interstate and follow the directions on my car's navigation system until I arrive at my destination. I drive slowly along the road, causing the motorist behind me to honk the horn and pass me, before I put my turn signal on. I turn onto a long, paved driveway that leads to a substantial two-story home with an attached three-car garage. A dark red compact car is parked in the driveway. I pull my car in next to it and kill the engine.

Nerves race inside me as I stare at the immaculate home with dark brown siding and a stunning stone archway at the entrance. I gather myself, open the car door, and march up to the front door. I'm going to do this and get some answers today.

I ring the doorbell.

Footsteps hurry to the door and it opens. A middle-aged woman wearing a pair of sweatpants and a light blue T-shirt stands in the doorway.

"Hello," she says pleasantly, a curious expression on her face.

"Hi," I say, smiling. "My name is Zoey Montgomery. Is Craig home?"

"Craig, uh no, sorry," the woman says slowly.

"Um, is his father home?" I ask hopefully.

"No," the woman says firmly.

I frown. "Oh, well, this is awkward. I was dating Craig at school, and we broke up. He texted me and broke up with me and I..."

I sound like an idiot, babbling on about Craig. I should never have come here.

"Oh." The woman's expression softens. "I'm Martha. Would you like to come in, maybe have a glass of lemonade?"

"Yes, thank you." I follow Martha into the cool, spacious house and pause at a large family photo hanging on the wall over the fireplace in the family room. A young teenage Craig with his parents standing in front of a sparkling blue ocean. All smiling brightly as they look at the camera. I sigh, missing him again. I continue into the kitchen behind Martha. I am wondering who she is.

She walks to the refrigerator and retrieves a glass pitcher of lemonade, pours two glasses and motions for me to join her at the kitchen table. I sit and take a sip of lemonade.

"Zoey," Martha says, smiling. "Craig mentioned you."

"Really?" Hope springs in me. "When did you talk to him?"

"Oh, it's been months since we've spoken. Not since he took off to Europe. He's contacted his father a couple times though."

"Oh." My voice drops.

"Craig called home a few times before he left, and you're all he talked about," Martha says, seriously. "You broke his heart when you broke up with him. I think he was serious about you. I never heard him talk about a girl like that. I don't know if I ever heard him talk about a girl; he usually is so private about things like that."

Her words ring in my mind. *You broke his heart when you broke up with him.* I didn't break up with him. Why would she think this?

"Zoey?" The woman is speaking to me again.

"Yes," I say, still distracted.

"I've worked for Richard since Craig was fourteen, shortly after his mother died. You know Richard is a pilot and he's gone for long stretches of time. He wanted someone to always be here for Craig, so I also live here. When Craig went off to college things changed between us." Martha smiles. "We've been in a relationship for the last six months."

I look at her in surprise. "Oh, Craig never mentioned that."

She shakes her head, her eyes sad. "Well, he only found out about that a few days before taking off to Europe. Richard called him maybe a day before leaving school for spring break. It caused a bit of a rift between him and his father, and I think combined with your breakup, he needed to get away from everything. I feel bad that he was upset by the news."

I stare at her. I had left school a day before him to head home. Why hadn't he called me if he was upset about his dad? Did this information somehow impact him breaking up with me, but how? Feelings swirl inside me at her mention of him seeming to be serious with me and how much he talked about me. I know what we had together was special, but the other part confuses me. "I didn't break up with him. Craig broke up with me."

Surprise covers Martha's face. "Oh, Richard, that's Craig's father, said you broke up with him. That's why he quit college and is traveling across Europe."

"No!" I say it a bit too forcefully. I don't understand. Why would Craig say that to his father?

"Well, I'm not sure what happened with you two, but I know Craig sounded so happy when he spoke about you."

Sadness trickles through me at her words. I was so happy with him too.

"When will Craig's father be back home?" I ask.

"In two weeks. He has a few international flights; he was hoping to catch up with Craig when he's there."

"Where is Craig now, do you know?" I ask.

"Richard said in the last text, he was in France."

So, Craig is only communicating in texts with his father too?

"Has his father spoken to Craig on the phone or video chat lately?"

Martha thinks for a moment. "No, I think just texting. The last time they spoke on the phone was when Richard told him about us. He wanted to give him some space to deal with everything. Craig has money from his mother's life insurance, so we haven't been too concerned about him. We just hope he's enjoying himself."

I take another drink of lemonade, choking down the sweet drink. A sick feeling spreads through my body and it's not from the lemonade.

Something's not right here.

THIRTY-THREE
2024

Zoey

I take a bite of the banana nut muffin and a sip of my caramel macchiato, then a glance at the large coffee-mug-shaped clock hanging on the wall, its slow tick tock grating on my nerves. I want to get this meeting over with and am wondering now if I'm being stood up.

Pearl is ten minutes late.

I'm still mulling over my conversation with Martha. Why would Craig tell his father I broke up with him? And why hasn't he called, or video chatted with his father at least once in three months? Only texting seems so odd to me. Granted, if Craig's traveling, he may be in areas without service and his dad's a busy pilot, but come on, not one call in over three months, almost four. That isn't normal.

The front door of the coffee shop jingles open and Pearl walks in, still wearing a navy-blue polo shirt, must be a uniform of sorts for the grocery store, but no name tag. That's likely stashed in the large dark leather purse she carries. She nods at me and orders a coffee at the counter.

She walks over to me, coffee in hand, and sits down across from me.

"I don't think I ever asked your name," she says. "Or if I did, I forgot it."

"Zoey," I reply.

"Zoey," she repeats. "Thanks for meeting me."

"Sure," I say. A wary feeling settles in my stomach, unsure of how this meeting will go.

She looks a little less scary under the dimmer, cozier light of the coffee shop. For one thing, she's not wearing her usual scowl, which makes her appear a bit friendlier. She's just a small, older woman, nobody I should be frightened of, so I guess I'm overreacting, but there's something... her eyes, still sharp as ever, study me. And that rush of uneasiness floods through me once again.

"Sorry if I scared you earlier," she says. "I'm usually in a bad mood when I'm at work. Who isn't?"

I nod. "What did you want to tell me?"

"Well, I worked in the kitchen at the camp in the late eighties. Not a bad job, but the owners were terrible, especially Ed Jefferies. The temper on that man was awful, you didn't want to get on the wrong side of him. I don't know how his wife put up with him," Pearl states.

"So that was Mrs. Jefferies's husband," I say.

"Yeah, Rose Jefferies. She was okay, mostly." Pearl pauses. "But something wasn't quite right about her either, but I'm not sure what exactly. Probably living with that man for so many years."

"I only saw her briefly at a campfire one night. She was very upset," I reply.

Pearl cocks her head. "Oh, why?"

"Did you hear about the legend of The Man in the Woods, the serial killer? One of the counselors was telling a ghost story about it and she became upset about it."

Pearl scoffs. "Yeah, that's just an old rumor. In the seventies two teenage girls went missing from the camp. The police decided the girls ran off together; they called them deviants, what a thing to call two young girls who are missing, but the rumor grew that they were taken by The Man in the Woods."

My thoughts drift back to my conversation with Gayle about her missing sister. I hope she's successful in getting the police to open the case again. These girls deserve answers just like my aunt does.

I look at Pearl. "Was one of the girls named Nadine?"

Pearl nods. "Yes, Nadine and Marie. I guess you already heard the story."

"Parts of it," I reply. "But tell me what you know."

Pearl continues. "I was away that summer, but everyone was talking about it when I got back. It was in the local newspaper. The camp enrollment really went down. My mom hoped it would close. She never trusted the Jefferies family. Believe me, she wasn't thrilled when I started working there."

"How long did they own the camp?"

"Forever, as long as I remember; Ed Jefferies inherited the camp from his parents." Pearl looks at me. "Those people are twisted. You seem like a nice girl, and I just wanted to warn you to be careful, but if I were you, I'd just leave."

"Why do you think they're twisted, Pearl?" I ask.

She grunts. "Those missing girls? I wouldn't be surprised if Ed Jefferies had something to do with it. Not that I have any proof, just a feeling. It wouldn't surprise me one bit. Yeah, he's gone now, but that Sherry is a piece of work too. She's not right in the head. She always wanders around those woods at night, lurking about. She used to do that when she was a kid too. I used to see her slinking around, gave me the creeps."

Wynn pops into my mind and how he told me that he likes to walk around the woods because he finds it "relaxing." Did he learn this from Sherry? Do they wander around together? Goosebumps prick my arms.

A thought pops into my mind, and I can't believe I didn't think of it before this moment. She might know something about Aunt Heather.

"Pearl, when did you work at the camp?"

"Nineteen eighty-six until nineteen eighty-nine. Four years," says Pearl. She takes a long drink of her coffee.

"Do you remember a girl named Heather who was camping in the woods in nineteen eighty-nine?" I ask. "She wasn't a camper, but a runaway. Her boyfriend was a counselor. She was my aunt, and she went missing."

A deep sigh escapes Pearl. "No, I don't."

I grab my phone and pull up the photos I took of some of Mom's old pictures. "This is her, my aunt. Does she look familiar?"

"No!" Pearl snaps, pushing the phone away from me. "I don't remember any Heather."

I lay my phone on the table. Why is she getting angry? She was the one who wanted to talk about the camp. Why does everyone get so touchy when I ask about her? What are these people hiding?

"Please, Pearl, that's why I'm working at the camp, to find out what happened to my aunt. It's always been a mystery in my family." I pause. "I need to find out for my mom. Heather was her younger sister. Her only sister."

She purses her lips together and drinks her coffee in silence. "In nineteen eighty-nine I heard a rumor of a girl living in the woods, but I have no idea if it's true or if it was your aunt."

"Okay, what happened that year?"

Her gray eyes lock with mine. "All I know is that one day I was driving into work, and I passed Ed Jefferies pulling out of the camp. A teenage girl, who I'd never seen before, was in the passenger seat. She might be the girl in your pictures, but the girl looked older. Her hair was much longer."

"And then?"

"Jefferies abandoned his family. Nobody ever saw him again. Rumors were that he left his wife for another woman, other rumors were that he just wanted to live another life, nobody knew for sure what happened." Pearl narrows her eyes. "But who knows? None of that story ever really made sense to me. Why would Ed Jefferies leave the camp? He loved that place, seemed like he loved it more than he loved his family. He'd more likely throw them out and move the girl in than leave himself. But what do I know? I'm just an old woman with old stories. But I know there's something wrong with those people."

"I thought Mr. Jefferies died," I say. "Mel told me that."

"Nope, he ran off. That's what everyone said. Maybe he's dead now, I don't know."

I open my purse and retrieve the two old photographs, one of Aunt Heather, Jennifer and Sherry and the other two girls, Nadine and Marie. I lay them on the table. Pearl stares at the pictures.

"Do you recognize any of these girls?" I ask. "Other than Jennifer and Sherry."

She picks up the photos, one in each hand and stares at them. She looks up at me.

"Yes, I recognize all of them," Pearl says in a serious tone. "Where did you get these?"

"I found this one"—I point to the photo of Aunt Heather— "in the basement of the Jefferies' house and the other in a storage room in their garage."

Pearl's eyes harden and she holds up the one of my aunt. "This is the girl I saw drive off with Ed Jefferies. She looks older here than the other photos you showed me. And she's wearing that white swim top. That's what the girl in Jefferies's truck was wearing that day."

Adrenaline courses through me. So it's true. Aunt Heather ran off with Ed Jefferies. So many more questions flood my mind. If this is true, what happened with her and Dean? How did Jennifer and Sherry take the news of their friend running off with their father? My mind is spinning trying to grasp the possible solution.

"And these girls." Pearl pauses, holding up the picture of Nadine and Marie. "These are the two girls we were talking about, the ones who disappeared from the camp. The runaways, or deviants, as the police determined. One thing you need to know about that family is that they can't be trusted. None of them."

A chill runs up my spine thinking of Nadine's fringe vest and all the other personal items that likely belonged to her and Marie, lying in the dusty box in the garage. Discarded. The girls would never use them again because they were gone. I tell Pearl about the items in the box where I found the picture of the girls.

"I spoke to Nadine's sister, Gayle, and she remembered a vest I found in one of the boxes. It was a favorite of Nadine's. Gayle is going to see if the police will re-open her sister's case."

"Like I said, they're shady, they're all liars in my book," she replies, her steel-gray eyes serious as we talk. "You should leave, Zoey. Those people are nothing but trouble."

"Why are you telling me all of this, Pearl?" I ask. "You don't even know me, but you told me to leave that first day I met you. Why do you care?"

She shrugs. "You remind me of my granddaughter, and I don't trust that family. I never have and you seem too... trusting."

I smile at her. "Thank you for helping me. This information puts the pieces together for me."

Pearl stands, picks up her coffee and turns toward the door. Then she swivels and looks at me one more time, the deep scowl back on her face. "I warned you and that's all I can do. Don't trust any members of the Jefferies family. Not one."

And then she walks out of the coffee shop.

THIRTY-FOUR

1989

Heather

Light rain falls most of the morning and I spend most of the time writing in my notebook. I decided to start a story about a teenager who runs away from home. I remember how my English teacher said to write what you know and I'm an expert on that story.

After a couple hours, I tire of the story and take my notebook outside to write a letter to Jess, since the rain stopped about an hour ago. I tell her what Dean suggested about running away to New Jersey and eventually getting married. Even when I write the word "married," I smile. One day I'll be Dean's wife and he'll be my husband. Maybe we'll have a cute little house with a front porch and a back yard. A real home where people love each other and are kind to each other. A home like Gran's house.

And Jess could come live with us too.

I'd have the two people I love the most with me.

I'm lost in my thoughts as I write, sitting in my sagging

camp chair, slightly wet from the rain. My words flow so fast and easily.

Then a man's voice startles me.

"Who are you?"

My head snaps up and my pen drops onto the ground. A tall man with blond hair and piercing blue eyes stares at me from the other side of my tent.

I recognize his voice.

Jennifer and Sherry's dad, Mr. Jefferies. I quickly stand and drop my notebook into the chair. "Uh... my name is Heather."

Mr. Jefferies cocks his head to the side, continuing to stare at me. "Hello, Heather, I'm Ed. I own this camp."

His voice is friendly, not angry like I overheard inside the camp store. I relax slightly.

"Hi," I say shyly.

He steps closer to me and points to the tent. "Are you living here?"

Nerves prick every part of my body. If he tells me to leave, I can't do anything, I'll have to leave. "Yeah, I'm sorry."

He stares at me for a moment, and I awkwardly shift my weight to my left side under his scrutiny.

"Why?"

"I... uh... I... ran away from home," I stutter.

"And you set up a tent here."

I nod.

"By yourself?" he asks, his stare hardens.

I hesitate for a moment, but I don't want to mention Dean and get him in trouble. He might even get fired. "Yes, by myself."

"Hmmm..." Mr. Jefferies says. His voice is deep, but not unkind. "Well, stay here for now. I have to think about this. I guess things were bad at home if you ran away?"

I nod. "It was bad."

"Okay, well, like I said, stay here for now." He smiles. "Bye, Heather."

"Thank you," I say, relief fills me.

"Ed." He meets my gaze.

"Thank you, Ed," I say and watch him walk away.

I let out a sigh of relief.

He comes back two hours later with a bag of food and a brand-new sleeping bag. He stands in front of me with a wide smile on his face. His face is relaxed and friendly as he looks at me.

"Heather," he says, still smiling. "I thought you could use these."

I return his smile. "Thank you. That's very nice of you."

He tosses the sleeping bag into the tent and sits the large brown paper bag on the ground next to the cooler, then runs a hand through his light, almost white, blond hair. He's younger looking than I expected after overhearing him at the store and how Sherry and Jennifer talked about him. I thought he'd be an old man, with wrinkles and a pot belly, like Harvey; instead he is rather handsome and fit for a middle-aged man and he smiles kindly at me. I don't know why Sherry and Jennifer always say their father is so mean. He doesn't seem that way.

He moves closer to me. "And I thought about it. You can stay here as long as you like. I've been in tough spots before too."

"Oh." More relief spreads through me. "Thank you so much, Mr. Jefferies. That's really good news to me."

"Call me Ed." He grins. "We're friends now, right?"

"Yeah." I giggle nervously. I don't know what else to say.

A yellow monarch butterfly lands on a tree branch by where we are standing. I admire its delicate markings, bright yellow edged in black. Ed follows my gaze.

"Beautiful, aren't they?" he remarks. He holds out his finger and the butterfly moves onto it.

I look at it perched on his finger and he looks too, twirling his finger around. I'm surprised it stays there.

"Delicate and free, just flying through this world, living and breathing while it can until the end. We can learn a lot from butterflies," he says thoughtfully. He holds up his finger and shakes it off and we watch it fly away.

"Well, I have to get back to work." He moves closer to me again, this time reaching out and touching my cheek for a brief moment. "You don't have to worry about being caught. You're safe here. And if someone comes looking for you, I'll send them away."

"Thanks, Ed, but I doubt anyone will come looking for me here," I say. I'm glad when his hand stops touching me and drops to his side.

He grins at me and walks away.

I listen to his footsteps as they become fainter and fainter, then look at the bag of food he left for me. A bag of apples, a big bag of potato chips, a bunch of bananas and a package of Tootsie Pops. I unwrap a cherry-flavored one and pop it into my mouth.

I'm surprised Ed is so helpful and doesn't have a problem with me staying here. I mean, it's a huge relief because now I don't have to worry about being caught here. I lift my hand to my face where he touched me.

Unless there's something more he wants from me.

THIRTY-FIVE
2024

Zoey

My head is buzzing with the information Pearl gave to me. I sit in my car for a few minutes before starting the engine as I digest everything she told me in the coffee shop. I'm glad I decided to meet with her; she has given me more information than anyone else since I arrived at Camp Medley.

Did Aunt Heather run away with Mel's grandfather, Ed Jefferies? It certainly seems that way. I want to believe that she made it out of the camp, and is living a great life somewhere, but why wouldn't she have contacted Mom at some point? This knowledge is kind of shocking and not the direction I thought my investigation would go.

The photos of Nadine and Marie haunt me. Two questions still bug me though... if they ran away why wouldn't they take their personal items along with them? And if they were abducted why were the items stored in the Jefferieses' garage? None of it makes any sense.

Except the one common denominator.

Ed Jefferies.

He was running the camp during both time periods. Mel said his parents owned the camp, so he grew up here, and was probably running it in 1974 and I know he ran it in 1989.

Did he do something to those girls?

Did he run away with Aunt Heather? Did he do something to her too?

So many questions swirl in my jumbled mind. I'm glad to have some answers now, but the questions still aren't completely answered. Unfortunately, Pearl isn't the one to ask now, but someone much closer, like Sherry or Jennifer, and neither of them want to talk to me about anything.

Should I tell Mel? If Heather and Mel's grandfather ran away together, she was the cause of him abandoning his family. That's not going to win me any points with Sherry or Jennifer, but surely, they would know what happened with their father and Heather, right? And didn't Mel say that her grandfather was dead? I honestly can't remember with all the information moving around in my mind.

Maybe I'll ask Mel about him, just casually. Although, she may not know what happened. Jennifer probably told her he was dead to avoid any embarrassment. My mind travels back to Pearl's words again, this time that she couldn't imagine Ed Jefferies leaving the camp, but if he didn't, what happened to him and my aunt?

I drive back to the camp, my head spinning with all the information I gathered this afternoon about Craig and my aunt. I park at the camp store because I meant to stop and get some gum at the store, but forgot. I pop inside and buy two packs of spearmint flavored, then head back to my car.

Jennifer is walking into the store as I'm exiting.

"Oh, hi, Jennifer," I say.

She gives me a tight smile. "Hello, Zoey. How are you?"

"I'm okay." I pause. Should I say something to her? Apologize for my aunt running off with her father and breaking up the family? Maybe I should because I'm sure that's a hurtful topic for her, and I keep bringing up bad memories for her with every question I ask.

"That's good," Jennifer murmurs, continuing into the store.

"Jennifer, may I talk to you for a moment?"

Her eyebrows rise. "I suppose so."

"Um, could we maybe go over here?" I point to a picnic table a small distance away from the store. "It's a little more private."

"Hmmm... why do we need privacy?"

I don't answer but quickly walk over to the table, and she follows. We sit and consider one another.

"I'm sorry I was bringing up old memories for you, probably bad memories, when I was asking questions about my aunt. I didn't know the whole story, but I think I know some of it now."

"Don't worry about it." She waves me off. "It's fine."

I lower my voice. "I know now that she ran off with your father, and he left your family. I didn't mean to upset you; I only wanted to get closure for my mom. I apologize for any pain I may have caused you."

Jennifer's mouth forms a tight line. "Yes, thank you. I appreciate your apology. Is that all?"

I watch her stand up and see her eagerness to leave.

"Yes, that's it," I say.

Jennifer nods and walks away. I sit for a few minutes and then an idea pops into my mind. I wonder who told Mom that Heather was picked up by her dad? I pull out my phone and type a quick text to Mom.

> Who told you Aunt Heather's dad picked her up?

A few minutes later a response arrives.

> Rose Jefferies, the camp owner.

Heather

"He brought you a new sleeping bag?" Dean asks incredulously. He opens the tent flap and looks inside with his flashlight. He arrived a little after nine according to my watch, and I immediately told him about my encounter with Ed Jefferies.

He shakes his head. "I don't know, that really surprises me. He can be okay, I've never had an issue with him, but he has a short temper, and I would think finding you out here would make him angry."

I shake my head. "No, he wasn't mad at all and said I can stay here as long as I want."

"I mean that's good, but kind of shocking," Dean says. "Well, I guess everything is good for now."

He grabs a soda from the cooler. "Want one?"

I shake my head and poke the campfire, adding another piece of wood. "Do you think I should tell Sherry and Jennifer?"

"Tell us what?" Sherry asks, emerging from the trees. She

carries a small cooler. "We brought some ice-cream cups. They were left over from dinner tonight."

"Oh, yum, thanks," I say.

"What did you want to tell us?" she asks again.

"Your dad was here today," I say.

"What?" Jennifer gasps.

"Yeah, he said it was okay if I stayed here. He wasn't mad or anything," I say. "He even brought me a new sleeping bag and this bag of food. He was really nice to me." I point to the paper bag.

Jennifer looks inside. "Hey, these are my Tootsie Pops. I couldn't find them anywhere this afternoon. He must have taken them from home and given them to you." She frowns, obviously irritated her treat was given to me.

"Oh, take it back," I say to her. "I didn't know it was yours."

"No." She pulls out an orange pop. "I'll just take this one. Dad will wonder why I have it. He'll know we hang out here with you. I don't know if that would make him mad or not."

I shrug.

"No, no, no!" Sherry yells, listening to everything. "You'll have to move your tent."

"It's okay, Sherry," I say. "He said it's fine if I stay here."

"You have to move your tent!" Sherry screams. "You can't stay here!"

And with that, she stomps away, disappearing into the woods.

I turn to Jennifer. "What was that all about?"

"She's kind of weird about Dad," Jennifer says quietly.

"Why?" Dean asks.

Jennifer shrugs her shoulders.

I toss and turn on my sleeping bag, trying to get into a comfortable position. I always sleep so much better when

Dean's here beside me, but he left early, setting his alarm on his watch, about an hour ago, at four thirty in the morning, to get back to his cabin. They were going on an early-morning hike so he figured he could get things ready for that, or more likely he'd sleep another hour or so and then scramble before they left for the trails.

I throw the blanket off me and lie on my back. I sigh, wishing he was still here with me. I aways sleep better with Dean beside me, holding me, hearing his heart beat beside my own. I miss him already and he hasn't even been gone an hour.

Yes, I'm totally in love.

A sound reaches my ears from outside, but I'm not sure what it is. Maybe Dean is back? I quickly unzip the tent and poke my head outside. Sunrise will soon be here, but now darkness still lingers in the woods. I listen for the sound, and it comes again. Tinkling, a light and delicate melody that comes from deeper in the dark forest.

What is that? Where is it?

I crawl out of the tent and stand outside, the world quiet except for a breeze that ruffles the trees and the soft tinkling song interwinding among them. A pretty cadence drawing me to its source, but I'll wait a bit until I explore.

Finally, about twenty minutes later beams of sunshine trickle into the darkness allowing me to travel through the trees without a flashlight. It's dead and I need to buy some new batteries.

The tinkling continues as I move along. Birds start their early-morning chatter, and I enjoy hearing their voices all around me. Sunlight dapples through the leaves above me creating pretty designs on the trees. I'm walking farther than I realize. I stop and look around.

I'm getting close to that spooky little cabin, I'm sure of it. I should turn back, but I'm so close now. The tinkling melody must be close by. I pass another large growth of ferns and just beyond them hangs a wooden windchime blowing in the breeze.

I close my eyes for a second, enjoying the closeness of the light tinkling sound, especially in the deep quiet of the early morning.

I move toward it and examine its craftsmanship. The slats of wood are roughly cut, and a few slivers of metal also hang beside them. I look at it for a few more minutes. An etching of a butterfly is on one of the wood slats. A simple construction that creates such a pretty sound.

I wonder who put this here?

I glance around to see any sign of someone. I don't see anything unusual, but someone had to place the windchime here. Was it to mark this spot for some reason, the sound beckoning a hiker to this specific location? Or maybe there's another reason.

Is someone else staying in the woods too?

THIRTY-SEVEN
1989

Heather

Dean and I are walking back from the pool. It's his afternoon off, so we spent some of it swimming, but it was so full, which makes sense on such a hot July day, we decided to go back to the tent early. It's great when he has an afternoon off, and we can spend more time together other than just at night when he stays with me.

We walk slowly, holding hands, and everything's so calm and peaceful, perfect. I glance at him in his red swimming trunks and white T-shirt, his dark blond hair longer than he normally wears it, and my heart soars with love. There's nobody else I love being with more than him in the entire world. Not even Jess. Nobody.

"I love you," I say to him. My voice is low in the quiet surroundings.

He looks down at me and grins. "I love you more."

We always say those words to each other, and I don't remember how it started, but I love it; it's our thing.

A thought pops into my mind.

"I found something in the woods yesterday," I say as we walk along the path.

"What did you find?" he asks.

"A windchime."

He stops walking. "A windchime, where?"

"Past my tent, deeper into the woods. It was hanging on a tree. I heard this tinkling sound, so I checked it out."

"That's kind of strange for a windchime to be hanging on a tree in the middle of the woods," he remarks.

"I thought so too. I thought maybe someone else was camping out in the woods, but I didn't see anything."

"Why don't you show me where it is," he suggests.

"Okay, hopefully I remember." I laugh. "Let's go."

He bends down and picks a few black-eyed Susans along the path and tucks them in my hair beside my right ear. I smile and touch them.

"How do they look?" I ask.

"Very sexy." He grins.

"They are one of my favorite flowers," I reply. "But I didn't know they were sexy."

"Only on you," he teases.

We walk back to my tent at a quicker pace this time and break off to the right into the woods. I think we're going in the right direction, but then we get lucky because a breeze picks up and the tinkle of the chime calls us, as it did for me before. We move faster now and eventually, we reach it.

It hangs in the tree as it did yesterday, rough wooden pieces mixed with metal, and a butterfly etching on the top of the middle wood slat. The sunshine beaming through the trees shines off the metal creating shadows in the darker parts of the woods. Dean and I search the area but there's no sign of anyone else staying in the woods, just a lonely windchime dangling in the breeze.

"Still is odd," he says, staring at it. "And I don't like the idea of it hanging here making noise. It could draw someone to your campsite."

"Yeah, that's true," I reply. "Let's take it down and take it back to the tent. Maybe if we get our own place sometime, we can put it on our porch."

Just saying the words "our place" gives me a thrill and excitement runs through my entire body. This is really going to happen for us.

He laughs and wraps his arms around me. "I love when you say 'our place.' Can you imagine how awesome that will be? Just me and you."

I kiss him and he kisses me back. I snuggle into his arms.

"It will be the best thing in the world," I say. I can't think of anything I want more than a home with Dean.

Jennifer and Sherry show up at the tent shortly after ten. They brought a huge bag of popcorn and a six pack of beer. We all sit around the campfire on my fern squares that I made into little mats for seating. It's amazing what you can craft from nature when you have all day to work on a project.

"Ugh, movie night was a disaster. The projector wouldn't work right, and we only got to show half of the movie. Mom's going to call someone to fix it tomorrow. Everyone was complaining, but what can we do if something isn't working? Nothing."

"Yeah, Dad was so angry at Mom because I guess there was a problem with it before and she should have had it fixed earlier," Jennifer chimes in. "It was a disaster."

"That's why we'll hang out here for a while," Sherry says, giving her sister a look. She places a handful of popcorn into her mouth. "Maybe all night."

Dean and I share a look. Neither of us wants them to stay all night. We have other plans that only involve the two of us.

"I'm sure it will blow over," Dean says, taking a swig of beer. "It's only a movie."

Jennifer and Sherry share a look again but neither says anything. We all sit in silence eating popcorn, drinking beer and poking at the dwindling fire with long sticks. Sherry hasn't been coming around as much as before since I told her about her father finding my tent. She hasn't mentioned it again either, so I'm fine not talking about it. Although, she's a little more stand-offish than before, but whatever. I didn't do anything; I'm relieved her father didn't tell me to get out. It's a big relief, no matter what she thinks about it.

Sherry gets up to add more wood to the fire. She walks over to the wood pieces stacked at the side of the tent, but stops, glancing at the object lying beside the cooler.

"Why do you have that?" she asks in a sharp voice.

"What?" I ask. Her tone surprises me.

She points to the windchime lying on top of a plastic bag. "That."

"Oh, we found it in the woods," Dean explains, staring at her.

Jennifer gets up and walks over, examining it. "Why would it be hanging in the middle of the woods? That's one of Dad's windchimes. He makes them."

Music swells from my small boombox and I turn down the volume, suddenly realizing how loud it's playing. There's rustling in the trees on the end of the woods that leads to the narrow stone lane. I whirl around and see Ed Jefferies emerge from the trees carrying a blue cooler.

"Hi, Heather," he greets, a wide smile on his face as he walks toward me.

"Hi," I reply. Uneasiness circulates in my stomach. I wonder why he's here. Is he going to tell me I have to leave?

He holds up the cooler. "I was in town and stopped for a burger. Thought I'd bring you one too. Hopefully the cooler kept the food warm and the milkshake from melting."

"Oh, that's nice," I say. And a milkshake sounds good. Like really good. "Thank you."

"No problem." He grins. I notice he has a blanket under his arm. He places the cooler on the ground and spreads out the blanket. He opens the cooler and pats the blanket for me to sit. "I thought we could eat together."

The uneasy feeling trickles through me again, but I sit on the far edge of the blanket, and he sits down, close to me, but not uncomfortably so.

"We better hurry," he says, handing me a paper-wrapped cheeseburger, container of fries and a cold milkshake with sweet vanilla ice cream dripping down the side. "That milkshake won't last long in this heat."

I take a sip of it, and it tastes so good. It's been a while since I had a fast-food burger and fries, so I hungrily dig in.

"These are good burgers," he remarks.

I nod, pop a couple of French fries in my mouth and take another gulp of milkshake. He's quiet for a few minutes while he eats his food. Then he clears his throat. I don't know what to say, but I'm wondering why he decided to visit me today. Maybe he changed his mind about me staying here. Uneasiness continues to filter through my body.

"How long do you think you'll be staying here?" he asks, staring at me. "I mean, it's okay. You can stay as long as you like. I'm just curious of your plans."

"Um... probably a while," I say, my voice wavers. "If that's okay."

"Sure, I told you it's fine." He nods. "Like I said, I was only curious. I'd like to check in on you here and there, just to make sure you're okay."

"Yeah, sure, but I'm fine." I meet his gaze. "I can take care of myself."

He holds my gaze for what feels like an eternity and then moves closer to me. "I'm sure you can. You seem like a very special girl."

I sit very still. It's awkward sitting here with him. I hope he leaves soon.

"I have two daughters," Ed says. "Sherry and Jennifer. They're about your age."

I nod, not sure if I should say I met them already. I decide to just listen to what he says about them and not offer that information.

"They work at the camp, usually in the dining hall," he goes on. "Jennifer is very reliable; she's a good girl. Sherry is a bit more difficult. She always has been."

"How old are they?" I ask even though I already know. It seems like a good question to keep him talking.

"Sherry's seventeen and Jennifer is sixteen." He looks at me. "How old are you?"

"Sixteen."

"Yeah, you're around their age," he says. "Do you have any sisters or brothers?"

"I have a sister," I reply wistfully.

Ed nods. "Does she still live at home?"

I shake my head. "No, she moved out. She's eighteen."

"So then you were stuck at home with your parents."

"Uh, my mom and stepfather."

"I see." Ed's gaze settles on me, and he watches me for a long time.

His attention is so intense I get uncomfortable. I don't know if he's waiting for me to say more or if he's only watching me. Either way, it's awkward.

Then he clears his throat, places the trash into the cooler

and stands up. "Well, I better get back to work. Bye, Heather. It was nice talking to you."

"Bye," I say, watching him disappear back into the woods.

Zoey

"Wow," Mel says. "So, my grandfather ran off with your aunt? Eww... that's so gross. How old was he? He had to be ancient."

"You said your grandmother is seventy-five, right?"

Mel nods.

"So if they were about the same age back then, your grandfather was around forty."

"I think they were, so yeah, he was ancient."

"I wonder what happened to them?" I muse.

"Do you think they're still alive?" she asks.

I shrug. "I don't know. I don't understand why Heather wouldn't have contacted my mom though. That part doesn't make any sense."

"Did you tell your mom yet?"

"Not yet, but I'm going to after we're done talking. She's going to be really surprised." I look at Mel. We're sitting on the small front porch of the cabin while the girls have some free time before bedtime. I must share my news about Craig with someone. "Something else happened today."

Her eyes widen. "What?"

"I went to Craig's house. He wasn't home, or his dad, but I talked to their housekeeper."

Her eyes darken slightly. I notice her hand starts tapping on her knee.

"Really? Why would you do that? What did she say?" she asks.

"I can't move on with the way things ended between us and I'm glad I went. He told his dad that I broke up with him! Can you believe that?"

A strange look flits across her face, then she frowns. "But he broke up with you, right?"

I nod. "And you know what else is weird? He's still in Europe and he's only ever texted his dad. No phone calls or video chats, isn't that strange?"

Mel is silent, then responds quietly. "Sure is."

"I just miss him so much," I say. "I thought he was the one."

"Oh, Zoey." Mel puts her arm around me. "I'm so sorry this happened."

"Thanks," I say, hugging her back. "I'm glad I went though. I finally feel like I'm getting some closure about the breakup. Well, maybe not closure, actually, it kind of brings up more questions for me."

"Just take it one step at a time," she replies gently. "And I'm here to talk about it anytime."

I smile at her. "Thanks, you're a good friend. Well, I'm going to take a walk now and call my mom."

"Oh, wait," Mel says. "I wanted to tell you that I have a doctor appointment tomorrow afternoon about the sleepwalking. It's my usual day to stay with Grandma, but I think Sherry will be able to take my place."

"Oh, that's great," I say. My mind scrambles. With Mel out, maybe I could spend some time with her grandma. Despite the dementia, Mrs. Jefferies may still remember something about Aunt Heather.

"You know, I'd love to stay with her. My grandma has a lot of health issues too and I'm used to that kind of thing," I offer. Hopefully Mel goes for it. I'm lying. I only have one grandma, my dad's mom, and she's very active and usually travels for many months of the year.

Mel is thoughtful. "Oh, that would be great."

"Uh... what about the girls?" I suddenly remember.

"They can join Sarah and Mae with Cabin Nine at the lake for the afternoon. I know they won't have a problem with that. You'd really be doing me a favor, because Sherry does have a busy schedule." She pauses. "This will work out so much better."

"Oh, sure, no problem!" I reply. An idea springs into my mind. Maybe I can ask Mrs. Jefferies about Ed. I'll have to be very tactful though, I don't want to upset her. I won't mention my idea to Mel though. She probably won't go for it and maybe I won't either. It depends on how Mrs. Jefferies is feeling tomorrow. Mel says she has good and bad days, so hopefully tomorrow will be one of her good days and she'll remember something about that time. I have some answers now but still don't know where Heather is or if she's still alive. Mrs. Jefferies might have some answers that will help me finally solve this mystery.

"Thanks so much, Zoey." Mel gives me another hug. "Now go call your mom."

I'm noticing how bright the moon is tonight, white slivers through the trees, as I chase Mel, once again, through the woods. This behavior must stop and I'm so glad she has a doctor appointment to have this issue checked out. I can't be chasing her out here every other night, it's ridiculous. I have a flashlight this time, quickly grabbed off the nightstand by my bunk bed after I heard her tumble loudly out of the cabin door.

Why am I the only one who hears these disturbances? I'm tuned into Mel and her noises like a mother to her baby's cry. I wish I was tuned into my own sleep rather than her bizarre nighttime adventures. I know it's weird, but I have to follow her. I worry she's going to hurt herself out here. I wonder if Wynn is lurking among the trees tonight too and shiver thinking of the possibility.

She's moving fast tonight, not the normal stiff movements of the previous nights. Her body moves in a fluid, almost normal way and I wonder why she moved so zombielike on the other nights. She travels down the stone lane, past the maintenance shed and then turns onto the trail leading into the woods. She's moving somewhat slower on the trail, and I can easily keep her in my sights, but I hope she stops walking soon. Or at least that she slows down a little more.

But she doesn't.

Deeper and deeper into the woods she hurries now as if she's late for an appointment with someone. Why is she moving so fast tonight? I'm struggling to keep up with her and I'm the one who's awake!

A thought pops into my mind. Maybe she is awake and that's why her movements seem more normal. And if she's not sleepwalking, I don't need to follow her. She's on her own if she's awake. Maybe she is meeting someone in the woods. Maybe Brett? Maybe someone else?

"Mel," I call, but she keeps walking.

"Mel!" I yell louder.

She pauses for a moment, only slightly turning toward me; her head cocks halfway around as if she's listening so I know she heard me. I stop and watch her neck turn at a snail's pace toward me.

Crick.

Crick.

Crick.

I can almost hear the bones in her neck move.

I tremble. She can hear me, but is she awake?

But then she swivels her neck back and breaks out into a run.

What the hell is she doing?

I run to catch up with her, silently regretting coming out here. Is she sleepwalking, or awake and playing some weird game with me? Unnerving thoughts of her and of Sherry fill my mind. My car accident, was it really an accident? Is Wynn lurking around here tonight too? Sweat runs down my back as my feet pound the dusty trail and fear spreads through me. My thoughts race from the dark consequences of me being out in the night with Mel and maybe others lurking about.

Watching me. Playing games with me.

I shake off the foreboding thoughts. Mel's my friend and she has a problem. I can't let her run out here alone in the dark. She doesn't even know what she's doing. Everything will be fine.

I don't even know where we are; I've never been this far into the forest on this side of the camp. The forest is thick here and I say a quiet thanks for the flashlight I have, as without it, I could barely see where I was walking. The noises are louder here too, screech owls and a coyote howl, although at a distance, thank goodness, mixing in with the other nighttime insects and creatures who call the forest their home. Their buzzing and melodies create a dark marching song as I fly along the trail after Mel.

Then the path stops, and we come to a clearing in the trees. I step out into the opening, searching for her. A dead smell permeates the air, swirling and penetrating my clothes with its hideous stink. A large white sign sits atop a post lodged into the ground.

CAMPERS ARE NOT PERMITTED PAST THIS POINT.
AUTHORIZED STAFF ONLY.

I look up from the sign and see a small lake, almost more of a swamp I determine once I turn my flashlight in its direction and shine on it. I survey the area with my bright light, trying to hold my nose from the stink. Why does it smell so bad out here? Thick green algae covers the lake, a couple dead fish lie to the side, mostly just bones atop rotting flesh, and a tall weed row springs on its sides. I lift my light higher, it looks like another path on the other side, or possibly a road, it's much wider. I direct the light back to the still, stagnant water and gasp.

Mel is stepping into it.

"No! Mel!" I scream, dropping my flashlight. It lands on the ground with a thud and switches off.

But Mel doesn't heed my calls; she continues into the murky green water. The moonlight shines down on her as she walks into its depths.

I race to her, grabbing her arm, even though I know it's not a good idea to touch her while sleepwalking, but I can't let her drown herself! I try to pull her back, but she remains steady and does not budge.

Be careful, a voice says inside me. *It may be a trap.*

But I can't let her drown!

She stops and I lessen my tight grip on her arm, hoping to gently guide her out of the lake. She doesn't look at me though. Her body, rigid now, faces the water. A lonely howl fills the quiet night, the coyote calling for his pack.

Goosebumps ripple up my arm and I try to guide her out of the water.

"Come on, Mel," I say, trying to keep calm even though my racing heart is anything but calm. Now that I'm right at the water, the smell is overpowering. The stench of death surrounds me.

Her head turns slightly, not facing me but a slight cock to the left, her long, blonde hair, almost glowing under the bright moonlight, concealing her face.

Her neck turns again.

Crick.

Crick.

Crick.

A guttural sound escapes from her lips. Her neck has turned more toward me, but her long hair still covers her face. She doesn't move, but instead, she grabs me with both hands and pulls me down.

Hard.

"No!" I scream as she tries to pull me into the water, her grip tight on me. Her hair hangs in her face so I can't see her eyes. She seems to have superhuman strength as she grips me and takes me farther into the dark, still water. I stumble and go under the stench-filled water for a moment, fighting my way up while she continues to push me down with all her strength.

"Mel!" I scream again as I gasp for breath, still trying to wrench myself away from her iron grip. I flail about and try to grab her.

She slows and her hair is swept away from her face, and I see her eyes. Open, like last time, but different.

Alert.

She stares at my arms with purpose it appears, not the glassy, unknowing look from the other nights. She seems to know exactly what she's doing to me.

More terror fills me.

Is she awake?

I think she is.

She jerks me forward and down, trying to push me under the water again. I slip again and go under for only a second, quickly struggling back up. Pieces of stringy plants, I hope it's only a plant, hang on my head as I gasp for breath.

She will *not* drown me!

I kick her leg hard, summoning all my strength, and she winces, losing her grip on my arms, momentarily. She reaches out again, though, and grabs hold of one arm, but looser this time. I'm not messing around now, and I punch her in the face. At this point I don't care if she drowns in this fucking swamp.

She's not going to take me with her! I have to get away from her.

She recoils and stumbles back and again I catch a glimpse of her eyes. Open and anger filled now. I finally pull away from her and hurry out of the smelly water, leaving her there.

I run into the woods, but I don't go back to the camp.

I hide among the trees in a dark pocket that hides my presence but gives me a view of the rotting swamp and Mel as she emerges from the water. She's bathed in moonlight as she trudges from the murky swamp in her once-white pajamas, now green with sludge, as are mine. Her hair still bunched around her face like a creepy horror-movie character.

She walks in a normal fashion, not like the other nights, out of the water and is pulling off the algae clumps and weeds from her clothes and hair.

Would she do that if she was sleepwalking?

I doubt it, but I'm not sure.

Then she walks over to where I dropped the flashlight, turns it on, and heads for the trail. I stay in my hiding spot and watch her as she passes me walking with her normal gait.

What the hell was going on there?

Did Mel just try to kill me?

My heart races and I sit hidden among the ferns, lying close to the ground.

Time passes and the only sound now is an owl hooting in the distance. My clothes are soaked and despite the warm air surrounding me, I shiver. Tears run down my face as I think about all that has happened. Mel and I are friends, why would she want to hurt me? I can still see the anger in her eyes when she couldn't pull me under the water. How could she do something like that to me?

Part of me can't accept that Mel tried to hurt me. We've become close in a short time, why on earth would she want to kill me? Goosebumps form on my arms and I pull my knees up close, wrapping my arms around them, trying to gain some warmth.

Maybe I'm wrong, could she have been sleepwalking? But her eyes, her manner of walking were different tonight. It was *so* different tonight. I rock back and forth thinking of how hard she shoved me under that dirty water, her hands strong and unyielding.

I fumble for my phone in my back pocket to call Mom. I need to talk to someone. I need to get out of this insane camp. Everybody here is crazy! My hands shake and then I realize my phone isn't working. It's soaked from being underwater in the swamp. Tears sting my eyes once more.

I shove my phone back into my pocket and sit in the darkness. Alone.

THIRTY-NINE
2024

Zoey

I pull on my black running shorts and secure my hair in a high ponytail, then take off down the few steps of the cabin's porch, jogging down the stone road to the trail that winds around the protected garden area. Mel and the girls are still asleep, it's barely light outside, and Mel still slumbers in her filth from last night. Eventually, I went back to the cabin and sat outside until I heard snoring, then went and got some clean clothes to take a shower before I went to bed. Not that I slept a wink. I only lay in bed staring at the bunk above me wondering why my friend tried to drown me. Sickness still fills me when I think about what happened last night. I considered Mel a good friend, and while I can't be completely sure that she wasn't sleepwalking, I certainly can't trust her. I considered if she has some type of dual personality, I kept seeing the nasty look on her face last night, but that theory is kind of outlandish.

I want to call Mom, but I'm going to wait until I speak to Mrs. Jefferies. I came here to solve a crime and that is what I'm going to do. If I want to work in criminal investigations, I can't call Mom every time I'm in danger; I must figure it out myself. However, I've detailed everything that has happened and all that I know about Heather's case in an email that I sent to myself, and even though I didn't want to, I sent it to Mom's email too, telling her if she doesn't hear from me tonight to call the police. She checks her email sporadically, so hopefully she gets it by tonight. I'm thankful my iPad is working. In case anything happens to me, the authorities will know everything about this twisted camp.

I don't want to think that the Mel I know would purposefully want to hurt me. Why would she do such a thing? It doesn't make any sense to me. We're friends, or at least we were.

I wonder what her face will look like this morning after my punch.

She's unstable, that's for certain.

My feet pound the ground, sweat beading on the back of my neck. The steady rhythm gives me clarity of mind and I increase my pace. I reach the beginning of the trail and turn onto it. The quiet of the forest soothes me and my quick solid strides strengthen me as I move along in the leafy haven, only a few slivers of sunlight dappling in throughout the trees.

It's only been a couple of days since I spoke to Gayle, Nadine's sister, but I hope her questions will spur a police investigation of the camp. She knows that vest was her sister's and that she would never leave it behind. I also know such things take time, unfortunately, and I feel I'm running out of time here. I'll speak to Mrs. Jefferies this afternoon and, after that, I may leave. I don't feel safe here.

I reach the protected garden, the secret garden. I stop and catch my breath until it evens out, and I look over the white vinyl fence at the beautiful flowers and plants growing inside. A large, healthy growth of black-eyed Susans covers a substantial section of the garden, meticulously cared for and stunning in their beauty. Other flowers in the garden burst in red, pink and purple. Deep, lush green plants, Hosta plants and wild grasses lie among them giving the space a balance of color and greenery.

A movement by the back catches my attention. A person by the shed at the side of the space. A man wearing a blue baseball hat enters the garden with a hose, spraying the flowers. He's humming a familiar tune as he goes about his work.

Mr. T, Mel's father. Aunt Heather's former boyfriend, Dean.

There's something calming about watching him toil. He's very focused on the task as simple as watering plants, and I suppose that's why the garden is so immaculate. It's important to him, you can tell by the care he gives to it.

I'm about to say hello, thinking about asking him something about Aunt Heather. He must have cared for her; he was the reason she came to this camp in the first place. I ponder on how to phrase it, so he doesn't get angry and clam up, like Jennifer and Sherry. I'm certain he knows something, maybe the entire story of what happened that summer. But I also don't know what, if any, role he played in my aunt's disappearance. I must be careful with my words.

But I don't get the chance...

Wynn grabs my arm and puts a finger to his mouth, then motions me to follow him, which I do, but pull my arm away first. I have a question to ask him too.

He leads me farther into the trail, past the garden where Mr. T works. He walks in silence, repeatedly running his fingers through his messy black hair. He stops abruptly and motions for me to follow him into the woods, and I do, and he stops at a grove of large hemlock trees.

"What's going on?" I ask him.

His eyes are sharp. "I saw you last night."

My eyes widen. "You mean when Mel tried to drown me?"

He holds my gaze. "Do you think she was sleepwalking?"

"I don't know, but why didn't you help me? I think she might have been trying to kill me!"

He flips his hair out of his face. "I was going to, but you got away from her so I stayed hidden. You gave her a good punch."

"Why were you in the woods? Were you following us? Did you ever see her do something like that before?" I demand, my questions coming in rapid fire.

He shakes his head. "No, and I told you I like to walk around the woods at night. It's... relaxing."

I raise my eyebrows. "Yeah, real relaxing."

"She was fucked up last night." He sighs. "Mel's always been a little different, but... I think she was really trying to hurt you last night."

I'm not sure how I feel about this verification that Mel may have tried to kill me, but Wynn saw it too. I'm not imagining it.

"And why do you think so?" I ask. "Why would she want to kill me?"

He holds my gaze. "That's what I wanted to ask you. You must know something about her, some kind of dirt. What do you know?"

A shiver races through me at his words.

What does Mel think I know?

And it must be bad if she wants to kill me.

FORTY

1989

Heather

Now knowing that Mr. Jefferies, Ed, is okay with me living in the tent, I feel more comfortable leaving my campsite more often. I don't have to stay hidden so much. This knowledge gives me a little rush of extra freedom and I relax a bit. I don't have to worry anymore.

I'm walking from the pool, wearing my white bikini and my cut-off jean shorts. As I travel along the stone path to the camp store, I touch the twenty-dollar bill in my shorts pocket. It's the only money I have in the world. I'll buy two notebooks at the camp store today, but I have to make sure to write tightly in them because I won't buy any more. I'll save the rest for if Dean and I run away together. It's something I can contribute until I get a job.

He'll ask his parents next week, then we'll know what we're going to do. I hope they say yes, yet more of me hopes we do run away together. Just me and Dean together forever doing what we want to do. I smile at the thought. Our entire lives are ahead of us and as long as we are together, we can do anything.

I hear a vehicle driving up behind me and I move farther to the side of the road. A truck slows down beside me and then stops.

"Heather," a male voice greets.

I turn and look at the driver. Ed Jefferies.

"Hi," I say, slightly uncomfortable although I'm not sure why.

"Get in," he says, smiling. "I have to go to the store; you can come with me."

I shake my head. "No, I'm just going to the camp store for some notebooks."

"Then definitely get in. I have to stop at the pharmacy anyway, notebooks will be cheaper there." He laughs. "Believe me, I mark up everything in the camp store. Everything in there is overpriced."

I hesitate, but I want him to let me stay at the camp. If I refuse to go with him, I might make him angry, and he'll tell me to go. It's just a ride to town to the pharmacy, no big deal.

"Okay," I say, opening the truck door.

He grins and we continue down the stone lane. The truck is clean, and a pine-scented air freshener hangs from the rear-view mirror. The truck pulls onto the paved road that goes past the main house, where the Jefferies family lives. Another car passes us, leading into the camp; a woman wearing a baseball cap is driving. I look at her, and she looks back at me.

He turns left onto the main road, and we drive for a few minutes. I'm now acutely aware that I'm only wearing a bikini top with my shorts and wish I had put on a T-shirt as I catch a few sidelong glances Mr. Jefferies gives me. The air conditioning in the truck chills my arms so I fold them over my breasts.

"Nice day," he remarks, his large hands gripping the steering wheel.

"Yeah, it's a nice day."

"Were you in the pool?"

I nod. "Great day for a swim. The water felt great."

"It sure is a nice day for that, wish I had time for a swim, but many things to get done."

I shift in my seat. "It's probably really busy running a camp."

He flashes me a friendly, knowing smile. "You're right about that. My list is never-ending, but I enjoy the work."

I relax a bit at the regular conversation we're having. It was nice of him to invite me along on his trip to the store. My nerves dissipate.

"We'll stop at the pharmacy first," he says. "You can get your notebooks there, then I need to stop at the beer distributor."

"Okay."

We drive another ten minutes or so until we arrive at the pharmacy. We get out of the truck, and he heads to the pickup counter at the back of the store and points out the stationery aisle, where I go to pick out my notebooks.

Ed was right. The notebooks are almost half the price of the ones in the camp store. I smile as I select a blue one and a red one, then hurry up to the cashier. She rings up the purchase and I dig out the wrinkled twenty-dollar bill from my pocket, but Ed is suddenly next to me, already handing her the cash.

"You don't have to do that," I say, looking at him. "I have money."

He shakes his head. "It's just a couple bucks. No big deal." He takes the bag and hands it to me, then we head out of the store.

"Thank you, Mr. Jefferies," I say. It was nice of him, but I wish I'd paid for it myself.

"You're welcome." He stops at his truck, opening the passenger door for me. I get in and I feel his eyes roam over me, only for a moment, so quickly I'm not exactly sure it happened, then he closes the door. "You're a special girl and I like to do nice things for special girls."

An alarm goes off in my mind at his words. Did he mean those words in a friendly way, or did they have a darker meaning? He isn't like Harvey with his gross jokes and invading my personal space, but there is something about him that I'm not sure about, yet he's only been kind to me. He gets into the driver's seat, and we drive farther into town, stopping at the beer distributor.

"You just stay here, Heather," he instructs me.

I nod and watch him get out of the vehicle and disappear into the store. A few minutes later he emerges with a case of beer and a brown paper bag. He puts the case in the truck bed but brings the bag in the front of the truck.

"I got a treat for you." He smiles. "Well, a treat for me too. Look in the bag."

I peek inside to see a six pack of peach wine coolers. Jess used to sneak them into her room and I tried one a long time ago. It was good. But why would he get this for me?

"Oh," I say.

"It's peach wine coolers," he explains. "These were refrigerated so they're nice and cold. I'll have one with you when I walk you back to your tent."

"You don't have to do that. You're busy," I quickly say, now regretting getting into the truck with him. "Just park at your house and I'll walk back by myself. I took enough of your time, Mr. Jefferies."

"I told you to call me Ed." His eyes darken. "Don't you follow directions, young lady?"

Fear races through me at his sharp tone.

"Uh, yes, Ed," I say quietly.

He stares at me, then laughs. "I'm just joking with you." He reaches over and gives my knee a squeeze, his hand lingering for a moment. "What a special creature you are."

I smile shyly and sit very still in the seat staring ahead, my heart pounding inside my chest. Something is not right here. We drive and he talks about the camp and how he likes baseball and asks me if I like any sports.

"I like to play volleyball," I reply.

"Sure, volleyball is fun." He nods. We turn into the camp and head back toward the pool but take a different stone lane than Dean uses. This is the one that goes past the creepy cabin, but Ed stops way before we reach that spot, close to my tent in the woods.

"Heather, I'm sorry if I offended you or scared you," he says earnestly. His blue eyes search me kindly. "I just thought you'd like the peach wine coolers. They're a treat."

I nod quickly. "Sure, they sound good. I like peaches."

A wide smile crosses his face. "Great, come on, let's try them."

Maybe I'm scared for no reason. Either way, I'll have to try one drink to please him. I don't want him to tell me to leave the camp if I make him angry. Or get Dean into trouble. I just want to get out of this truck!

He picks two out and opens them, handing one to me.

"Should we walk back to my campsite?"

He shakes his head. "Nah, let's just sit in the AC for a bit." He turns the fan up in the truck and the cool air blasts over me, feeling amazing. "I have to get back to work, but I can have one or two drinks with you."

I smile awkwardly and I suddenly remember how angry Sherry had gotten the other night when I told her about meeting her father. If she would see us here, she would flip out. I take a sip of the drink. It's sweet, peachy and good like I remember, but I don't want to drink too much.

"My wife always liked wine coolers," Ed is saying. "I guess she still does, but we don't really like each other." He lets out a rueful laugh.

I don't say anything because all I'm thinking about is how to get out of this truck and back to the safety of my tent, although is my tent a place of safety now? I'm not sure.

"Drink up, girl." He winks at me. "Might as well enjoy the good moments in life, and I must say sitting here in this cool truck with such a beautiful girl who's as sweet as this drink is pretty pleasant."

I manage a weak smile, but I want to get out of this truck. Now.

"I should let you get back to work," I say, eyeing his large hands and hope that he doesn't touch me again. I clutch the bag containing my notebooks and the almost full wine cooler to my chest. I reach for the door handle.

Ed puts his hand out, stopping my reach. His gaze travels briefly down my body. Again, I wish I was wearing a T-shirt instead of this *damn* bikini top. "Has anyone ever called you beautiful before? Has a man ever called you beautiful? Because you are."

Silence hangs between us, thick as molasses, and I don't know what to say to him. Then he moves away from me shaking his head. "I'm sorry, Heather. I'm not being respectful of you. It's just that... I'm dealing with a lot in my life right now and I enjoy talking to you. You're very easy to talk to, but I don't want to make you uncomfortable."

The vibe inside the truck changes, relaxes a bit and I let out a breath. "Okay, thanks, Ed."

His eyes brighten when I say his name and he flashes me a smile. "Of course, and it's probably a good idea if I go back to work." He pushes the brown paper bag toward me. "Take the rest of these, I'll just finish the one I opened."

"Thanks, bye," I say, opening the truck door. I hurry into the woods while the truck idles behind me.

I feel his eyes on me as I disappear into the forest.

FORTY-ONE

1989

Heather

I breathe a sigh of relief when I reach my tent. I plop down the bags and go into the tent to retrieve a T-shirt and pull it on. If Ed Jefferies comes back, I want to be covered up; it gives me a sense of security.

Probably false security.

Even though it's hot, I still crawl inside the tent and lie down on the sleeping bag. Despite the heat, goosebumps prickle my arms thinking of the ride back with him. He's not as obvious as Harvey, but something is off about him. I don't want to be alone with him again. Ever.

I bury my head in my pillow. Everything was going so well, but now, do I have to worry about him? Will he hurt me, or is he just kind of strange?

Why can't my life just be easy?

I only want to be safe, be with Dean and write in my notebook and things were working out, finally, for me, for us. One of Gran's favorite sayings was that God doesn't give us more than we can handle and gives the hardest struggles to the strongest warriors. I don't know about that one. I'd rather be a weak warrior with easy struggles. It's not fair to have to fight or worry about everything.

I take a deep breath. It's good to think about Gran, looking down on me from heaven. I wish she was here with me right now. But if she was still alive, we'd be at her house, probably making Toll House chocolate chip cookies. And Jess would be there too. I'd tell her all about Dean and she'd want to hear all about it. At bedtime, Jess and I would crawl into the queen-sized bed in Gran's extra bedroom, cover up with the old, thick flowered quilt and whisper to each other until we fall asleep.

Tears fill my eyes, and I sob into my pillow.

Shortly after seven that evening, after I tell him about Ed Jefferies and the ride to the store, Dean paces around the campsite.

"You can't stay. I don't trust that guy and he's acting so friendly with you. That's not him." Dean frowns. "We have that damn midnight scavenger hunt tonight. I'm going to have to go back around eleven to help with it. I won't be able to stay with you."

"Mr. Jefferies will be helping with that too, right?" I ask.

Dean nods. "Yeah, probably."

"I'll be okay."

"Maybe you should stay in my cabin tonight. Tomorrow I'll call my parents and if they say no, we'll head out to New Jersey."

"Really?" I jump out of the camp chair to hug him.

"Yeah, if they say no, there's no sense in staying here. I'll get a job at the garage, and we can get settled."

"Oh, I'm so excited about this!" I smile, joy filling me. Everything will be fine.

"So am I." He grins, kissing me. "So, you'll sleep in the cabin tonight?"

I frown. "Won't that be weird? I don't want to disrupt the whole cabin."

Concern crosses Dean's face. "You can't stay here, Heather. What if he comes back?"

"He's not going to come back tonight. He'll be busy with the scavenger hunt and it'll be late. He'll just go home to bed."

Dean's quiet for a moment. "At least, let's move the tent deeper into the woods. If he does come out here, he won't know where you went. He'll probably think you left the camp."

"Okay," I agree. "Let's move everything."

So we do. Tent, sleeping bags, camp chair, cooler, backpack, pillow. I don't have much and though we move much deeper into the woods, it doesn't take long.

"Why don't you come with me to the scavenger hunt?" Dean asks. "Then we can come back here together."

I shake my head. "I'm tired and have a headache. When you leave, I'm just going to sleep. I don't feel like going to a scavenger hunt."

Dean frowns. "Do you think you'll be okay?"

"Yes, I will," I say, smiling at him. "Don't worry about me."

I turn on the small boombox and "Crazy for You" by Madonna comes on. I grab Dean's hand and twirl around in the moonlight.

"Dance with me?" I ask.

"Love to." He flashes me a wide grin and wraps his arms around me.

We sway in the dark, dancing to our song, music playing on low volume, moonlight shimmering between the trees, our bodies molded together and the sweet scent of honeysuckle wafting in the air. If there is a heaven, which I'm certain there is, I imagine it would be just like this.

The song ends and "If You Leave" by OMD comes on.

Dean hugs me tightly and kisses me. "It's almost eleven," he says. "I have to get back and help with the scavenger hunt."

"Okay," I say, smiling at him.

"I'll be back as soon as I can," he says. "I'd turn off the radio and don't put the flashlight on. That way nobody will know you're here."

I nod.

"When this song is over."

He nods and kisses me again.

"I love you."

"I love you more," I reply. A few minutes later, the song is ending, and I watch him disappear into the dark forest, the final strains of the song playing.

FORTY-TWO

2024

Zoey

I'm inside the big green house with the shiny white shutters with Mrs. Jefferies. We sit in the sun-soaked living room. The AC is blasting, and she complains she's cold, so I hand her a cardigan lying on the back of a chair, which she quickly puts on. She eases back into the leather recliner, and I sit back onto the comfortable sectional sofa next to it. I'm propped on a bright red pillow reading a cozy mystery book to her and about half an hour into the story, she drifts off to sleep. Not surprising, cozy mysteries usually put me to sleep too.

I place the book down on the coffee table and wander over to the picture window overlooking the lake. The house is quiet, and I enjoy the peace, even though my mind is running at a breakneck speed. My conversation with my mom last night still echoes in my mind. Telling her Pearl's story was bittersweet, and she feels the same as me: If Heather ran off with Ed Jefferies, why hasn't she contacted Mom after all these years? It doesn't make any sense.

I still don't know what the hell was going on with Mel last

night, even after talking to Wynn. When I got back to the cabin, she was in her bunk, dirty and stinky from the gross swamp. I took a shower right away and put on clean pajamas, but she lay in her stench all night. I certainly wasn't going to wake her up after what she tried to do to me. This morning, after I got back from my run and encounter with Wynn, she appeared confused why she was so dirty, and I told her what happened, but I'm not convinced all her confusion wasn't an act for my benefit. Her eye was slightly black and blue from my punch; I thought it would look worse than it did.

She apologized profusely, but I can't get the look in her eyes last night out of my mind. She wasn't dazed or confused that time; her hands gripped my arm with purpose. And Wynn witnessed everything. He's known her his entire life and if he thinks she was trying to hurt me, I should believe him. She was trying to kill me, I'm almost certain of it. Is she a sleepwalker? Yes. Was she sleepwalking last night? I don't think so.

Then the real question...

Why would Mel want to hurt me? It couldn't be the questions I've been asking about my aunt, could it? She seemed as interested in the story as I am. I don't think that makes sense, but I also don't have any other theories as to why she would try to pull me underwater last night. Unless she was sleepwalking and me yelling at her made her aggressive. Perhaps she felt threatened. I don't have any answers, but the way she picked up that flashlight and the normal way she walked doesn't add up in my mind; it was different from the last time. And that split second I saw her eyes, so focused and aware, not glassy or looking through me, but purposeful. And that flash of anger later.

I'll have to do some more research about sleepwalking. I do know that I will not be following her anymore. She can run through the woods like a wildcat for all I care. Let Wynn traipse through the trees watching her; he's obviously often around the woods at night. What a weirdo. I'm starting to think this entire family may be unstable.

Maybe Mom is right, I probably should leave here and be done with it. But I know I'm so close to finding out what happened to Aunt Heather. I never should have followed Wynn into the woods; I should have talked to Mr. T instead. I'm sure he knows everything and if he ever had real feelings for my aunt, I'm sure he'd tell me what happened. I know one thing for sure, I'm done with Mel. Whatever was going on last night, I want no part of it. No, Mel is on her own now. I'm not going to be her babysitter anymore. I'm staying tucked into my safe bed at night. No matter what else beckons me in the dark night.

I turn away from the window and stare at Mrs. Jefferies still asleep on the recliner, a soft fleece blanket pulled up over her small frame, chilly even after pulling on the sweater. I still wonder why she lied about Heather leaving with her father. Should I ask her about it? Will she remember anything now?

Probably not.

Jennifer's words warning me not to upset her mother and how she wouldn't remember anything from that long ago ring in my ears. I think about the words, but I also think about the way Jennifer said them.

She was worried. Maybe worried her mother would remember and tell me everything? This might be why Jennifer was so adamant that I didn't ask her mother any questions.

But... I'm going to try. She might know where they went, maybe even knows where Aunt Heather is right now. I mean, really, what do I have to lose?

I sit down on the sofa again and look at the book I read to Mrs. Jefferies earlier, while continuing to debate in my mind about asking the questions I so desperately want the answers to. The clock on the wall does a slow tick tock, providing perfect background noise to my swirling thoughts.

The recliner leg lift goes down and Mrs. Jefferies throws off the blanket.

"Oh, I'm so hot," she says, looking at me. "Who are you?"

"I'm Zoey, I'm your granddaughter Mel's friend."

"Mel, oh yes." She nods. "Sweet girl."

I'm just going to go for it. "Mrs. Jefferies, do you remember that girl who ran away with your husband? I'm her niece. My mom never knew what happened to her and that's why I'm here. Do you have any idea where they went?" I quickly ask in a rush before I lose my nerve. "Why did you tell my mom that she'd been picked up by her dad?"

Wow, that was a mouthful. I had to say it in a rush, or I probably wouldn't ask. So much for being tactful. I look at her to see if she understands. I hope I haven't overwhelmed her or upset her, but I need some answers.

She meets my gaze, her eyes clear and alert. "Heather. Why are you here? You can't be here."

"Why?" I ask, allowing her to believe I'm Heather.

Mrs. Jefferies goes silent but tears slowly run down her face.

Oh no, I upset her. I shouldn't have said anything, but she remembers Aunt Heather. She must know something.

"Mrs. Jefferies?" I ask gently.

She is turning to me now. "Why did you come here? This isn't a safe place!"

She's shaking now. I touch her arm lightly. "I'm sorry, I don't want to upset you. It's okay, we don't have to talk about it."

Mrs. Jefferies looks at me, her tears drying, her gaze clear. "You never should have come here."

Mrs. Jefferies frowns as she stares at me. "You know what will happen! My husband was an ugly man. He was pure evil and darkness. Did you come back from the grave to haunt me? Why do I have to tell you what happened, you already know."

I stare at her, unsure of what to say.

She sighs. "Well, I guess if you're going to haunt me, you

want all the details. I owe you that much. He molested other girls in the past, shortly after we got married. I was so stupid marrying him, but he was handsome and charming, and I was young and naïve. I never could have imagined this is what he was. And his temper..." Her watery eyes became glassy. "He was a terrible man to live with."

"Yes, go on," I say gently.

She shakes her head and stares at me for a long time. "You're not haunting me for what I did, or rather, didn't do?"

I shake my head. "No, I just want to know what happened."

Dementia is a cruel disease, playing tricks with people's minds, sometimes confusing places and people. Sometimes mixing past time frames with the present. I must be careful to keep Mrs. Jefferies calm, but I want to hear what she has to say about Aunt Heather.

She stares at me, her eyes glassy now. "They were just kids, all of them. Do you know that old ghost story they tell about The Man in the Woods around the campfire?"

I nod.

"That's my husband, Ed Jefferies. He's The Man in the Woods. The monster that everyone sits around and tells ghost stories about is real. A real live monster."

Then she bursts out in tears. "I don't want to talk about this! I can't talk about this!" She grips the arms of the recliner.

"I'm sorry," I say in a soothing voice. I want her to continue, but she's clearly very upset. Maybe if I can get her to calm down, she'll start talking again.

The front door opens and slams shut. Mel walks into the living room.

"What's going on?" she asks, her hands on her hips.

"She's very upset," I quickly say.

"Hold on, Grandma, I'll get your medicine." Mel disappears to the kitchen, and she comes back with a glass of water and two pills. "Here, take these. You'll feel better."

Mrs. Jefferies takes them and takes a drink of water. "Oh, I don't want to talk anymore."

"Okay." Mel helps her out of the chair. "Let's go back to your bedroom. You can take a nap, the pills will help you."

"All right, honey," she agrees, and the two disappear down the hallway.

I head to the front door and walk out. I don't want to talk to Mel.

FORTY-THREE

1989

Heather

I must have drifted off briefly, but it doesn't last long. A slight, cool breeze enters the tent as I toss and turn on the sleeping bag. I can't get comfortable, so I sit up and rub my head; remnants of a headache still linger. I step out into the inky night lying outside. I stretch for a moment and stare up at the patch of stars above me in an opening between trees. Their luminous beauty makes me smile, and I can't wait for Dean to join me again so we can enjoy them together.

My gaze shifts down and I notice a light to the right of my new campsite. I wonder where it comes from? It's higher than a light from a tent or a flashlight, more like a light in a house window. I look around. We moved much deeper into the forest this afternoon, away from the pool, to be safe.

An idea stabs me.

I'm closer to that weird cabin I found a few weeks ago.

I stare at the light, blindingly bright in the black night. It must be coming from the cabin; there's nothing else around here, at least that I know of. Goosebumps prickle on my arms, and a slight breeze ruffles the leaves of the trees. I remember the screaming whispers I heard at the cabin the day I discovered it. *Go away! Go away!*

A twig breaks behind me and I turn, but nothing is there. A screech owl lends an eerie melody to the already creepy night. Dread infiltrates my body and mind, although I don't know why. I'm standing alone in this dark forest. Nobody knows I'm here except Dean. I hope he comes back soon.

Please come soon.

Another twig breaks. I see a movement from the corner of my eye. I don't know what it is, but I feel the urge to run so I do. I run as fast as I can into the dark woods. My feet are bare against the forest floor and the rough ground digs into their tender flesh, but I ignore the pain. Something is following me. I hear its heavy breathing and its footsteps moving behind me.

This is no animal.

A person is behind me.

A person who doesn't say anything, but moves quickly, gaining on me as I increase my speed.

Sharp sticker bushes prick my bare legs and low tree branches whip my face. Blood runs down my legs. I push myself to go faster, but you can only run so fast in the woods in the dark. At least whoever is behind me isn't using a flashlight. The darkness envelops me in every corner as I move forward. There is no light here.

My heart races, adrenaline fueling me as I continue to run with only moonlight to guide my way. Sweat drips off my face. Who is out here? Who is chasing me? Is it him? I should never have stayed here alone.

Run.

Run.

The forest seems to become still and every sound I make, lumbering through the trees, thunders inside of it. How am I going to hide if I'm making so much noise? Ahead of me is a large hemlock tree with a massive trunk and low-hanging branches.

I'll hide there.

I slip underneath the low branches and stand behind the wide tree trunk.

Please let this person, this thing, whatever it is, go away. Please go away, I continue to pray in my frantic mind.

Now that I've stopped running, the night is quiet, serene almost except my heart that races inside my body. I take a few silent breaths to try to calm myself. I'm going to be fine. Everything will be fine.

A twig behind me breaks, but before I can turn around, a large hand clamps down over my face, and I smell chemicals on a rag that now covers my mouth. I slowly lose consciousness, but I don't fall.

He has me.

My eyes flash open under the bright spotlight shining on me. Terror seizes me as I try to move but can't as my arms and legs are tied to a bed. A twin bed with a plain white comforter.

I'm inside the weird cabin.

I try to yell, but there's a rag in my mouth. My eyes flick to the tall man standing over me.

It's him.

Ed Jefferies stands towering above me. He's wearing the same T-shirt and jeans he wore when he took me to the store earlier in the day. Was that only today? It seems like a lifetime ago.

"You're not going anywhere, Heather," he says, his lips curling into a wicked smile. "So, I wouldn't even waste the effort. You're all mine now."

I ignore his words and try to scream and move again, but I remain in the same position. My mind scrambles for ways to get loose and get away from him. My heart races and sweat drips down my neck. How am I going to get out of here! Please someone help me!

"It's no use," he says in a calm tone. "I've told you, Heather, you're not going anywhere."

His eyes dance with anticipation and madness.

I continue to struggle, but I can't move. I don't know how I can get out of here. Get away from him.

"That's the thing, once I make a choice, well..." He pauses meditatively. "Maybe that's the wrong term because I've always felt the girls choose me in a strange way," he continues in his calm voice. He stares at me with piercing blue eyes. "Once I have a girl, she never gets away."

Fear floods me again and my brain struggles for ideas, anything to break free and run out of this cabin. Run fast as hell away from Ed Jefferies.

Ed towers over me with his hands brushing against my face, then his long fingers trail along my face, touching my earring. Without a word, he unfastens the right one, and then the left, holding both earrings in his hands.

His lips curl into a disturbing smile. "My souvenir. I'll put them with the others. I know you're hoping your boyfriend will show up to save you, but he won't," Ed says. "I already have a plan for him."

Somebody, please help me! I scream in my mind. Get me out of here! This is more dangerous than I imagined. Ed Jefferies isn't just a pervert; he's a psychopath.

"Oh, your boyfriend posed a problem, but I've got that handled. I made some changes to scavenger hunt night, and it will last much longer than usual. We'll be all done here, and I'll toss your tent and everything in my truck. He'll look for you, but he won't find you. I already placed some pot in his bunk bed tonight and will alert the police tomorrow morning. My daughters always have a stash around they think I don't know about. Then he'll be gone too, although not permanently, like you."

I swallow, but barely any saliva is left in my parched throat. The ripples of fear coursing through me now flood my body in strong waves.

He walks away from me, over to the side of the room, next to the door. I notice dark shades are now pulled over every window in the small cabin.

Tears trickle down my face and I keep struggling.

My body shakes in spasms. Is this really going to happen to me? Is this the end?

I do the only thing I can... pray. I don't have any other options. I can't move. I can't even speak.

"Oh, I almost forgot my bag." Ed unlocks the door and walks outside, then returns carrying a brown bag. He unzips it and retrieves a camera from inside it. When he reenters the cabin, I notice he forgets to lock the door. If I can just get loose somehow, I can run, I know I can.

"Don't worry, sweet Heather." He runs a hand up my leg. "It'll be over soon."

He looms above me, staring into my eyes. I close them.

"Open your eyes," he tells me. "Look at me."

My body shakes but I keep my eyes closed.

"Open them," he says sharply.

I slowly open them and meet his gaze. His cold, ice-blue eyes slice through me. No compassion, only deadness of spirit. Harvey's face flashes in my mind. His rough laugh when he'd make some gross joke, his body purposely brushing against mine, his eyes always watching me, dead eyes just like Ed. A different man, but the same.

A predator.

"Good girl," he says, touching my lips.

A sick feeling engulfs me and I squeeze my eyes shut again,

pushing everything away. Help me. Someone help me, I scream in my mind.

But nobody will come, and I lie on the bed wishing I could exit my body and leave it lying here and run away, far away from this perverted weirdo. Murderer. I can't move, but I want to distance myself mentally. I can do that.

I have to do that. It's my only escape.

A wave of calm washes over me and comforting words of one of the Psalms fills my mind. I hear the words in my mind. I hear Gran's voice reading them to me.

Even though I walk through the valley of the shadow of death,

I will fear no evil,

for you are with me;

Your rod and staff, they comfort me.

My mind fills with thoughts of Dean, Jess and Gran. Dancing with Dean in the moonlight only hours ago is the main image in my mind. I won't be Dean's wife; I won't be a writer; I won't even become a woman.

I'll remain a teenager forever.

I will die soon.

Here in this small bed, in this creepy cabin, with this disgusting, evil man.

There's so much I'll never do in life, but I have lived. I was loved, and I've given love. I've had pain and I've had joy, and soon I will have no more breath in my young body. I will be extinguished, my earthly body lying in the dirt next to those other poor girls. He can take my body, but my soul remains alive and will go somewhere else. A place of light and love.

I feel him hovering over me, his breath hot on my neck again. Then his large hands around my neck, and I slowly slip into darkness.

I'll be seeing Gran soon.

FORTY-FOUR
1989

Dean

Trevor and I organize our campers into small groups for the scavenger hunt. Now that our groups are together, we'll soon be ready to start. I walk over to Jennifer, who's handing out the activity map. I just want to get this damn thing over with and get back to Heather. I should never have left her at the tent. I should have insisted she come with me. I don't trust Jefferies. I keep looking around for him, but I haven't seen him yet.

"I'll take five of those," I say to her.

"Okay, here." She places the papers into my hand.

I glance over to Sherry standing on the small porch of the camp store, handing out small flashlights to all the campers. She glares at me. She's been acting like a jerk since Heather said Ed Jefferies stopped out at the tent and more so when she saw the windchime.

"So, Sherry is still mad?" I ask.

Jennifer looks over at her sister. "I guess, but it's not her fault."

I stare at her. "What do you mean?"

She shrugs and looks at me. "I don't know. What's wrong with you? You seem upset or something."

I sigh. "Your dad came to see Heather today again. He was acting weird."

Jennifer moves closer. "Like what?"

"I don't think we can stay here anymore," I say.

Jennifer places the papers on a bench and grabs my arm. She leads me over to the side of the store where it's more private. "You know I said Sherry was upset, but it wasn't her fault? I think she's jealous," she whispers to me.

"Of what?"

Jennifer presses her lips together. "I shouldn't tell you this."

"What?" I demand. "Tell me."

Jennifer looks at me a moment before continuing. "Our dad goes into Sherry's room late at night. My room is right next to hers."

My eyes go wide. "What?"

"And I think he does sex stuff to her. I want to tell Mom, but Sherry won't let me. It's so gross and I don't know what to do about it. I think she's jealous of Heather."

Panic rises inside me thinking about her alone in the woods right now. "Fuck, she's not safe alone in the woods tonight. I knew it," I yell. "Where is your father now?"

Jennifer shakes her head. "I don't know."

Adrenaline and anger race through me. I never should have left her alone. We should have left here tonight! Why was I so stupid?

I turn away from Jennifer and run as fast as I can into the woods.

To Heather.

I have to save her.

. . .

I reach her campsite, but she's not here. I struggle for gulps of air and soon my breathing calms.

Where is she?

The cool night air wraps around me and its whispers envelop me. I turn to the right and see a dim light in the distance and head in that direction. Worry pounds my brain and sweat runs down the back of my T-shirt. She has to be okay is the only thought pounding my brain as I run toward the light.

She has to be okay.

I want to cry, but I won't allow myself. Crying won't help me or Heather. But I will allow the anger inside of me to build. White-hot rage runs through me with each step I take bringing me closer to the light in the darkness.

Fucking Jefferies.

He better not have touched her.

I reach a clearing and a dilapidated old log cabin sits a few feet away from me. Dark shades are pulled over the windows, but some light shines through. A toolbox and shiny red shovel sit on the rickety front porch.

I creep up the stairs, grab the shovel and turn the doorknob. Surprisingly, it opens.

Heather lies naked on a bed, her arms and legs tied to it. Her eyes are closed and her body limp. Dark bruises are around her neck. For a moment everything stills. The physical and emotional pain of seeing her like that stabs me over and over again. Then the rage takes over. Hot, burning, seething murderous rage.

Jefferies stands with his back to me, his finger tracing down Heather's breastbone. He lets out a low groan.

I strike, raising the shovel above me and I hit him in the head, the back, the head again until he falls over. I continue to hit him over and over again, kicking, hitting until he lies in a deep pool of his own sticky blood. The side of his head is dented. I drop the shovel.

He will never hurt anyone again.

He will never move again.

I step over his corpse, untie Heather and remove the rag hanging from her mouth. I cover her with the white blanket, crawl under it and hold her close to me. Her body is still warm and so soft as I gather her in my arms. I bury my face into her long, dark hair.

And I cry.

FORTY-FIVE
2024

Zoey

I hurry down the sidewalk of the Jefferies home to the gravel road and then move onto the trail leading further into the woods. I need to think. Mrs. Jefferies wanted to tell me more and it's obvious that she knows what happened to Aunt Heather.

My thoughts are racing as I travel along the path, then I hear music playing. I look up and see Mr. T, still working in the protected garden.

Dean. Heather's boyfriend. It's time to ask him for the truth.

I march up to the garden, rounding the back where the gate is open. Dean is watering a lush growth of black-eyed Susans. He turns off the hose and spins around. Surprise jumps in his eyes when he sees me.

"Oh, uh, Zoey, right?" He smiles at me.

"Yeah," I reply.

"Can I help you with something?" he asks. He lays the hose on the ground.

"You were my aunt Heather's boyfriend," I say. I wait for his reaction. All I see is sadness in his eyes.

"Yes," he says.

I'm surprised by his honest answer.

"Tell me what happened to her."

He points over to a shade tree. "Let's sit over there. I'll tell you everything."

We move under the tree and sit down on the soft grass. This is going to happen. I'm finally going to find out everything.

"I spoke to Mrs. Jefferies. She was confused and thought I was Heather. She said it was her husband's fault that she's dead."

He nods. "He was a pedophile and a murderer. He knew Heather was hiding in the woods." His voice wavers. "And I left her alone that night."

I wait for him to continue.

"After thirty-five years, I still remember every vivid detail. I don't think it will ever leave me. How could it? Something that traumatic stays with you forever. It weaves itself into your very fiber and lingers, its sickness traveling through your body, never wanted, but always present," he says, staring at the ground. "But I still have the good memories too and I hold them tight to me, making them a deeper part of me than the rest."

Dean stares at the garden, his mind miles away. "The love I felt for her was unlike anything I've ever experienced. All-consuming and unbelievably exciting. I've never stopped loving her."

I watch Dean's expression as he talks and it's obvious that he still loves Aunt Heather very much.

"I know it's not fair to Jennifer, but I never lied to her," he goes on. "She knew exactly how I felt, and she accepted it even though I know she didn't like it. Jennifer and I gravitated toward each other after everything happened. We could talk to each other, there are no secrets between us. We leaned on each other.

"Jennifer told me her father had been molesting Sherry, and I ran so fast to get to Heather that night. She was in the woods and I left her there alone! I left her all alone because of a stupid scavenger hunt!" he cries. Tears run down his face. "I found them in that rundown cabin and Heather was... dead."

My heart leaps. "The cabin on the side road?" I ask. "What did he do to her?"

He nods. "He strangled her." His eyes darken. "And I killed him."

"Oh..." I look at him.

I notice he's lost a lot of weight since the first time I met him. He looks gaunt and sickly. Carrying around this secret has to be devastating to him.

"I kept working at the camp after everything had happened. I was fueled by the feeling that I couldn't leave Heather alone. Rose Jefferies needed the help and I'm good at fixing things; I'm skilled at that type of work and the camp always has something that needs fixing. I don't regret being with Jennifer, but I know I was never fully in the marriage and that's not fair to her. Although at this point, none of those issues matter." He clears his throat.

He points to the garden. "I try to keep this garden perfect. It's the least I can do for Heather. She deserved so much more. I probably spend too much time out here, pruning, watering, mulching all the plants and bushes, but I have... I want to. I want everything to be perfect here around Heather's resting place. Sherry has a section in the back that she claimed. She thinks her father is buried there, but his remains are under that rotting mulch pile. Exactly where that evil monster belongs. He deserves so much worse."

I stare at the garden. Aunt Heather and Ed Jefferies are buried... here?

"Jennifer told her mother about Heather and they, along with Sherry, followed me that night. Mrs. Jefferies knew about some of her husband's issues in the past, but she thought it had stopped. She was firm in protecting me. She didn't want me to go to jail for murder, so we created this garden and the story of Ed Jefferies leaving and Heather's father picking her up," Dean says flatly.

I'm still staring at the meticulous, beautiful garden. Aunt Heather has been here for all these years, in this camp. My emotions are swirling around inside me. I'm happy to finally know the truth of what happened, but it is such a heartbreaking truth.

"I could never let go of Heather. Even though I eventually married Jennifer, she was the only one I could talk to, the only one who understood everything, and I thought I loved her, but I never gave her all of my heart. I never was the same person; trauma changes you and it was comforting to have someone who understood that change because it became a part of me. A broken person. Functioning, but broken. But my heart could never completely open to Jennifer," he chokes, more tears running down his face. "It always belonged to Heather."

He stands up, tears streaming down his face. He wipes them away, but more fall. "I can't talk about this. I'm sorry, Zoey."

I touch his arm. "Thank you, Dean."

I walk away from him, my thoughts swirling with all the revelations. Aunt Heather is buried in the protected garden, the secret garden. She's been so close to me the entire time.

I stare at the ground as I walk back to the cabin on the lonely trail. So many thoughts crowd my mind as I move along. I have to call Mom and it's time for me to leave this camp. I hope my phone is dried out from last night. My step quickens and I run into a tree branch, a spiderweb brushing against my skin. I stop, swipe it away and rub my hands on my shorts. Footsteps move behind me, and I turn, wondering if Dean wants to talk some more. The path is empty behind me, but something hits me in the head and a searing pain shoots through it. I stumble and fall onto the ground. Another hit and more pain stabs my head.

Then the world goes black.

I try to open my eyes slowly. They feel so heavy it takes what feels like a long time to open them fully and look around. I'm in a bedroom decorated in muted gray and a pretty lavender. I'm lying on a white canopy bed. My hands are tied to the bedpost and my legs are tied together with rope.

What the hell is going on?

Muffled voices are in the hall outside, but they quickly go quiet. I survey the room more closely as I try to loosen the ropes restraining me. A white framed photo sits on the nightstand next to me. A younger Jennifer and Dean, and a young Mel smile back at me in front of the Cinderella Castle at Disney World.

I stare at Dean thinking of all he told me only what, minutes, hours ago? I'm sure not much time has passed, but sunlight filters through the curtains so it's still daytime.

This must be Mel's bedroom. What are they going to do to me? Who knows I'm here? Mel! Mel knows and I breathe a sigh of relief. They won't do anything to me. Mel will find out I'm here and we'll sort everything out, but then images of last night fill my mind. Mel trying to shove me under the swampy water. Holy shit, what if this is another plan to kill me? She didn't succeed last night, so now what, this is a second chance to knock me off? Why? What did I do to these people, or are they all insane?

I struggle with the wrist restraints, trying to wiggle free.

Where is Mel? As much as I don't trust her, I do know her the best of everyone here. I thought we were friends. Surely, I can reason with her, understand what she's thinking, and we can work something out. I pull harder on the bed, too hard, because it knocks the picture frame and something hidden inside the frame falls, hits me on the side of the head and lands with a thud on the far end of the bed.

A strangely familiar object. I stare at it for several minutes.

Is it?

No, how could it be...?

My head aches both from the impact and getting knocked out earlier, but I don't have much time to dwell on the pain.

The bedroom door opens and Mel stands in the doorway. She closes it behind her.

"Mel!" I exclaim. Hope springs in me. "Untie me! Please!"

She walks over to the bed and stares at me. The room is silent as we stare at each other, then the air conditioning kicks on. She looks away.

"Please, Mel!" I beg, pulling on the ropes. Then I stop. "Why did you knock me out on the trail?"

She turns back to me and now the weird smile is on her face again. "No, that was Aunt Sherry. She's supposed to be here, but Wynn needed her for something."

I glare at her and yank on the ropes again. They are loosening. "Let me go, Mel."

She glances at the familiar phone lying on the bed next to me. A phone with a Philadelphia Eagles cover on it. I shudder.

Her eyes meet mine and she frowns. "So you know."

"Why do you have Craig's phone?" Anger seethes inside me and I want to jump on her, but I can't move. I know she did something to him, but how? Why?

She moves closer; her face contorts into the creepy smile I've witnessed a few times before. Now I know why she looked at me in this way. She wants to hurt me; she has to hurt me according to her logic. "You never should have come here, Zoey."

FORTY-SIX
MARCH 2024

Mel

My head still buzzes after those shots I had earlier at the bar. It was such fun seeing Kayla and Marci tonight, but I should have taken up Kayla's offer to stay at her house. She only lives two houses down from the bar. I shouldn't really be driving, but I'm not drunk, just buzzed.

I grip the steering wheel and focus on the road ahead. It's so dark and lonely on the road that leads to the camp. Only fields and dark forest occupy it, and the dim glow of the camp is the only source of light. Usually, I rather enjoy the darkness. I don't have to pay as much attention to the road because there are hardly any cars on this back road, only locals or people who want to avoid the interstate and would rather take a leisurely drive than arriving at a destination in the fastest time. I only need to be careful of deer that may streak across the road unexpectedly, but I'm used to watching out for them.

I think.

I'm so hot so I turn down the windows and let some cold air

into the car, which instantly gives me a jolt of alertness. I can't wait to get home; I'm feeling so tired now.

I swerve, thinking I saw an animal cross the road, but on second look, I was wrong. I grip the steering wheel again. I guess I should pay more attention in case a deer decides to jump out onto the road. I don't want to get into a wreck.

A car is parked alongside the road, and I glance at it momentarily, then turn my eyes back to the road, but my reactions are slow.

Too late.

I hit a large form.

A deer? I peer at the form lying across the road, unmoving.

No.

A person.

I jump out of the car and stand over the man lying on the road. He's not moving. His fly is open and I'm guessing that's why he pulled his car over, to take a leak at the side of the road.

Why didn't I see him?

Because you're drunk, you idiot, I say to myself.

I poke his arm gently. "Hey," I say.

No response.

Fuck. What am I going to do? I lean down to see if he is breathing.

He is not.

Shit, shit shit! I should call the police, but... I've been drinking. I'll go to jail for murder. My mind is twisting in a million directions, but I have to think fast. What am I going to do?

I can't call Mom or Dad, they would call the police, but Aunt Sherry might have an idea. She's always been a little different. She likes to make her own rules. Yes, she'll know what to do in a situation like this. She'll help me.

I quickly text her.

I'm right: Sherry knows exactly what to do and we move fast getting the man back into his car, then she drives him to the protected garden area in the camp, hands me a red shovel and tells me where to dig.

Everything happens so fast, and before I know it, I'm standing on the fresh dirt that covers the man's grave and Sherry is hurriedly dumping a pile of dark mulch on the area. Luckily it is a warm March, so the ground is soft.

Did I really just kill a man I hit with my car?

Did I really just bury him?

My phone buzzes in my pocket, another text. I pull out the phone with an Eagles phone case. The man's phone.

The girl again. Zoey. I guess his girlfriend.

I quickly type a text to her, breaking it off. After all, her boyfriend is dead. She needs to move on.

Then I follow Sherry to dispose of the man's car in the lake, not the swimming lake, but the back lake, more of a swamp really, full of algae and rotting plants, that nobody ever goes to. I don't know how Aunt Sherry knew how to do all of this so fast; it's as if she's done it before, but I'm thankful for her knowledge.

My problem is solved.

FORTY-SEVEN

JULY 2024

Zoey

As Mel tells me the story, rage builds inside me. She's lost in her storytelling and barely looking at me, and I keep pulling on the ropes and one is almost completely loose.

She killed him.

She killed him.

And Sherry drove his car into that disgusting swamp, the swamp Mel tried to kill me in last night!

FUCK!

I give my right hand a good yank and it loosens completely, allowing my hand to become free.

"It wasn't my fault, really," she says. Her eyes are wide, possibly regretful, or she's pretending, I can't be sure. "I didn't mean to kill him."

"But you did!" I yell at her. "You killed him!"

Her face darkens and now she gives me her full attention, moving closer to me. She hovers over me, her blue eyes sharp and focused, her breath smelling of onions, and her lips curve into the weird smile.

"And now I have to kill you too," she snarls. "I'll make sure I do it right this time. Then when Aunt Sherry comes back, we'll dump you in the swamp."

Her hands go around my neck and she squeezes, crushing my windpipe. I grab her long hair with my free hand, yanking it as hard as I can, catching her by surprise.

"Stop!" she yells, pushing my hand away. She jumps on top of me, straddling me, one hand squeezing my neck, the other holding down my free hand.

I struggle to breathe, but manage a few breaths. She shoves my arm under her knee and now both her hands are around my neck. My air is limited and decreasing quickly. I'm getting weaker.

Is this how I die? Just like Aunt Heather. At the hands of the same person who killed Craig.

I'm fading in and out of consciousness and then a commotion is around me.

"Get off of her now, Melanie!" a stern voice instructs.

I gasp as Mel's grip loosens and air returns to my lungs.

"Dad!" Mel yells. Dean pulls her off of me and I continue to gasp for air. Slowly my breathing returns to normal. Police sirens wail outside the house as Dean unties me.

The paramedic assessed me, and my vital signs are normal and there's no visible injury, other than some bruising, but they will take me to the hospital in a few minutes for a full examination.

"Thank God you sent me that email," Mom is gushing to me. "I'm so glad you'll be okay." She squeezes my hand.

I squeeze back. "I love you, Mom."

"I love you, honey," she says, tears welling in her eyes.

I smile and close my eyes as I rest on the paramedic cot. Thank God indeed, and that Mom called the police as soon as she received my email. Even Pearl contacted the police for a wellness check on me when she saw Mel and Sherry buying rope at the store and overheard them whispering my name.

And thankfully Dean showed up when he did. He saved my life.

FORTY-EIGHT
2024

Zoey

The protected garden is the gravesite for Aunt Heather, Ed Jefferies and Craig. The police brought in cadaver dogs, and the remains of five teenage girls were also found by a rotted old cabin deep in the woods. All the bodies are being carefully exhumed. My mom is packing up my clothes in the cabin, and we'll stay at a nearby hotel. Craig's father will be here tomorrow, and we are making proper burial arrangements for Craig and Aunt Heather. Gayle, Nadine's sister, will also be arriving here tomorrow.

I wish I could have kept Craig's phone with me, but the police needed it for evidence. I mourn him. I loved him, I still do, but finally knowing what happened gives me some peace. He loved me too. His phone code is the basic 1234, yes, ridiculous, but he said he'd forget anything else. Lucky for Mel, because she guessed the code and kept up this charade of him traveling through Europe, randomly texting his dad, friends, etc., eventually they would have investigated more, but it had worked for her up to this point. His screensaver is a picture of the two of us, happy and in love. I know it means he felt the same about me, but also that Mel knew who I was the entire time.

The rage I have for her simmers in every fiber of my body.

She killed Craig. My love.

The anger still boils inside me, but it's over now. I got the answers I was looking for when I arrived here, answers for Mom, and answers for me, although I didn't expect what I found. At least we will have closure, not the never-ending wonder of what happened. We know their stories, as sad as they are, but we will hold our loved ones in our hearts and minds forever. They will never die there.

I stand by the meadow now, in the woods hidden from view, watching everything unfolding in front of me. I stare at the white tents covering the bodies, the forensic team still working on exhuming all the parts of the people we loved. The camp was evacuated, all the campers are gone and most of the staff. Sherry, Mel and Dean are all in jail waiting on bail to be announced. Jennifer and Mrs. Jefferies are still here, on house arrest, because of Mrs. Jefferies's fragile health, and Jennifer is her caregiver.

The shock of Craig's death still hasn't fully hit me and the thought of never seeing him again fills me with such a heart-breaking sadness. We were in love and had a bright future together.

The thought of him being here, buried in the back of the protected garden the entire time I've been here, is insanely chilling to me. What Mel and Sherry did fills me with a white-hot rage, and it takes all my effort to maintain some kind of calm right now. I'm so glad both are in custody; if they were here, I don't know what I'd do.

I like to scroll through the pictures of us on my phone, and I don't know, it makes me feel close to him. Reminding me that what we had was real.

One is taken at a hayride around Halloween. One of the fraternities had arranged it and there was a party afterward. I love how we look in this photo. It was cold that night and we both wore turtleneck sweaters, his dark brown and mine red. We're snuggled under a blanket as we lie in the hay. The wagon is crowded but the way we look at each other it seems as if we are the only two there.

I look at this photo several times a day.

It makes me happy.

And sad.

We could have been so much more, but I'll remember him always. He was a beautiful part of my life for a short time. And I will make sure Mel and Sherry have consequences for what they did to him. I will show up to every court date, sentencing and parole hearing. I'll never let them get away with what they did.

They took away the man I love.

As I watch the forensic team exhuming the bodies, sadness fills me. I went to the jail yesterday to visit Dean, and he told me more about Aunt Heather. And I thanked him for saving my life.

Dean is a good man, albeit a sad and broken man, but he loved Aunt Heather. I could see it in him when he talked to me, heard it in his voice. Mel's grandfather, Ed, took her from him just as Mel took Craig from me, and if I was in the same situation as he was in, I'd likely do the same.

I'm glad I solved Aunt Heather's disappearance, but didn't realize how personal it would become. At least we now have answers.

A rustle in the trees behind me causes me no alarm, only curiosity. I turn to see Wynn walking up next to me.

"Hey," he says.

"Hey."

He points to the meadow with all the activity. "I told you this place wasn't right."

"You did." I look at him. "Did you know about everything?"

"Nah, I know my mom is fucked up, she always has been. And I knew about the car she and Mel drove into the back lake, but that's it. Those two always kept secrets. I guess my whole family did."

I nod. "Where will you go now?"

He holds up a duffel bag. "I'm getting out of here. Gonna stay with a friend for a couple months until I turn eighteen, then I don't know. Maybe move someplace warm. Florida. California, not sure yet."

"I hope that works out for you," I say. "Hey, give me your phone."

He looks at me, then hands it over. I tap in my name and number under contacts. "Give me a call sometime. We're friends now."

He grins and takes his phone back. "Friends, okay, that works."

"Good luck, Wynn."

"Thanks, you too." He flicks his long black hair and turns to leave.

I watch him walk away and then I do the same.

EPILOGUE
OCTOBER 2024

Dean

Three months have passed since my arrest. I've been out on bail for two months while I await sentencing. Jennifer and I are waiting for our court trial, Jennifer's mother died a month ago, and Sherry was denied bail after assaulting a police officer. She'll be in jail until her court date and probably for many years after. Mel, too, my sweet baby girl, was denied bail at this time because of the multiple charges against her. Tears well inside me thinking of her in jail, thinking of what she did. How could my kind, beautiful daughter commit such horrible acts?

Now I lie in the hospital bed we purchased for Jennifer's mother months ago, the one with the remote to move it up and down, making it easier for a sick person to get comfortable.

I am a sick person.

I was diagnosed with pancreatic cancer this spring and my prognosis was grim, even if I did the treatments available. I refused all treatments. I don't want to fight it; I'm ready to go. Maybe this is my punishment for not keeping Heather safe so many years ago.

I'll never forgive myself for leaving her that night, not protecting her, but I always loved her. I still love her. The agony in my heart and mind will never forget that night or the pain of never seeing her smile again or holding her in my arms.

My phone beeps from the table by the bed and I pick it up.

> Thank you, Dean. This means so much to me and my mom.

I smile and lay the phone back on the table. I sent Zoey all of Heather's notebooks and her half-moon earrings, white opal, that she always wore. I kept them all these years because they were the only tangible items to remind me of her. Not that I needed reminders; I thought of her every single day, but now I won't need them.

I try to get comfortable in the bed and take a sip of cold water from the glass that sits on the small table by the bed. My favorite station that plays eighties music plays softly next to me on my phone. Our song comes on. The one Heather and I danced to at the Winter Dance when I was seventeen and she was sixteen. I lie back on my pillow, smiling, remembering my arms around her, her sweet scent, how she looked at me. And the last night we danced in the woods under the moonlight. I remember everything about her, even after all these years. She was so special to me.

Heather took a part of my heart that nobody could ever touch, not even my wife, and that's my fault. Heather was the one I wanted from the moment I saw her walk onto my bus so many years ago. She was the one I wanted to marry, the one I loved so *damn* much. The one I couldn't keep safe, that's my fault too. A fact I've told myself about every single day since her death.

Even bright spots in my life, the happy moments, marrying Jennifer, Melanie's birth and watching her grow up, were still dimmed by the absence of Heather. That's probably the wrong thing to say. She was never absent in my mind, only in the physical state; she lived on in my memory forever.

I cough and my frail body shakes.

The doctor says I probably won't make the night. Jennifer just left the room in tears, and I spoke to Mel a short time ago on the phone. We said goodbyes and then I wanted some time to myself. I love them and I will miss them, but it's my time to go. My time with them is soon over and I hope I leave some happy memories with them both.

And Mel... I failed her too. I tried to be a good father, but I guess I didn't succeed. How could she have run over Zoey's boyfriend, killed him, and not have reached out to me for help? It was an accident. Yes, she was drinking and there would have been consequences for that, but she just buried his body with Sherry's help. Plus, she tried to kill Zoey too, and may have succeeded if I hadn't intervened. A sob escapes me. All I can give her now is my love; she'll have to figure out the rest on her own. After all, I've many choices I regret too. Part of me wonders if evil travels through bloodlines. Mel has the blood of Ed Jefferies coursing through her veins.

A heavy sigh escapes me. So many regrets. And all of them come back to Camp Medley. I've wished so many times that I never came here, never worked as a counselor, certainly never brought Heather here. But none of that matters now and, strangely, I welcome the quiet peace of death. I'm not scared at all; instead I feel anticipation like I felt that night at the Winter Dance when I picked up Heather at her house. The anticipation of being close to her, near her, with her. It's all I ever wanted and while it's said there is no one soulmate for a person, but rather several possible compatible matches throughout a person's life, I don't think that's true for me. She was the love of my life. Even after thirty-five years have passed, I still remember every detail about her.

And I always will.

It was always Heather for me even if life and death separated us physically, no one and nothing could separate the bond, the love between us.

Like the air we breathe.

Or the blood pumping through our bodies.

It was life. In its purest form and its most beautiful—even in the presence of evil, that love lived on. I lay my head back into my pillow and stare at the ceiling. I close my eyes and smile.

I'll be seeing Heather soon.

A LETTER FROM THE AUTHOR

Huge thanks for reading *No One Saw Her Go*. I hope you enjoyed Heather's poignant story and Zoey's search for answers for her family. If you want to join other readers in hearing all about my new releases and bonus content, you can sign up for my newsletter.

www.stormpublishing.co/sally-royer-derr

If you enjoyed this book and could spare a few moments to leave a review, that would be hugely appreciated. Even a short review can make all the difference in encouraging a reader to discover my books for the first time. Thank you so much.

I loved writing the dual timelines in this story. Heather, a young woman struggling for survival and independence, and Zoey on a quest to find answers about her aunt, her mother's long-missing sister, were both such strong, interesting characters. And the summer camp setting gave incredible creepy vibes to this story!

Thanks again for being part of this amazing journey with me and I hope you'll stay in touch—I have so many more stories and ideas to entertain you with!

Sally

ACKNOWLEDGEMENTS

Thank you to Oliver Rhodes and the entire fabulous team at Storm Publishing for sharing my work with your audience. A special thanks to my editor, Emily Gowers, who has an amazing insight into my books and working with her is an absolute joy!

Thank you to all my incredible readers. I appreciate your support every single day!